DEATHSPEAKER
Hunt

Casey Fry

Acknowledgments

It is difficult to tell, at some points, whether I wrote this story or if the characters climbed out of the pages, stole my keyboard, and told the tale themselves. I probably owe them a lot more credit than I'm willing to let them take, but I think even Ricker at his most cynical will agree that there are a few people to whom we owe a lot of gratitude.

Thank you to Crystal Breon, for reading the story as it was born, for her enthusiasm at the turning of every page, and for discussing assassinations over lunch dates.

Thank you to my wonderful editor, Chelsea Haire, for her excitement every time I typed a new roman numeral.

Thank you to Dottie Martin, for being there at the beginning, and for watching the characters and story grow.

A huge thank you goes out to my parents, Mike and Sandy, for teaching me to reach for my dreams, even if it means defying gravity and growing wings. Thank you to my brother, Dustin, for always being there, and for being an inspiration on so many levels.

A big thank you goes to Cindy Freland of Maryland Secretarial Services, Inc for her help in the publication of *DeathSpeaker*.

There are so many people who helped in the formation of this novel, from mere excitement to a random comment that sprung an idea. I cannot possibly thank you all by name and still leave room, and time, for you to read the story. Please know that you have my sincerest gratitude, each of you, for all the help you've given, and every smile offered.

Some say that the DeathSpeakers existed long before the wars began. They claim that the first came long before history was being recorded – that he was the first person to ever order someone else to kill. They say that they, more than all of the other PlagueCursed that have risen since the wars paved the way for the Dark Plague, reflect the true nature of humankind. That it is inherent within our species, our main prerogative, to destroy others, sheds light on what the future holds for our species if it is true that within all of us, there lies a DeathSpeaker.

DEATHSPEAKER
Hunt

Sarah,

Merry Christmas!

I hope you enjoy the story.

I

"Where did the boy sleep?"

The walk down the corridors of the church she called her home never seemed as long to Annabel as it did now. She kept her pace as calm as she was able, but her movements were still quickened by her eagerness to be rid of the man who walked the stone path beside her.

She glanced at him as she walked, but his gaze had yet to stray from the stonework of the floor before him. It was not a humble or pious intent with which he focused his eyes, but a stubborn refusal to meet her gaze that he had enacted from the moment he appeared at the threshold of the church. His eyes remained a mystery to her by his own will, but he did not hide his appearance and she studied him as she had not dared to when she'd first met him at the door.

Hair the color of slick mud was swept backward across his skull in scattered and unruly locks, as though he had before been walking miles against the wind. The skin around his eyes was wind-burnt, red from the harsh weather that seemed a constant in the world.

Annabel's eyes were drawn from the firm line his lips were drawn into, down to his neck. The skin of his throat had been bared purposefully. She could see the clasp that normally bound his cloak tight around his throat. If she looked closely enough, it appeared to resemble the head of some animal. It was of crude design, however, as though made by the hand of a child, and it was impossible to tell what sort of creature it had been meant to represent.

It was not the clasp that had her attention, however, but the black tattoo-like design that curled across the skin of his throat. It was this that he had bared for them to see. It stood out against the pale of his flesh, shaped like the wings of a bird, half-unfolded, but jagged, as though sprouting thorns.

It was his Mark: a denotation of what he was. As much a man as a human was an animal, the winged Mark was a warning to all who saw it. It told that he was a DeathBreather, a human who had been altered by the Dark Plague, rather than destroyed by it. Annabel knew more about him than what that blemish on his skin detailed. He bore a warning toward others that he was PlagueCursed, but there was no Mark to warn them of what choices he had made in life, and what he had become by them.

Annabel knew. She walked down the hall briskly, with him matching her gait step for step. With the clasp of his cloak undone, only the strap of a strangely-shaped leather parcel across his back held the brown fabric closed around his chest. Annabel did not ask what was in the parcel. She was certain that it was some form of weapon that he used in his line of work, and she had no desire at all to learn anymore about that. She already knew why he was here, and that in itself was too much.

"In the servant's quarters, where all of our young charges make their beds."

He grunted in reply, but offered nothing else. Annabel pressed her lips together to keep herself from speaking her initial response, but she could not stop her eyes from narrowing in his direction.

They walked in silence for a time, the only sound the echoing of their footsteps against the

6

stone walls. The path was a long one, for the church was both old and large, but it was familiar to Annabel. As they walked, she did not need to study the murals chiseled into the walls to know the scenes. They passed kings rising up over other men, men with multiple limbs, humans with the wings of giant birds or the heads of animals, a great dragon breathing flame, and a scene seeming to consist of a great ball of light shining down on the world. As they walked on, more scenes were shown, of war and peace, kindness and cruelty. Annabel did not pay much mind to them now. The familiarity alone gave her some comfort, and further strengthened her tongue.

"We could not have simply left him to die."

"It would have been far less dangerous for you if you had."

She was unsurprised that he didn't even bother to look her way. She already knew what his opinion on the matter would have been from what he had chosen to become in this life. Still, the way he spoke, so bored with any manner of resistance she would show even in her words, gave her a glimpse of him through the eyes of those unfamiliar with his kind. For a moment, she could see why people so feared the very mention of his name. Death meant so little to he who cared nothing for the life of a child.

"We are not interested in the *safe* route through life." Her tone was scathing and she could hear the righteousness blazing within it. She should have checked herself, but what he was and what he *stood for* disgusted her too much to try overly hard. Her tongue snapped like a serpent from between her teeth, "but rather the more fulfilling and *right* one! Our Lord—"

"I'm not here to listen to children's stories, madam. Kindly keep your heathen god's teachings to yourself."

Annabel's mouth snapped shut with an audible click. Her gait hesitated on a step, surprised by the interruption, and the exasperation in his voice. It was the first bit of emotion she had heard uttered from his lips other than boredom. That fact did little to stem her ire. She narrowed her eyes at him, hazel irises nearly obscured by her lashes, before she harrumphed loudly and continued down the hall at a quick, angered bustle that was further accentuated by the habit she wore. To her further ire, her companion kept an easy pace with her.

Annabel knew that he was dangerous, but she had no fear of him. He had physical power, with whatever weapon he had strapped to his back, but he had no faith or belief in the things that could not be seen, and so he could not touch her. Still, he angered her so, for she knew the young boy he sought. She had cared for the child, held him close when life had offered him no chances for reprieve. She knew the innocent boy this *man* intended to find and kill, and because he was here to see the Father and not her, she could do nothing to stop him from finding the boy.

The corridor came to an end at a simple wooden door. The brass doorknob was tarnished by the years. Annabel stopped before it and knocked quietly, before turning to face the assassin.

She gazed at him coolly and tried to ignore the sensation of many-legged things crawling over her skin beneath her habit. She knew she wasn't successful in hiding her surprise when he finally glanced at her and their eyes locked. He did not have the dark, near-black eyes that she had expected from a murderer. His irises were a rich aquamarine, the color tales told the seas had once been, before disease and pollution turned them as black as oil and killed everything that lived within them.

Annabel swallowed her shock and tried to school her face into an emotionless expression like the one he had focused on her.

"Father Thomas is waiting for you."

Her voice did not come out in a sneering tone, but trying to halt her lips from curling back in disgust was like trying to stop paper from turning black at the whim of a flame. This man before her wore the perfect disguise; eyes that told of life, and a heart that brought only death.

The expression on the assassin's face did not change from its cool indifference, and he moved by her with the fluid grace native only to the deadliest of creatures. He did not touch her, or come close to doing so, but as he brushed by, the dry air of the church wafted against her, as though his soul was reaching out as he passed to slide demonic hands over the flesh of her body, and sink his tainted being beneath her skin.

Even once he had passed through the ornate door and into the room beyond, she could not stifle a shudder and the urge to brush her hands down her arms. Once he had closed the door behind him, Annabel broke into a run from the hall, moving as swiftly as she could down the stone corridors, as though she could outrun the foul sensation that cloaked her.

She knew, in her heart, that such a speed was not attainable by creatures of a mortal world. The feeling of insects swarming over her, of snakes slithering about her body, of some foul, indiscernible, dripping substance oozing over her would never leave her now. The image of those two aquamarine eyes, rich as life, would remain blazoned in her mind for all eternity. So, too, would the hope burn within her heart that the child he sought would die a swift death, for within those eyes, it had become clear to her that death would come for him regardless of anyone's wishes to the contrary.

~*~

The room that Ricker stepped into was sparsely decorated, but unusually bright. There were four windows that made up the majority of the wall to his left, reaching from floor to ceiling. The curtains that hung from a thick metal rod above them were heavy and white, as was common, but they were pulled to the side. The glass panes had clearly been crafted in such a way as to magnify the light that filtered through them, for Ricker had rarely seen the sunlight shine so brightly.

The meager furnishings within the room consisted of a small bed with thin white sheets and a square pillow. A small bookcase sat near the bed, overflowing with books of all sizes, though a cursory glimpse told Ricker that most of them were quite old. As rare as books were, this did not surprise him, but the amount present on the shelf seemed vast for a mere priest to have in his possession.

A well-used lamp hung from the ceiling in front of the bookcase. Ricker could smell the kerosene in the air, though in the wake of the sunlight in the room, the flame had been snuffed.

To the other side of the lamp from the bookcase was an armchair. It was currently occupied by the person Ricker had come to see.

The man sitting in the armchair was regarding his visitor with a passive, patient look, clearly content to allow him the time that he desired to study the room to its fullest. As best Ricker could tell, Father Thomas was a short man, and large about the waist, though he doubted that the priest's large size was caused by having been so well-fed.

While members of the church in times prior to the final war had oft been as corrupt as any of the madmen who ran among the people, in these times, harsh and nearing their end, those of the church were forced to make many sacrifices. Some were small and simple, but others took a great amount of effort or personal strength, leading there to be fewer members of the churches that remained, but faithful members, all.

It was clear to Ricker that Father Thomas was not a healthy man. His skin had a waxy sheen to it, slick with sweat and slightly yellowed. His eyes were sunken into his head, a look accentuated by the black bruising that surrounded and hung liberally beneath them. His irises might once have been a dark brown, but were now a dull yellow that did nothing to hide the intelligence within them. The unnaturally bright light filtering in through the windows reflected off his scalp, now all but bare, with only a thin halo of greying hair, as though he had already been claimed by the Heavens, despite his lingering mortality.

"Master Ricker," the man greeted, and despite his obvious illness, his voice was strong. He spoke as though the two had been long-acquainted,

11

and not as though they were meeting now for the first time. "I trust this is not a social call?"

"Father Thomas," Ricker bowed his head slightly in respect. He did not ask how the man knew his name. He was bothered more by the jovial greeting, and the smile that stretched the waxy skin of the man's face. It was akin in his mind to being greeted by a corpse, happily, as though they were meeting in a place where they both belonged. Regardless of his frequent acquaintance with death and those about to die, Ricker found it deeply disturbing.

"Do you, Ricker? One would never have guessed such a thing; you're so eager to kill."

"I believe you're here to discuss young Mortimer." Father Thomas leaned back in his chair with an easy smile, folding his hands in his lap. Ricker saw then that the man's fingers were thick and bloated, the tips and under his fingernails the color of blueberries.

Ricker turned his eyes away from Father Thomas' hands and straightened to his full height, clasping his hands behind his back. He regarded the man before him with a solid expression.

"Yes. I want you to tell me where he is."

Want wasn't really a part of it. Ricker expected to be given the information that he had come for. He was a hunter of monsters, not men, and he would not raise his hand against Father Thomas if the information was refused him, but he knew it wouldn't be. Not for a DeathSpeaker.

"As it would be an insult to your intelligence to ask why you wish to find him, I would instead ask what you intend to do once you have accomplished this small thing."

"Small thing? Is murder such a little sin as to be ignored by the churches? It did not used to be so…"

Ricker tilted his head just a fraction and scrutinized the man before him, willing the voice that penetrated his concentration to be silent. He did not need the distraction, not now.

It was no surprise that Father Thomas knew his intentions; there was no mistaking them. Ricker's name was known to many across the western lands he traveled. In some places, he was synonymous with that area's Boogeyman, and in others, he *was* their Boogeyman. A hunter of monsters, a slayer of DeathSpeakers, an assassin – he was a professional at killing, and everyone who recognized his name was aware of it.

For Father Thomas to ask what Ricker planned to do after he had killed the DeathSpeaker alerted the assassin to the fact that the old man wanted something. For a priest who was dying, not much could be offered by one of Ricker's trade, and some things he had been asked for by others, he would not give. He was a slayer of *monsters*.

"If that is how you allow yourself to sleep at night. What little sleep you get…"

"Mortimer's guardian was a foolish creature."

Ricker did not allow his expression to shift, but he pondered if what the priest wanted would come up directly, or if the man intended to try and fool him into agreeing to something. Ricker's quest to slay all DeathSpeakers was a self-appointed one, but he was occasionally called upon when other monsters reared their heads and could not be slain by those haunted by them. That did not mean that he was in the business of doing favors. Especially

13

not for people who had so far allowed him to believe something that was untrue.

"I thought you were his guardian."

The old man scoffed, and the gesture he made with his hand was less dismissive than it was cutting, as though he wished there were someone there that he could strike with it. Ricker wondered briefly if the old man were to prefer the DeathSpeaker, or its guardian.

"No, I am not. That duty was taken by Father Fabula – one of the few who were willing to abide such a horror near them. Due to my standing, the duty would have befallen me upon Father Fabula's death, but the child left the monastery that same night, and so I need not concern myself with it."

So the DeathSpeaker's guardian is dead, then. "I was told that the boy had not yet reached his tenth year."

"No, he has not." Father Thomas' bloated fingers interlaced in his lap again, giving him the image of a calm creature, but Ricker rather thought otherwise. "I am to understand that this fact won't change your intentions?"

There was a shrewd gleam in the man's eyes that was not diminished by their yellowing. Ricker had the impression that Father Thomas was not a man to be trifled with, although it escaped him how the priest could do harm to anyone in his current state.

"The greatest of harms do not come from creatures like you, Ricker, who take up arms against others. There are better ways to hurt someone. But you know that, don't you?"

14

"No!" At Father Thomas' curious look, Ricker raised a placating hand and closed his eyes. *Enough of you. I do not need your council.*

"So you think."

Enough!

"Very well. I will leave you to your homicidal intentions. For now."

The echoing voice that rippled through his mind faded away, and Ricker lowered his hand, opening his eyes to see Father Thomas watching him with undisguised interest.

"My apologies. Of course, my intentions are not altered by the age or status of the boy. He is a DeathSpeaker, regardless of whether he bears his wires. You need not be concerned with that.

"Although, I find I am curious: why did you permit the DeathSpeaker to remain here if you despised him so?"

The curiosity on Father Thomas' face lingered, to Ricker's irritation, but he said nothing. Eventually, the priest recovered his interest in the topic at hand and moved on.

"Unfortunately, our god does not see things as we see them. He is so distanced from our world that He looks down upon us and sees the great tapestry that is our whole existence. He is unable to focus upon one specific creature or another, and so cannot understand, as powerful as He is, what horror DeathSpeakers can cause. Our god, we know, is all-seeing. His greatest power is His most fearsome limitation, I'm afraid.

"By His decree, killing is prohibited by those of the church – even the killing of such creatures who would cause our deaths with little conscience. The hands of those of us who stay within these walls for others must remain clean.

15

Regardless of my own personal opinions towards their kind, or even the opinions of the majority of the church, our lord's decision remains stalwart, and so we must abide by it."

"And this is why you called upon me."

Father Thomas glanced toward the door. "I did not call upon you, Master Ricker. If you'll recall—"

"I was asked to come by Brother Frederick," Ricker said, nodding knowledgably. His lips curled up and he glanced up from his slightly bowed head at Father Thomas. As the man turned back to him, Ricker bared his teeth in a feral smile. "No doubt, he was asked to contact me by the head of his church. That *is* you, isn't it?"

Father Thomas cleared his throat, looking away from the assassin's face. Ricker chuckled lightly.

"I would ask you to do something for me, once you have handled the boy."

Ah, and here it is. Ricker gave Father Thomas his full attention, a curious look upon his face.

"In his foolishness, Father Fabula gave the boy something that belongs to the church. It is a necklace, bearing a pendant the likes of which you are not likely to see again in your life."

"Is it valuable?"

"In times past, one would have been able to trade it for the livelihood of ten profiting farmlands." Ricker's eyebrows shot up in surprise. "In times past," Father Thomas repeated. "The gem might be mistaken for a ruby of the purest crimson. I assure you, it is no such jewel, though it is worthless in such a class, anyway."

That wasn't entirely true, Ricker knew. Oh, Father Thomas was not wrong in the fact that a gem of any purity or size would have a value that was almost nil in comparison to what it would have been centuries ago, before the wars that destroyed the lands. Back in those times, value was judged by the amount of money one had – a value demonstrated by pieces of paper with varying numbers upon them, to denote rank.

No such system continued in this day and age; the time of paper bills and metal coins was over. The inability to find food and water that was not poisoned by the plague had caused the world to fall back on trade, those who had goods and skills that were beneficial could trade them for their needs. A gem that was beautiful and no doubt worth a great deal in other times would have little value in a world that put value on the necessary things in life.

That did not mean, however, that everyone would hold this view. There were some people, in the distant places, who would still place value on such trinkets. If one knew where to go, such a gem could still be sold for a high price – whatever the owner wanted, in fact, be it ten profiting farmlands, or a herd of three generations of healthy cattle.

Not that it mattered to Ricker. He had no use for a shiny trinket, and less still for farmlands or cattle. It had been years since he had lived in a place where such things would be of value to him. All that he needed could be got by other means; means that he already had.

"It appears as a jewel, then, but is not so? You wish me to fetch a worthless rock from the neck of a small boy?"

17

This time, it was the priest who chuckled. "I wish you to recover an artifact belonging to the church from the throat of a corpse, Master Ricker. There is nothing more to say of it than that."

"And nothing more that you *will* say, I take it."

"Need I tell you more?" Although the man spoke his words flippantly, Ricker thought he must be rather desperate to keep the truth of the false gem a secret.

"Only what worth there is to be had by me for recovering this... stone. I have no need for jewels or trinkets, Father. In fact, there is not much that I *do* have need for, so while my curiosity is peaked, I see little reason to burden myself with another journey into your *lovely home*."

Father Thomas smiled, and there was no mistaking the gleam within his eyes. The priest was sly - one who held his cards close to him, until such a moment that it would be most beneficial that he show his hand.

"I happen to know, Master Ricker, of three other DeathSpeakers who have made homes of the churches across the world. If you are kind enough to bring this pendant back to its home, I'll draw you a map."

~*~

Leaving the church behind him was the best thing that Ricker had done recently. Only once it was completely beyond his sight did he feel well enough to relax. He wasn't sure why, but part of him had been expecting to glance back and see the bloated, jaundiced, living corpse that was Father

18

Thomas, following behind him like a walking shadow of death.

"How ironic that we are in a valley..."

"Shut it, Shadow." He grimaced at the soft laugh that surrounded him and poked a stick into the fire, wishing he could use it as a brand and slap his witty companion with it a few times.

"You could try, of course, but I imagine you wouldn't appreciate the result as much as the idea."

He sighed. "You're in a disgustingly cheerful mood today."

"And you, my dear Ricker, are as cross as you have ever been. I find the consistency soothing."

Ricker watched as the shadows thrown by the flickering flames writhed. "Restless?"

"I am disappointed in you. As usual."

"Hmph."

"So eager to kill. So eager to slay..."

"Enough, Shadow. You spoke your piece earlier today."

"Oh, I have only begun to speak my piece. It is a large diatribe ranging from the foolishness of mankind in general to your blatant and prejudiced stupidity."

He resisted the urge, strong as it was, to roll his eyes skyward. Years spent in the company of this vocal shadow had allowed Ricker to become accustomed to the brash opinions offered when they were least desired. Unfortunately, even after so long a time of practice, he was still unable to remain unaffected by the words the shadow spoke that cut too close to festering wounds.

When Ricker had first been spoken to by the ghost, he thought that he had finally lost his mind.

Only he could hear the words that echoed inside his head as though they were uttered from the furthest end of a long tunnel. The creature that lingered by him despite his reluctance to such companionship was not a figment of his imagination, however. Shadow had once been a living human being, but the times in which he lived were not kind, and his life ended sooner than it would have otherwise, or so the creature said. He would not tell Ricker what happened after he died, or who he had been before he was murdered; he only knew that Shadow had remained as a spirit on the world, able to speak to those he chose to, and take form in the shadows of living creatures, a mere silhouette of the person he had been when he passed.

For whatever reason, the ghost had chosen to follow Ricker around as he traveled across the northern regions. It wouldn't be so bad if the ghost didn't insist on complaining excessively about Ricker's line of work, and everything that it entailed. It grew increasingly annoying as it continued, and as Shadow was *already dead*, there was nothing Ricker could do to cease the spirit's whining.

Not that he would have ended Shadow's life were he alive. At the very least, though, he would have been able to gag him.

"You should sleep."

"Are you concerned for me, Shadow?"

"Someone needs to make certain you do not drive yourself into unconsciousness. You will certainly make no effort to do so yourself, and thus I am left to suffer the responsibility."

"How positively horrid for you."

Shadow did not speak, and Ricker frowned, his eyes scouring the ground for a familiar-shape. A dark patch of long, frazzled mane caught his attention, and he found the top of his companion's head, decorated in a large top hat. The black shadow of a face was blank, which was unusual.

"Are you asleep?"

A sigh drifted through his mind like an exasperated breeze. *"The dead do not sleep."* Two eyes opened in the silhouette's face – almond-shaped sockets of pure white light contrasted against the darkness of the shadow's form. *"Sleep, Ricker. You will need it to find this DeathSpeaker."*

"I thought you were against my hunting the boy." He chucked another two pieces of wood on the fire and watched sparks leap for the sky.

"You will hunt him regardless of my opinion, and you will find him, regardless of any interference. And there will *be interference."*

Ricker glanced at the shadow to see his eyes had closed again, the fingers of his left hand clutching the rim of the top hat. "How do you know?"

"Because I am meant to. Now, sleep."

The eyes of the dark creature remained closed, and he knew he would get no information from Shadow. Unable to contest the good advice of the ghost, Ricker slept.

II

The dirt was like silt and rose up in a brown cloud around their feet as they made their way through the deserted town. Houses and buildings that might once have been shops were charred black from a fire that had long since gone cold. What buildings remained standing did so precariously, edges white and flaking in the hazy sunlight, while others lay in heaps of rotting rubble on the ground.

Decades prior, the town had flourished, filled with farmers who worked the fields and raised animals bred for safe consumption. Water poisoned with death would eventually move into the area and nourish the grasses on which the animals fed. One of the heifers would eat grasses that flooded her system with poison. Her calf would suckle on teats tainted with death, and the feces dropped by these calves would be spread over crops to help fertilize them. Bane would grow and bloom, and the farmers would pluck death from vines and stalks, and they'd eat toxic vegetables, and feed them to their cattle.

And death spread like wildfire in a windstorm.

"They burnt this town t' the ground when the plague came again, didja know that?"

Trudging across the dusty, ash-strewn ground, a tall, thin man looked back at his captive, dark strands of hair hanging in his face. The boy he tugged along stumbled behind him, silent as a dead wind. He kept his eyes focused downward, his head bowed, and the man just turned around and kept walking, pulling the boy behind.

"A coupla them that wasn't too sick knew what was hap'nen. They locked alluh the townsfolk up in their homes, and they lit the town up. One giant fireball ya could see from the mountains – a bonfire o' human corpses ya could smell for *miles*. The people who set the fires kilt themselves so they wouldn't pass the plague, an' they died fast. But there was some people still alive in those buildings."

The man turned around again, and this time his thin lips were stretched in a smile that bared yellowed teeth. "They didn't die quick." He giggled a high, quick laugh that cut through the silent air of the ashen town. The boy flinched away from the sound, but the man's long fingers kept a tight hold on his wrist, and he pulled the boy forward with a sharp jerk that had him flying into the man's arms.

He twitched as a long arm curled around him, thin fingers gripping the back of his neck in a too-tight grip. The man leaned down and grinned at him, breathing rancid breath into his face. He tried to turn his head away, but the fingers on the back of his neck tightened painfully, and the man reached up with his other hands and ran the tips of his dirty fingers over the wire that sewed the boy's lips firmly together. The grin stayed firm on the man's face.

"But people like ya... yar different. "Ya got the Dark Plague, but it didn't kill ya. It *can't* kill ya. Yar worse than dead. Yar Plague-Cursed."

The boy said nothing, and the man eventually released the hold he had on his neck and grabbed his wrist again, pulling sharply to make the boy walk fast behind him. The fingers that were wrapped tight again around his wrist were painful, but the boy gave no indication.

He'd been a prisoner for two days now, dragged across a countryside he did not know. He

23

had no shoes to wear, and the terrain they traveled was often harsh. The boy's feet hurt from being cut and from dirt being caught in healing wounds. He could not voice a complaint for the wires that bound his mouth, but even his face remained stoic in the wake of the man's treatment of him. Oh, he had shed tears. His eyes still burned and his face was sticky from the tears that had dried on them, but they had been shed in grief, rather than pain. The memory of his master's final cries and the pungent scent of blood as sharp as its crimson color cut his memory, but the tears he had shed for the man who raised him had been mocked by his kidnapper.

Mortimer did not know the name of the man who held him captive, nor did he know the real reason for his abduction. From tales the man had told him in mockery of his current state, the boy only knew that his kidnapper was working for someone else, fetching a wire-bound DeathSpeaker for his master. For what reason, he did not know, but he knew he would find out.

Twice now, he had tried to escape, and twice he had failed. Like his tears, the man who held him captive had mocked his attempts as both foolish and futile, and he had not tried again.

He had not given up yet, but it was clear that the man who held him was prepared to hold a small boy captive, and aware of what advantages his size would give him. He had been prepared both times that the boy attempted to escape, and making a third attempt from nothing would likely have the same result. He didn't know if he would ever have a chance before they reached wherever the man was taking him, but the boy would be on the lookout for his captor to let down his guard. He didn't know where he would go if he got free – he didn't even know where he was – but he would run, far away from the man who held him and his waiting master.

"My master's gonna fix that for ya, Mort," the man said, as he pulled the boy along. "He's gonna take the curse offa ya."

Mortimer kept his eyes on the ground as he was forced to follow the man, refusing to look up to see the unpleasant grin he was sure was on his captor's face.

"He's gonna make ya all better."

Two days ago, his master had been killed, and the life of silence he had planned to live in the church was taken from him. In less than a week, he would turn ten, and the wires that bound his lips would unwind, leaving him free and able to speak.

And when a DeathSpeaker speaks, all who hear die.

III

"She was born with her mouth sewn shut. Oh, sir, please... how can this be?"

His mouth was set into a firm scowl as he walked beside the chattering man. The other was wringing his hands in nervousness as he continued to talk, begging for an explanation as to how his daughter, his new baby girl, could be such an abominable creature.

"Does she know?"

"My wife?" The man looked at him, eyes wide and hair in disarray. "N-no, no. Em- the baby... she didn't cry, you know. She couldn't. The wire—"

"Let me see it."

Ricker followed the man into a small room set off from all the others. It was sparsely lit with candles, no fireplace here to provide either warmth or light. A table sat in the center of the room – the only piece of furniture. Upon the table, wrapped in a blanket, was the newborn baby.

He stepped up to the table and stared down at the creature. The face was pink and smooth, a waft of hair standing almost straight up from an otherwise bald head. The tiny nose was upturned slightly, similar than the man's who stood behind him. Two tiny pink lips were held fast together by a thin, shining black wire sewn through them. The baby had been born in such a way, as all DeathSpeakers were. It was their Mark.

"Leave me with it." There was no movement behind him and Ricker turned to glare at the man, who was staring at him in confusion. "Are you deaf? Leave me."

"Why?" Ricker's eyes narrowed and the hands started wringing again. "Right, right, yes. I'll just be – outside, then." The man quickly fled the room, shutting the door tightly behind him. Ricker waited a moment, watching to make sure the door was not going to open again, before he turned back to the table. Slipping his hands beneath the folds of the blanket, he picked the child up.

It was not a chore for him to find the right way to hold it. It would not be the first time that he held a child. One hand under its back, the other supported its neck as he held the small body against his chest. He stared down dispassionately at the thing in his arms. Blue eyes stared back at him, overly-large and too innocent. His own eyes narrowed.

He held the child for a moment, fingers moving gently over the soft skin. He did not look in those large blue eyes, but kept his focus on the wire binding the child's lips together. His fingers were gentle as they moved, slipping over delicate skin. He supported the child's neck with a gentle hand. He was careful to be always gentle. Gentle as he held them, gentle as he smoothed their skin, and gentle, so gentle–

Snap.

–as he killed them.

Ricker opened the door and stepped back into the hall. The other man was waiting for him, still looking nervous and confused. Ricker handed him the bundle of blankets in his arms and the man took them gently – so gently.

"My condolences to you and your wife, sir. It is never easy, to lose a child."

The man's eyes flashed to the blankets in his arms. His eyes widened before his head snapped up

again, but not like the child's head had. "You-
you—"

But Ricker turned around and walked away,
out of the house and away from the wails of a
mother who had never felt the breath of her child,
and a father who would keep his secret.

He clutched the severed wire in his hand. He
had secrets that he would keep, as well.

Ricker bolted into consciousness, throwing himself to his feet with a shrieked curse. He screamed as he attacked the fire ring, kicking ash and hot coals across the ground until there was nothing left of them to kick about and then he stormed back and forth madly, like a caged beast, snarling curses.

When he had found some semblance of calm, he turned to find Shadow reflected against the ground, sitting in a cross-legged position and appearing to be sipping from a teacup. He released the teacup, seeing as Ricker's tantrum was done. It was whisked back into another shadow from which it had been formed and the shade placed his hands delicately in his lap.

"Nightmares again, Ricker?"

"Shut up, you smarmy bastard."

"Ah. A bad one, I see. Which was it this time, Ricker? The newborn baby whose neck you broke? Or perhaps you're remembering the death of an older child. Do you still dream of coming home to find a pair of dead blue eyes?"

Howling, Ricker leapt at the shade, landing heavily on the ground and slamming his fists into the dirt. Shadows writhed beneath him like a bed of serpents as he clawed at the ground, his teeth snapping in rage and spit flying from his mouth as he snarled curses he did not remember thinking. He tumbled across the ground, flinging dirt into the air as he kicked and scratched at the earth until he had dug trenches with his heels and broken his fingernails into a cracked and bleeding mess on each hand. Lying on his stomach, he breathed heavily, each exhale sending up a cloud of dust that scurried away from him.

"Damn you, Shadow," Ricker whispered.

He saw the darkness beneath him move, and then Shadow stretched out before him. His face was just inches from Ricker's, the white eyes not glowing quite as brightly as they had the previous night. Ricker watched the silhouette of a top hat being delicately replaced on the shadow's head.

"I'm afraid your tirade offers little in the way of effect, Ricker. I am, after all, already dead." Ricker said nothing in reply to this, though Shadow waited, making a show of dusting off his arms. *"I was merely asking for the purpose of helping you to accept that you still do have a conscience – gods know how – and that you should, of course, listen to it."*

Ricker pushed himself to his feet as the shadow dusted off the back of his tailcoat. After he had brushed off his leggings, the shade moved to match Ricker's stance – straight-backed, his arms crossed over his chest. He paused a moment before speaking again. *"I daresay that memory cost you a fair bit of guilt. That's not to mention the original action, itself."*

"Do you have anything of worth to say this morning, Shadow, or should I just tune you out?" Ricker's voice sounded weary now, rather than annoyed. This did not stop Shadow from speaking his mind.

"Well, I suppose I could tell you that you talk in your sleep – mumble, really. Do you have something against blue eyes, Ricker?"

Cursing under his breath, Ricker grabbed his bag from the ground and slung it over his shoulder, before turning away from Shadow and striding off.

"I should probably mention, of course, that there was someone here last night."

Ricker stopped and took a moment to think before he turned around to face the shade. He had to look at the ground, of course, because there was nothing here for the shadow to be cast against. "Someone?"

"They did not come close enough for me to see them," Shadow said, and his tone now lacked the flippancy it had previously contained. *"I have some freedom to move in your shadow, but it is still bound to you and I dare not move too far from you without breaking our connection."*

The connection was not necessary for either of them, Ricker knew. Although Shadow insisted on burdening Ricker with his presence, the ghost had… existed for some length of time before they had encountered one another. Ricker rather thought his own life had been a great deal less complicated before the shade had entered it.

Shadow kept himself close to Ricker, however, and did not allow the man to be free of him. Oh, the shade would argue that it was because the connection allowed him to speak mentally to Ricker whereas he otherwise would have been forced to speak aloud, but he knew better than that. He did not know the ghost's real purpose for hounding him so fiercely other than sadistic enjoyment, but the shade remained regardless of Ricker's failure to understand.

"Did you see which way they'd gone, at least?"

"I do have eyes, Ricker." He ignored the ghost's tone. *"Nearing dawn, they headed south of here."*

"Near dawn... we shouldn't be far behind them, then." Ricker studied the sky, even though he knew that he rose every morning just past the sun's breaking the horizon. He turned his attention to the ghost again. "You're sure you don't know who they are?"

"I said they were too far away for me to see them," Shadow said, studying his hand as though bored with the topic. *"You did not ask who they were."*

"Shadow..."

"Although, I can't be certain of their identity. Still, to see a man with a young boy as his companion... and the firelight did glimmer nicely off of those wires."

"Shadow! The DeathSpeaker was here last night and you didn't wake me?"

"I thought you needed the sleep."

"Sha..." Ricker cut off his exclamation with a growl, grinding his teeth together as he paced back and forth. "South of here, you said."

"That was the direction they took, yes. If memory serves, it will take us toward the Undeadlands."

Ricker grunted in affirmation, but said nothing else.

The Undeadlands. Certainly not the most pleasant of places to find oneself in need of traveling. The name was something of a misnomer; there was nothing there that had died and come back, and no zombies roamed the wastelands that

31

the world had become. Rather, the Undeadlands was made up mostly of forest. Although the forests might appear to be dead at a glance, life had grown to thriving proportions there, and it was for that reason that the Undeadlands was reluctantly entered. Miles and miles of forest, filled with plants that had evolved to survive nuclear fallout, the Dark Plague, and then a world where there was not enough sunlight to sustain the vegetation of ages before. Ricker would be lucky if he only managed to run into some new type of poisonous vine.

He didn't say anything as he turned and headed off. The sun tried futilely to burn through the hazy sky on his right as he made his way southward, following whoever had been there the night before.

"You realize that it's possible you're walking into a trap."

Ricker muttered something low under his breath. Shadow didn't seem bothered to not be spoken to directly.

"They'll know, of course, what you're after, now that they've seen you. Your presence is not something easily mistaken. He will have seen you and know you are coming after the DeathSpeaker, and he will do all he can to stop you taking the boy."

"You told me last night that there would be interference." Ricker didn't look back to see Shadow nod. "You did not tell me it would be enough to stop me, and I can assure you that it won't. I will end that DeathSpeaker, and I'll even take the damn necklace back to Father Thomas. We'll have three more to hunt down after that."

"How lovely, these dreams you have of infanticide."

32

Ricker pinched the bridge of his nose lightly, before dropping his arm and glaring at the ghost. "I won't be stopped."

"You're right, Ricker. One such as you must stop themselves." Ricker rolled his eyes and kept on walking. *"You must find the strength to stop yourself."*

~*~

The journey southward held little in the way of interest. Ricker had chosen to ignore Shadow, and the shade, for his part, had accepted this and kept his comments (mostly) to himself.

Rarely, Ricker would pass a bit of vegetation that had attempted to grow in the dead land, shriveled and dry as beetle husks poking out of the ground.

As he walked, the dust of the dead earth rose up around him, as though mimicking the lingering smog that clouded the skies even years after the wars had gone. It obscured everything behind him from view, including the shadow that followed in his wake. It was in these moments that Ricker wanted so very desperately to speak up and ask the ghost a question, for when the dust blocked his eyes from finding even the glowing white gaze of that dead creature, Ricker felt more alone than he ever had before.

He did not speak, however, for he knew the consequences of such an action. The shade would reference the weakness again some time in the future, were he to do so, as a form of blackmail or teasing, and Ricker would not show the ghost one of the only cracks in his armor that the incorporeal creature could manipulate. So he kept silent and walked the lonely path through dying lands in search of the man and boy that Shadow had seen that previous night, burdened by the presence of the ghost, and his silence.

"There is a town in the distance."

And his lack of it.

"A town?" Ricker asked, stopping for a moment to shield his eyes from the still-blinding rays of the hazy sun. "How can you see so far?" He scanned the horizon but spotted no signs of a village nearby.

"I am dead, Ricker," the Shadow replied, deadpan. *"I am not so bound as you by the limitations of the living."*

"Oh, how jealous I am of your immobile heart."

"'tis not immobile, Ricker. It must merely be moved by means other than yours."

Ricker scowled at the insult. "How far is this town?"

"We should reach it by nightfall." Ricker sighed in defeat and began walking despite the protestations of his feet. *"That's much better than by sunrise."*

"If only *I* could float."

"Next we see a river, I will be sure to properly teach you how."

"You'd like it very much if I was dead like you, wouldn't you, Shadow?"

"As they say, my dearest Ricker – misery loves company."

"Then may I find someone else soon who will join me in bearing your presence." He scowled at the mirth in the shadow's laughter and walked on.

As it happened, they arrived shortly before dusk. The town itself was quite small, but the farmlands that surrounded it made up for that, stretching for miles in all directions. Wooden fences placed in the ground by hard work alone surrounded the pastures that Ricker had to traverse as he made his way following Shadow's direction. Eventually, the pasture he had been walking through ended at a fence that bordered a dirt road, and Ricker began to follow that toward the village he could see in the distance.

At one point, they were passed by a large wagon. The man sitting on the seat of it was holding a set of reins. The cow harnessed to the wagon let out a loud mooing as they passed, waving its head in Ricker's direction as though chastising him from walking down the same path the wagon was traveling.

As the wagon passed, Ricker glanced into the back of it. It was filled heavily with bright orange pumpkins. No doubt they were being taken to the nearest city, or perhaps another village, to trade for other goods. As large as the pastures were, and considering the size of the pumpkins, this village was probably prosperous, and Ricker suspected he would see yet more wagons before he left. Perhaps he could find one headed in the same direction and convince the driver to let him ride a while.

Despite the short distance to the town, the walk seemed long. Perhaps it was the silence, but it was only once he had walked miles down the dirt road and passed more cows than he cared to take a guess at that did he finally reach the village.

Farm villages were not rare in the world, but ones as large as this were not a frequent passing for him. In the wake of the Dark Plague, the animals had faired no better than the humans. Many had died, a great many species wiped out completely, with those that remained oft-tainted with disease that left them alive, but useless to the humans who had survived the wave of sickness. Ricker had heard of many farmlands over the years that had attempted to become a safe haven for those passing through; a place where people could gather to find home and safety in a world that rarely offered either.

More often than not, these villages managed to thrive for a time, only to find amongst them a single sick beast that spread disease as fire spreads across dead fields. Whole farming villages wiped out nearly overnight. Ricker had heard of it happening so often, in fact, that he did not look at this town, with its many healthy cattle, as a safe haven. Rather, his eyes sought out an hourglass in the skies above the village, so that he could count the grains of sand that remained to fall, telling the world how long this village had before it, too, collapsed into ruin.

"You have such faith *in people, Ricker."*

"I know what people are, Shadow."

"No, I don't think you do, actually," the ghost murmured, just before a pretty young girl in a tan dress walked toward him. Ricker kept his frequent scowl on his face as the girl neared him, and studied her closely.

She had short blonde hair that reached just to the base of her ears, and light green eyes that did not hold any suspicion for him.

"Good evening, sir," she greeted, stopping a few feet before him. "Is there something I can help you with?"

The girl appeared healthy. She was thin, with a bright light in her eyes, and skin that was pale, but with the slight glow to it that showed she spent much of her day in the presence of the sun's cool light. Ricker searched her face for a grimace of pain, her eyes for the yellow of jaundiced disease, or the pleading glance of despair, but he found none of the things he sought. Here before him stood a young girl with innocence still glimmering like rare gems in her eyes, and he found that he was drawn to her as he had been drawn to no one in years, and that he pitied her with more of a heart than he knew he still bore. He knew that all of the innocence she held within her young heart would cause her such pain when it was stolen away by the truth and cruelty of life.

"Do you have a room available?"

"A few left, sir, yes," the girl said, and took a step to the side, motioning at the building behind her. "The inn is above the tavern, sir."

The tavern and inn, Ricker saw, was one of the largest buildings in the village; it appeared that only the stable outranked it in size. The wood was worn by weather and many bodies slipping in and out of it over the years, but Ricker could see the craftsmanship was strong, the building well cared for. The second floor, where the rooms were, bore windows that were open to emit light as though it would warm and please the interior. The door to the tavern downstairs was closed, but still the scent of warm food wafted out and to Ricker's nostrils. He willed his stomach not to rumble, but his mouth, too, demanded something more substantial than dried fruit and jerky.

"What is the cost?" Ricker eyes, his eyes returning to the girl before him.

"The room costs nothing, sir." Ricker raised an eyebrow. "Those who pass through the village with peace are free to stay the night and travel in the morning. The food, sir, costs what you have to give."

"What I have to give. You ask for payment based on talents?"

"Well now, that should be easy for you." Shadow's voice echoed in Ricker's mind, mocking and disgusted. *"Simply ask the girl if there is anyone they would rather have dead and I'm certain you'll eat like a king."*

Mind your tongue, Shadow, Ricker thought fiercely.

"'tis a flapless, immobile thing, Ricker, like the hearts of some who shan't be moved as still they breathe."

"I have little to offer in the way of trade."

"What you have to offer shall be enough. Have you a talent, sir?"

"Death."

"I once turned my hand at the crafting of weapons."

The girl's eyes lit up brighter still, the excitement in them clear. "You were a Weaponsmith, sir?" Ricker merely inclined his head in response, the girl's delighted smile catching him off guard. "I shall fetch my father. He can speak with you."

The girl turned and rushed back to the inn, clearly pleased to be able to do so, and Ricker was quite surprised that it was out of excitement and not fear. A strange village he found himself stumbled into.

"You may wish to consider bearing your Mark."

"And why would I wish to risk my stay here by doing something so foolish?" Ricker kept his voice quiet as he spoke, his lips barely moving.

"Due to the fact that the discovery of such deceit after having let you into their home will not likely go well for you."

"You speak as though this discovery is doomed to happen."

"It is."

Ricker didn't have a chance to ask Shadow if the ghost thought himself a god, as the door to the inn opened again, and the girl stepped out and then stood to the side, waiting for a man to follow her.

The man's eyes were lime green like the girl's, his hair a pale gold, but those were the only similarities as far as he could tell. Where the girl was slender with pale skin and eyes of naïve belief, this man was a muscled creature with skin brown and red from heat and calloused work. Where the girl's gaze was innocent, this man's was hard, much like Ricker had grown used to seeing in those who had witnessed the true cruelties of life.

"I hear you're a Weaponsmith." The man's voice was a loud grumble, like the chug-chugging of an engine, or the low growl of a large, hairy beast; not something to anger, at the least.

"I was," Ricker corrected idly, "long ago."

"Have you still a hand for it."

"Two hands," Ricker said, flexing his fingers. The skin of his hands remembered the feel of leather, the heat of a forge, and the steady tingling that ran through his bones as he held a blade to a grindstone. "Neither of them knows how to forget."

The man nodded sharply, his matter-of-fact manner not allowing Ricker time to pause and ponder long. "You forge something for me and I'll feed you tonight and in the morning, ere you leave."

Ricker tilted his head slowly forward in a nod of acceptance. "What had you in mind?"

"I want a blade, Weaponsmith, strong enough to cut off the Mark of a PlagueCursed."

IV

The heat from the fire stirred the sensation
of warmth against the left side of Mortimer's back.
With his eyes closed, he could concentrate hard
enough to locate the exact point where the circle of
warmth ended. He could feel the heat from his
shoulder to just below his elbow, and just above his
left hip. It reached almost to his spine, on the left
side, and he thought some small portion of his left
ear was warmed by the distant flames. His
concentration broke the illusion of being warm at
all, however. The chill on his right side was too
great.

Mortimer shivered.

Behind him, there was a shuffle of
movement and then a loud sound as another log was
tossed onto the fire. Sparks erupted into the air,
mocking the stars for their hidden existence, before
winking out themselves. Mortimer tried to ignore
the tightening feeling that had been growing in his
stomach since he had been taken captive and stolen
away from his home in the church. There was
something wrong with him.

A stick clacked against the tree to the right
of Mortimer and he flinched away from it, jerking
on his bindings. His kidnapper laughed.

"Keep still, stupid boy!"

Mortimer had been shuffling, trying to find a
comfortable position, but it wasn't possible. Even
with his mouth still bound by the wires, his
kidnapper didn't trust him. He had forced Mortimer
to hold his hands together above his head so that he
could bind them to the thick limb of a long-dead
tree. The limb was at such a height that Mortimer

41

had to place his weight firmly on his knees, his back straight and tense, as any attempt to relax would cause the rope that bound him to dig painfully into his wrists.

His kidnapper had done this on purpose, he knew. The man had made it quite clear that he did not like Mortimer. Circumstances as they were, Mortimer felt the same in regards to his captor.

His dislike of the man who held him as a captive would no doubt escalate in the future to something more inclined toward loathing for all the man had done. Despite his present state, Mortimer still felt adrift within nothingness, a vast fog surrounding him as though he were caught in the web of a dream. The world about him, everything that was happening and had happened within the last few days was surreal in his mind, and had surely never happened.

It would hit him, eventually.

It would happen suddenly, like a blow to the chest, striking him down and dropping him to his knees. He would realize in a moment all that had happened, all that the man had done, all that he had lost. It would tear him from the confused haze in which he now dwelled and drop him into an icy river of realization, ruin him with anguish and understanding. Part of him knew that it would come, and the knowledge, however subconscious, of this monstrous comprehension rising swiftly toward his consciousness filled him with a sense of dread that Mortimer mistakenly took for being fear of his current predicament.

But all would be revealed in time.

"I s'pose yar wond'ren what my master 'tends to do with ya, boy."

Mortimer did not move his head. Faced away from the fire, he could not see the man from his position, no matter how far he tried to crane his neck. He could hear the grin in the man's voice, the pleasure he took in antagonizing his captive. Mortimer made no indication that he had even heard the man.

"He has plans for ya. He's been waitin' for me to bring ya to him, an' then'ee can put 'is plans inta action. He jus' needs yew, boy. Yar the final ingredient." The man chuckled, a low grumble of a laugh in the back of his throat.

"I do hope you do not make a pleasure of revealing his plans to *everyone*, Louis."

At the first syllable of this new voice, Mortimer had jerked in surprise, his bindings biting into his wrists. He heard, too, the heavy sound of a body hitting the ground. His kidnapper had also been surprised.

"Hester. Yar out late."

Mortimer remained still, hearing his only available sense toward the two people behind him. Listening closely, he could hear the slight tremor in his captor's voice – was he afraid of the woman who had arrived?

"I have no fear of the dark, Louis. Can the same be said of you?"

Her voice was distinctly feminine, rolling off a tongue as smooth as glass, and just as sharp. Mortimer could feel his heart vibrating in his chest, racing against the bonds that held him, as though if it beat fast enough, he could break free of them and escape the reach of this woman. She terrified him for reasons he could not directly place, but he could feel the terror well within his soul and he knew that she was someone he wished desperately not to be around. Only the wires that bound his mouth kept him from screaming, but it was his fear, and not his bonds, that kept him from fleeing.

"There's not a thing out here to fear and ye know that."

"Oh, I know well what lurks here." The movement of cloth and the sound of the earth beneath the weight of a human foot alerted Mortimer to the woman's nearness, but he didn't dare change his own position. He hardly breathed. "I see you have actually managed to complete your task. I would not normally be impressed, but as it is you..."

"Whaddaya want, Hester? I'm keepin' time."

"Must all of my actions contain an ulterior motive? Is it not possible that I came merely to check on you?"

"To spy on me, like. Ya don't hold any love for me, don't pretend ya do."

"I shall not burden you with any such lies. I will admit to much doubt in regards to your abilities. I did not think you able to complete such a mission without aid, though as you said, you are doing a remarkable job of keeping within your time limit. Master will be pleased."

"He oughta be. It weren't easy, fetchin' the boy."

"Come, Louis, you stole him from a church. You had not needed to invade a prison or barracks. Surely it cannot have been that difficult to stave off the priests that roam those stonework halls, or did you find yourself faced against some pious assailant? I would dearly love hear tell of your besting by a nun."

"I was told not to be seen, and I weren't seen but for the boy's keeper. Him I dealt with as I's told to, so ya can run on back to ar master and let'im know I ain't been caught."

There was a silence after this that held steady beyond their campfire. Even the forest was like death to Mortimer's ears, not a whisper of life beyond the tree he was held fast to. Only the sounds that linger even in death painted the silence of the world; the swish of the wind through leafless branches, and the crackle of the burning fire.

Mortimer's body quivered lightly as he stood on his knees. His eyes were focused on the tree before him, but he did not see it through the blur of tears that filled his eyes, and the memory that took his mind.

Mortimer stared down at his hand, uncomprehending. The scent of copper met his nose, burning in a flame that warmed his hands. They were scarlet-soaked, as hot as bathwater; Mortimer stared down at them, wondering when he had trailed his hands through paint.

"There ya are, boy. Bin lookin' fer ya." A hand grabbed the back of his robes and yanked hard on them, pulling him backward so he stumbled, his back ramming hard into another body. An arm curled around his stomach and he tried to pull away as a face appeared next to his, warm breath blowing on his right ear as the man spoke again.

"Yar a hard'n to find, boy, but no more hidin'." The man's lips pulled back, baring his teeth in Mortimer's face. "Ain't nothin' fer ya here, boy."

The man grabbed hold of Mortimer's wrist and forced him to follow as he began to leave the room. The man's hand slid over his skin, slick with the red liquid, and Mortimer felt the slightly heavier weight to his left sleeve. He glanced back, confused, as the man pulled him along, and saw his guardian lying on the floor, c-covered in pai-paint.

Mortimer closed his eyes tight as the man pulled him along.

Father Fabula was sleeping.

He... he was only s-sleeping.

Mortimer shivered, the smell of copper thick in his nostrils. His eyes were closed tightly as he tried to force the image of his guardian out of his mind. His left sleeve had fallen down to his elbow from the position he was in, but his right sleeve was sticking to the skin of his arm, held fast by a paint that had turned brown and begun to crack and chafe. He didn't want to remember why.

"You know what it is Master wishes the boy for, yet you leave him beyond the fire?" The woman's tone was reprimanding, and Mortimer could hear movement behind him. Her voice got closer as she spoke. "He will be ill if he remains so."

"Wha'see gonna catch? The Plague?" The man brayed at his own joke.

Mortimer's attention was on the woman, who had appeared at his side. In the shadows beyond the fire, he could not see much of her face, but her lips were held steady in a lack of expression, and her eyes glimmered hard amber in what they could catch of the firelight. Her hands were gloved with a rough leather that brushed hard over Mortimer's knuckles as she played with the ropes that held him.

"Why is he bound so, Louis? Do you fear him?"

"I dun fear wired lips, Hester, and ya know it."

"There is little reason, then, to leave him cold, faced toward the darkness." The woman undid the knot in the ropes and Mortimer pulled his arms away, sitting on his ankles as he massaged the red burns the rope had left on his arms.

"If'ee runs, Hester..."

"He will not run, will you, child?"

Mortimer glanced up at the woman through his lashes. He felt still, in his chest, the violent beating of his heart that told him he must flee her presence as quickly as a rabbit flees a fox. The frantic vibration of his heart told him, too, that he would never outrun her if he tried.

He shook his head.

"A wise child." Her voice had the sweetness of sugar dipped from a bowl of poison. She motioned toward the fire with one hand, and Mortimer tried not to scrabble as he made his way into the ring of light. He sat on the other side of the flames from his kidnapper, eyeing the man warily and holding his left wrist tightly. The man flashed him a rancid grin and Mortimer cringed, looking into the flames to try and escape sight.

"I see the boy does not hold the pendant." The woman knelt down on the ground near Louis, the position of piety not escaping Mortimer's notice. "I will be pleased to tell Master that you have failed him grievously and taken the wrong child."

"I ain't failed nothin'," Louis said, sticking a hand into his pocket and pulling out a necklace.

The cord was nothing more than a simple piece of leather, the two ends tied into a knot where they met. The middle of the cord was wrapped and knotted around a gem that outshone the fire and would make the hazy sunrise weep.

At a glance, it was a ruby; scarlet in color and gleaming like glass. Even a moment's study, however, revealed the gem to be something more. Where a ruby held layers darker than others, this gem bore no shadows. The crimson sphere would have shared the same shade as blood, but for the fact that it seemed to glow, both brighter and darker than the blood of a human. There were no scratches on it, but it was so perfectly shaped that it should have been impossible for the leather cord to remain wrapped around the upper part of the orb. Gleaming with scarlet light, it was a small star glowing in the palm of Louis' hand, but its pull was greater still than that of the sun, for Louis, Hester, and Mortimer were drawn to it, as all who saw it would be drawn to it. To take it, to use it...

"He did bear it, then, as Master said."

"Gave me a hard time, gettin' it offa him. The boy didn't wanna give it up. Started bawlin' when I pult it offa hi— ey!" Louis jerked violently away from the woman as she plucked the pendant from his grasp. "Watch where yar touchin'!"

Hester ignored him, holding the gem against the light of the fire and staring into it. "It is perfect," she said, her voice a quiet hum against the crackle of the fire. "It is just as he said."

"Ah, yeah, ar master told us right 'bout that. No'un gonna resist the glow of that'un. I kin sellit fer a good price even at the market, but I got someplace better I kin take it."

"What fool would buy a trinket when untainted food and water is so scarce?" Hester had pulled off the glove covering her left hand and now held the gem in bare fingers. Her amber eyes

48

glowed in the light of the fire as she studied how it retained its unearthly shine regardless of its proximity to the light of the fire.

"I got my places, and thar mine."

Louis eyed the woman's bare hand balefully, the longing in his eyes clear as they set upon the gem. Her eyes, however, were fixed with a deep fascination upon the jewel in her grasp as she rose to her feet and removed her other glove, dropping it to the ground. She cradled the false ruby in her hands as though it were a precious bit of water that she had but to drink to stave off all harm, her feet carrying her from where she had been standing before the fire, walking into the darkness that surrounded the little camp, concentration fully upon the jewel in her hands.

"Ar master said fetch the boy that had that pendant. He didn't say nothin' about wantin' it." Louis turned back to the fire in annoyance as the woman ignored his clear desire to have the stone back, glaring into the flames with furious exasperation.

"You are right, Louis. Master did not say anything to you of his desire for the jewel." She stopped behind him, slipping the jewel into her pocket as her eyes moved to the back of his head. "What occurs beyond its acquisition is none of your concern."

Mortimer flinched back as Louis suddenly stood. There was understanding and fear in his widening eyes.

Hester moved like a serpent.

Her left hand slipped beneath Louis' left arm and around his chest, as her right curled over his shoulder and grasped his throat.

Louis froze with a twitch. He made a sound like a hiccough of breath had been caught in his lungs by a mousetrap. For a moment, he was frozen in Hester's embrace, her arms curled about him, his face pale in fear.

Mortimer stared at the two of them, frozen in terror. His eyes were fastened to the face of his kidnapper, locked onto the wide eyes, the nostrils flared in fear, the mouth that hung slightly open revealing just the tips of his top teeth, yellowed. Mortimer watched as the light of the fire reflected in the man's eyes like a violent flicker of candlelight. The pale skin of the man's face greyed, as though the fire had dimmed, and then the lips moved as though speaking a quiet word.

A breath of air whisked out through silent lips, and Louis suddenly sagged in Hester's arms.

She released her hold on his throat and stepped back, her arm sliding out from around his chest. The corpse hit the ground with a heavy thud, but Hester stepped over the body as though it were a rotting log. Mortimer shivered as he watched her calmly pick up her leather gloves from where they lay by the fire and pull them on as though nothing had happened.

Just for a moment, he glimpsed a black circle on the palm of her right hand, the sphere appearing to have shattered outward, black veins splintering through her skin. Then her gloves were on, and Mortimer shut his eyes tight when she stepped in front of him.

"He was expendable, child."

Mortimer flinched at the title she gave him. It was the same word that his guardian had used to refer to him, but her voice held none of the warmth that had been present in Father Fabula's.

"I have need of you, child, as an angler a worm. They will come hunting you, and give themselves to Master's plan." Mortimer glanced up at the woman to find her lips had spread into a smile sharper than a sword made of diamond shards.

Hester grabbed hold of Mortimer's arm and pulled him to his feet. Tears flushed to his eyes as he tried to escape her hold, the image of his own face taking on the grey of death too clear to his mind's eye.

"I will come for you, child," Hester said, and Mortimer looked at her. For a moment, his eyes were drawn to her amber gaze as they had been to the pendant now held in her pocket. "I will come for you as Death comes for all her creatures." Her smile was monstrous. "Now run, Mortimer."

He stumbled backward, as his name echoed off her lips.

"Let me hunt you, child."

Mortimer turned and followed the shrieked advice of his heart, hammering in his chest.

"Run, child."

He ran.

V

Standing on hot stone, surrounded by the tools of his trade, Ricker closed his eyes and let the familiarity of the scene wash over him. The scent of ground metal met his nostrils, bringing to mind the sound of air rushing through hot coals, a blade sparking as steel met stone. The forge was before him, the red of the coals glowing so brightly he could see them through his eyelids. The heat wafted at his face, and in his mind he could hear the bellows blowing air, the coals lighting up golden, as though before him were a treasure chest, and the image of metal softening, glowing, until it was ready for him to work it. Ricker's hand tightened around the hammer in his right fist and he opened his eyes.

He had work to do.

There was a hammer in his hand and steel ore at his fingertips, waiting for him to make his decision. Should he craft a sword, long and double-edged, as sharp as diamonds, or a single-handed blade – a scimitar, dull on one side with curved death on the other? Better yet, a dagger, small and silent, like the tooth of a predator, gleaming with intent to rip and tear. Perhaps a simple knife would do, a handle to fit a man's grip, and a one-sided blade with a serrated edge fit for cutting through flesh and bone.

Ricker rubbed the pad of his thumb up and down the wooden handle of the hammer as he thought. There had been no request for any specific type of blade beyond its ability to remove the Mark of a PlagueCursed. That left a great deal to interpretation and didn't give him much boundary.

There were too many types of blades to choose from, but there weren't very many Marks.

The PlagueCursed had existed for centuries – humans born altered by the devastation wrought on the world. Throughout the centuries of knowing they existed, of fearing and hating them, there had only been six different types discovered, and each type with their own Mark to distinguish them to the eyes of others.

Ricker reached up and touched his throat, thinking about the Mark present there. Black as ink, it appeared as though perhaps a crow, mutated by the presence of his dark power, had settled, jagged-edged wings spread, upon his throat.

He sighed.

"You should reveal that, before they find out later of their own accord."

"I have no intention of revealing myself, accidentally or otherwise."

"No one intends to accidentally do anything."

Ricker pulled the chain to activate the bellows and allowed the sound of air rushing up through the forge to drown out anything more Shadow might have to say. He could continue to speak directly into Ricker's mind if he truly wished to be heard, but the ghost's current prattling was little more than obligatory teasing on his part.

The hot coals brightened, heat flaring off of them and wafting violently against Ricker's face. He squinted his eyes slightly against the sensation, familiar but missing for so long. In his peripheral vision, he saw Shadow flitting about on the floor.

"Made up your mind, have you?"

Ricker ignored the bait and picked up a steel ingot – a bar, much like what gold had been shaped into centuries prior, made of steel that had been melted down and cast into a form that made for easy transport. Using a pair of metal tongs with long legs, Ricker placed the ingot into the burning coals and leaned back against the support beam behind him, eyes closed.

This was such a familiar place, even though Ricker had never been here before. Not all forges were the same, but at the core, all good forges had similar equipment, the same potential to create great weapons, and the same feel about them. Like coming home.

Ricker opened his eyes to find the ingot was glowing bright orange. He removed it from the coals quickly, placing it on the anvil. Once it had cooled, he would put it back into the fire until it glowed with heat again, and then he would remove it to cool, before placing it back into the fire once more. The annealing process took a while, and to some people, could seem boring. For Ricker, however, the minutes of watching the metal heat and cool alternatively were the first truly peaceful moments he'd had in a long time.

The coals shuffled loudly as he placed the ingot back into them for the last time. The skin of his knuckles burned from his close proximity to the fire, and he was certain he could feel the hair on his arm being seared off.

Ricker glanced around the forge.

He'd taken a glimpse when he'd been shown where it was, but he had been distracted by the necessity of making certain he had the proper equipment. Now that he knew he had what he required and was in the process, he could take a moment to observe his surroundings.

The forgery was about as well-built as anything else in the town. Wooden boards worn by use and weather made up walls that wouldn't protect against the chill of the wind. Ricker was inclined to think that support beam he was leaning against had little to do with keeping the building steady. The shack might only be still standing because of the strength of the chimney that reached up through the ceiling from the coal pit where the ingot had turned a molten orange.

Removing the ingot from the fire, Ricker placed it on the anvil. Holding it down with the tongs, Ricker gripped the hammer tightly in his right hand and brought it down on the ingot.

The strike of metal on metal rang in Ricker's ears, white hot like a knife to his brain, and yet, too, cold. Ricker felt a chill race up his spine. He shook his head to quell the feeling of dread that filled him.

He brought the hammer down sharply again. There was a clang as the metal head of the hammer struck the ingot, making it ring against the anvil. The feel of the fire's heat was warming his chilled arms, so he ignored his breath of relief and brought the hammer down again.

The movements were as choreographed as a dance routine. Ricker's mind wandered as he worked, the rhythmic clanging of his hammer a drum march into memory. He thought back to the last time he had stood within a forge, crafting a weapon for a client. It had been a long time since he had felt the tools of his trade within his hands; too long since he had last used all that he knew to *create*.

The sound of boots on the stone floor of his workshop did not distract Ricker from the rhythm of his hand, as he brought the hammer down sharply

55

on the steel. Placed precisely over the edge of the anvil, the off-set section of the steel broke off. Ricker found himself smiling as the sounds of footsteps slowed, and he raised the blade to inspect it as a young boy stepped into the heat of the forge.

"I believe you have lessons to attend to."

He didn't need to look at the boy to know that there was a smile on his face, no doubt growing larger still. "You said you'd teach me how to create a blade today."

"Did I?" Ricker's lips pulled back from his teeth as his smile widened. "And what sort of blade would you want to create?"

"A basilard."

Ricker rolled his eyes. "Of course. You must be difficult, mustn't you?"

There was a giggle that made him grin. "Yes, Daddy."

The half-formed blade rang loudly as it struck the stone floor. Ricker let out a sound like a mewl and folded in on himself before dropping to the ground, a hand covering his face. His breath shook as he drew it in and he swallowed past the ash clogging his throat. He should have known something like this would have happened, using a forge after so long. He just wasn't used to the heat in the air, anymore, the sparks from the hammer strikes, the smell of shaved metal. It was... too much.

That was all.

Ricker rubbed his hands down his face, brushed the ash out of his eyes. He cleared his throat and drew a few steadying breaths.

It was just a knife. It wouldn't take him as long to craft as a sword, and then he could get away from the forge and find some fresh air, eat a hot meal, maybe get a drink of something stronger than water, if they had it here.

He could use something strong.

Ricker pushed himself to his feet, retrieving the cooling piece of steel from the floor. He placed it back on the anvil and found where he had dropped his hammer.

The sounds of metal striking metal filled the forge yet again. They would later be replaced by the hiss of water as a hot blade was rapidly cooled in a barrel, the scratching of a file on the edge, and the grinding of stone on steel.

Ricker continued to work, enveloped in the sounds of his trade, the heat of the fire, and the memory of what once had been. He would attribute his blurring vision and the wetness of his face to sweat, and it would never occur to him to wonder about the ghost that stood just beyond his peripheral vision, watching in silence.

~*~

The door to the inn creaked open slowly and Ricker stepped inside. It was not very late in the evening, but few people passed through the town and the inn didn't have many to house in addition to Ricker. He spared a brief glance at the tables and wondered how many of the patrons were locals keeping their seats at the bar out of curiosity about the visitors, rather than any need for housing here.

The small area in which there were tables for patrons to sit and eat was filled with the scent of roasting meat, the air thick with heat from the fire burning in the hearth to Ricker's left. The flames that licked at the blackened bricks of the fireplace left shadows dancing across the floor for him to traipse through.

Ricker ignored the stares that followed him as he moved toward the far end of the room, where he could see the bar that separated the dining area from the kitchens. The bar was long, stretching out nearly from one side of the room to the other, but the wood was unfinished and stained from alcohol and food that had been spilled onto it. Eventually, it would rot beneath the glasses it held and collapse onto the knees of the patrons and the aching feet of those who stood behind it.

Ricker eyed the three-legged stools that sat in front of the bar. They were short, as a necessity for their make, but also worn down by time and use, chipped in areas and burnt in a few others. His lip curling slightly, Ricker chose not to test his luck sitting down.

"Weaponsmith."

Ricker glanced up to find that the large man he had spoken to previously had come out from the kitchens. He gave Ricker a gruff nod of greeting and a searching gaze at his hands. Ricker resisted the temptation to roll his eyes.

"Innkeeper," Ricker said back, restraining his smirk as the man's eyes lifted up to his. The fact that he wasn't immediately corrected in his assumption assured Ricker that he had guessed correctly the man's profession. It was more than a little satisfying, too, to be able to turn the man's very to-the-point wording back onto him.

"There's a hot meal in the back," the innkeeper grumbled in his bear-like tone, "if you've finished my blade."

"Papa!" The young girl that Ricker had spoken to when he arrived in the town proper was standing behind her father, expression and tone one of exasperation. "He should still eat tonight. He might not be finished, yet."

"It's finished," Ricker said. There was a clatter as he tossed the newly-crafted weapon onto the bar. Not a loud sound, as would have been made by a heavy weapon, but yet more palpable because it was sustained. A heavy weapon would sooner have thudded into position, held fast by the force of its weight and gravity's call. The small blade that Ricker had created – for he had not created something at all large or long – hit the bar and rolled in a jumpy, bouncing fashion, until it did stop, slowing in a final spin on its hilt.

It was of a simple design; homely, in the way that the stained teeth of a hungry shark could be called homely. From the base of the cylindrical hilt to the tip of the blade, the knife was no longer than Ricker's hand. The blade itself was half the length of the hilt, formed into a fang-like shape, a smooth, easy curve across the top, with a sharper curve on the bottom that brought the knife to a sharp point. There was a small section of the bladed side of the knife, the inch closest to the hilt, which was serrated. The blade was fitted into a hilt made of wood, which Ricker had bound tightly with strips of leather to shield the wooden handle from the elements. In the light that flickered across the bar from the distant hearth's fire and what came from the kitchens, the hilt was a thing of darkness against the gleaming blade. It gave the already clearly-dangerous blade an appearance of ominous intent.

There was a moment of silence in which those behind the counter processed what they were seeing. The innkeeper recovered first

"Starve to death, Weaponsmith."

"I have done as you asked."

"You've crafted me a dagger when I asked—"

"You asked for a blade that can cut the Mark from a PlagueCursed." Ricker nodded toward the knife on the bar. "I have crafted you one. Now hold up your end of our bargain, or I will take my payment..." There was movement in Ricker's peripheral vision and he glanced to the Innkeeper's left. "...by other means."

"She's just a young girl!"

"What?" Ricker asked, his eyes flashing back to the innkeeper.

The man's fist lashed out with a suddenness that would have caught Ricker by surprise were he a lesser man. He shifted – minutely, but that was all that was needed – to the left, putting his weight on his left foot and reaching out to grab the blade from the bar. The innkeeper's fist impacted only air, and Ricker grabbed the man's extended arm, twisting it sharply until the man spun on instinct to try and combat the rise of pain.

"What the hell?" Ricker snarled, when he had the man bent backwards over the bar and his arm pressed lightly against the man's throat. He focused his attention upon the thumb of his left hand, which he had dug into a pressure point in the man's right shoulder, pinning him in place. His other hand held the knife that he had recently retrieved from the bar, the sharp edge pressed against the flesh of the innkeeper's inner forearm.

"We appear to be having something of a miscommunication," Ricker growled, his mouth just above the innkeeper's ear. "You asked for a blade that can perform a specific action, and I crafted it for you. I was offered board and meals, and I had expected to receive them. Instead, my work is left unrewarded and I am attacked. Someone has clearly not done their promised duty, and it doesn't seem to be me." He pressed the blade a little more firmly against the man's flesh, his skin turning white with blood loss around the edge of the blade.

"Perhaps the mistake lies in your paltry expectations of what I would be crafting. Were you hoping for a Falcata? The blade is too long to allow for the ease of movement you require. I would have crafted you a Kalis if I thought you intended to chop fish, but I believed you desired this blade for else."

He raised his eyes to meet with the larger man's, finding them still wide in surprise and perhaps fear. "Would you have preferred I craft you a Rapier? Were it any straighter, you would sooner sever a PlagueCursed from his Mark with a broom." He smirked. "But at least the hilt is pretty.

"Were I to know you would be so demanding after giving me so little to go on, I would have crafted you a Tachi and let you perform Sepukku and rid me of your egotistical *bitching*."

Ricker turned his attention back down to the blade in his hand and traced the tip of the knife over the skin of the man's arm. He heard the innkeeper swallow heavily, but was quietly impressed with his restraint.

"Now this? This is a skinning knife. It's not impressive in appearance, of course, but it makes up for that with its effectiveness. After all, most of the PlagueCursed you may encounter have Marks that taint their skin. In order to remove the Mark, it will be the flesh that you remove." He pressed the tip of the blade sharply into the man's arm and began to slowly trace it upward. The innkeeper let out a surprised breath at the feeling of his skin splitting, and Ricker watched a line of blood follow behind the blade, a drop sliding down the man's arm and leaving a pink trail behind.

"You see, skinning knives are used by hunters to remove the flesh from their prey. Part of the blade has a serrated edge to allow it to tear into the flesh, cutting an area in the hide were one can begin skinning. Of course," he added as an afterthought, "the tip is kept sharp so one can cut the abdomen of their catch, to expel the guts, when they need to carry the animal some distance. Humans are heavy creatures, you understand. Sometimes, it helps to lighten the load."

Ricker removed the knife from the man's skin, holding the slightly red blade in front of his eyes for inspection. "The blade is small because of your prey. You do not want to skin the whole hide of, say, a cow." He glanced back down at the innkeeper's face. "You want to cut off the skin of a PlagueCursed palm, or remove their tongue. The length of this blade allows for its easy manipulation." He laid the blade flat against the man's throat and watched his Adam's apple bob thickly as he swallowed.

"You see, you couldn't use a sword to remove the Mark of a DeathBreather and let him live, but with a small blade…" He moved the knife with a twisting, flipping grace over the innkeeper's jugular, never once cutting him, but allowing him to feel the fluid movements of the blade. "… you can maneuver easily into crevices, around obstacles, following a pattern." He pulled the blade back and smiled down at the innkeeper. "And people underestimate a weapon that is so very small."

Pulling back from the bar, Ricker allowed the innkeeper to stand up slowly. The man turned around and looked at him with a wary expression, wiping the thin line of blood off his arm.

Ricker held the knife out, hilt toward the innkeeper, the blade pinched between his fingers. "Of course," he said casually, "if you still believe I've crafted an inadequate weapon..." He raised an eyebrow.

"No, you've proven yourself quite well-informed about blades, Weaponsmith." The innkeeper hesitated only a moment, before reaching out and taking the blade. "I'll send my cook out with a meal for you."

"No need, Papa."

Ricker and the innkeeper both glanced to the man's left to find his daughter standing there, a plate of steaming food in her hands. She regarded her father with an expression that seemed to dare him to say anything, and when he looked resigned to her actions, she walked past him and set the plate of food on the bar.

"I hope you're not planning on attacking any of my other customers tonight."

"I haven't attacked a patron yet." He glanced from the plate of food to her face. "But I have no set intention."

The girl nodded at his answer as though it had been particularly wise. "That being said." She bent down under the bar and grabbed something from a low shelf. Standing up, she placed a large redstone mug on the bar and then turned around to fetch something from the counter behind her.

"Have you ever been here before?"

Ricker regarded the girl's back with a curious expression. It was not often that he was in a town, much less around people. It was more infrequent still that he was struck up for conversation. The girl was speaking to him, however; stubbornly, it seemed, against her father's desires, as she worked on uncorking a small, gallon-sized barrel.

"No," he said, eyeing one of the dubious stools, before settling carefully onto one with a grimace. "I have never been here before."

"You've missed out, Master Weaponsmith." The cork squeaked as she worked it free from the barrel and the girl turned back toward the bar. She balanced the barrel on one hand as she steadied it with the other. "Our barley season is over for the year, but we've a festival when harvest comes. Our inn is usually full, then, of course, not that most people make it to their beds come the end of the night."

She tilted the barrel, resting the side of it on splayed fingertips, and a dark, tea-colored liquid splashed out of the uncorked hole in the top. The girl had clearly performed such an action often, as not a drop of the liquid was spilled outside of the mug, and she filled it fully to the top.

Corking the barrel back up, the girl replaced it beneath the bar and offered Ricker a smile. "Enjoy your meal, Master Weaponsmith."

Ricker watched the girl walk back into the kitchens as he lifted the mug to his lips. The drink had a soft, sour smell to it, and when he tipped the liquid into his mouth, the cold alcohol bit at his tongue sharply, and Ricker swallowed the ale with the ease of much practice.

He placed the mug back on the counter and took up a fork, stabbing the thick slab of meat on his plate and beginning to cut it into smaller portions, his face caught in a thoughtful rictus.

"If you're that curious, you should just ask her name."

He resisted the urge to roll his eyes and swallowed. The meat was beef, tender and filled with juices. The heady flavors filled his mouth, a vast difference from what he had grown accustomed to eating during his travels. The meat had clearly been cooked slowly over a long period of time. Taking another bite, Ricker surreptitiously looked around to make sure no one was near him.

"I'm not interested in anything you're suggesting."

"I'm not suggesting anything," Shadow corrected snidely, *"but you certainly didn't jump to defy her father's accusations."*

"What accusations?" Ricker muttered sharply, scowling down toward the floor where Shadow held relatively still, but for the flickering movements allowed by the dancing flames in the hearth. He took up his mug again.

"That you were looking to take his daughter as payment if he didn't fulfill his end of the bargain." Ricker choked and planted the mug on the bar, coughing. *"Of course, he did swing a fist at you a moment later, so I suppose it would make sense that you were distracted."*

"Why in the *hell* would he even *think* that?!" Only the fact that no one was nearby kept him from being overheard, his voice rising in sharp disbelief and defensive anger.

"You don't exactly exude demure innocence." Ricker closed his eyes so he couldn't judge the distance between his forehead and the bar and try to lessen it. Violently. *"Of course, I knew you wouldn't do such a thing."*

Ricker eyed the mug for a moment, before picking it up again and quickly draining it. "Do you have such faith in me, Shadow?"

"Well, perhaps, but this was really based on a simple observation. Exactly how big of a hard-on did you get while lecturing him about swords?"

VI

Ricker woke up to the sensation of the blade he had crafted the day before ripping open his left eye socket.

This was not actually happening, of course, but the sunlight beating through the bars in the door's window mimicked the strength of a blade. Ricker found his whole body ached, and he stretched his arms over his head, trying to loosen his tightly-knotted shoulders. He struggled to free his mind from what seemed a mass of cotton and fog, as his eyes roamed the room he was in. He didn't recall going to bed the night before or... really anything at all, beyond the meal he had eaten and the sound of the mug he had been drinking from being refilled again and again.

And the room that he was in was less a room than it was a jail cell.

Ricker groaned.

It was a small room and square, maybe seven feet wall to wall. The ceiling above him appeared to be little more than a couple large pieces of wood nailed down on the boards that formed the walls. How it held together was anyone's guess, as the walls themselves were messily crafted, cracks present, boards rotting. The whole building might sooner collapse on top of him than keep him confined, and he wondered if they were so in denial of the sorry craftsmanship that they presumed the building could hold him, or if they expected his good grace would have him sitting happily on the cot, waiting for whenever they chose to release him.

"I question the supposed abilities of a man who can't hold his ale."

Ricker turned toward the sound of the voice, finding the innkeeper's daughter was standing outside of the iron bars that had been built into the wall opposite the cot. She was leaning casually against the wall, arms folded over her chest, amusement curling her lips into a smile. There was a red kerchief tied around her hair, knotted at the nape of her neck, and she was dressed in dirty work pants and a sleeveless shirt that had seen one too many days. This all came to Ricker in a short glance, which was all he could afford her attired posture. He found his eyes were once again drawn to hers – light green and full of such innocence it half made him want to cry.

"Only a fish can survive a river poured down his throat." Ricker stood up and walked over to the bars, squinting in the meager light that made its way through the boards of the cell walls. The girl didn't move from her relaxed position, watching him as he moved. If she only knew what he really was, she'd be far more fearful of him.

"I would have thought someone who could breathe death would have no trouble with a little alcohol." Ricker's hand moved to his throat before he could stop himself. Instead of the slightly-stiff, high collar of his cowl and his cloak clasp, he was wearing a plain, thin shirt, the neck piece cut into a V that displayed his Mark perfectly.

"*Where* are my *clothes?*"

The girl smiled at him with no small amount of amusement. "We decided it best to relieve you of them, since you were so willing to remove them yourself in the first place."

"*What?*"

"You don't remember? You seemed to think everyone needed a lecture on the way in which the world really worked. Things might not have been so bad for you if you hadn't been so disrespectful, violating our shrine and interrupting Mass."

"Mass..."

The last swallow of ale in mug number... in Ricker's latest drink, was doing a drunken lap dance with his tongue when he heard a strange chiming sound from behind him. Twisting on his rickety stool to try and find the source proved to be a foolish idea, as it nearly sent him sprawling face-down on the ground. Righting himself quickly and keeping the stool from toppling left him able to see everyone else react to the strange sound.

For everyone else present, the sound didn't appear to be foreign. The scraping of chairs and stools, the knocking sound of mugs and plates being placed on tables, and the murmur of people talking politely with each other was joined by the sound of the kitchen staff shutting down, a few of them slipping out past the bar and leaving by the door that Ricker had entered.

"Hey!" Ricker called to one of them, not quite sure whether they were a cook or a waiter, or possibly someone there to clean. "Can I get a refill here?"

The man he'd spoken to was younger than him by a good ten years at least, with dark hair that seemed to attempt defying gravity at every move the boy made. "The inn is closing for the hour, sir."

"Why?" Ricker demanded.

"Mass, sir." The boy pulled a cloak on over his loose clothing, fastening it at his neck. "You're welcome to come, sir. Everyone who visits Pasture is welcome at Mass."

"Welcome at Mass?" Ricker grinned. "I think I'll take you up on that offer."

The younger man smiled back. "Then follow me, sir."

Ricker groaned and slammed his head against the bars of his cell. His skull rang in response, two painful lines of pain ripping down his forehead, but he ignored it. "Damnit." It didn't take much for his mind to find everything that had occurred after that, splintered as it had been within his memory. He could recall the place of worship easily.

An open area, devoid of walls, the grass as green as the growing pastures – there were two rows of long, straight benches, built sturdier than the bar stools at the inn. The rows were positioned to mirror each other, the benches turned so that the end facing the center aisle between them was further back than the end facing the outside edge of the row. It allowed for everyone on the benches to have a clear view of the simple, wooden podium that was positioned at the front of the ceremonial area, facing where the worshippers would sit.

Behind the podium was a wooden table, eight feet long and made of a solid, sturdy wood. A dark green cloth hung down almost to the floor of the bar, and upon this sat small wooden carvings of animals, simple-framed pictures drawn by talented artists and children alike, the skull of a long-horned cow, the horns decorated with garlands of flowers that had been made from picking the blossoms that grew thick and beautifully around the base of the bar.

All of these things, the wooden trinkets and pictures and garlands, surrounded the heart of the shrine. Whoever had carved the statue had been a master sculptor, and now, sober and remembering the beauty of the sculpture, Ricker had a mind to wonder if the statue had been kept safe during the war those centuries ago and the chaos that followed, or if there had been a sculptor so talented still living after that great time of death. Ricker knew little of sculpting, but even he could recognize marble when he saw it.

The statue was not large, and certainly not to scale, for if it had been set on the ground it hardly would have reached Ricker's chest. Still, the representation was brilliant; it was clearly an effigy of a man dressed in a habit, hands folded against his chest. The hair was shown to curl slightly at the edges, and the face, so exquisitely detailed, showed a soft smile and eyes that seemed alive, brilliant and kind. Birds fluttered their wings in various positions on the man's habit, and a small creature – a squirrel – sat at the man's heels. Ricker thought, for a moment, that he could see the unfamiliar creature's tail twitch, but it had been nothing more than a trick of the light and a sculptor's skill.

Whatever speech of the world's true nature he had chosen to give those present at Mass, Ricker did not recall the words. They apparently had little worth against the memory of the expressions on people's faces. Everything from shock to concern to rage, and another emotion, something that he couldn't define but thought he had seen once, glimmering in the eyes of the ghost that followed him. The faces of those watching him had altered, terrified at his drunken madness, shocked at his daring, enraged at his violation of the sanctity of a place of worship. And whatever that other emotion was that he didn't want to define, glittering in the eyes of a few.

Looking back, it didn't really surprise Ricker why so many people had reacted in anger.

He'd had the audacity, first, to lecture the worshippers on the cruelties of the world, but his speech – whatever it had consisted of – paled in comparison to the impertinence he had shown by lowering his pants in the middle of Mass and relieving himself on the statue of their patron saint, Francis of Assisi.

Grimacing, head pressed against the bars of the cell, Ricker muttered under his breath. "Tell me someone punched me in the face for my stupidity and brought me here?"

He scowled when the girl laughed lightly. "You wouldn't remember passing out, I guess," she said flippantly, "but do you remember vomiting up your weight in alcohol beforehand?"

Ricker's head vibrated to the tenor of the ringing bars.

"You're going to give yourself brain damage."

So you are *here,* Ricker thought, eyes rolling to the left to find a shadow suspended on the floor of the cell. *I thought you'd left.*

In truth, the fact that Shadow had kept from speaking had caused Ricker to wonder if the ghost had taken serious offense at his actions the previous night and had left him for good. He hadn't been sure what he'd thought of that. His initial reaction was a sense of relief that the ghost had finally left him in peace. Still another part of him, a part that he had done his best to ignore, had felt betrayed by the shade's disappearance. That he was now back, and had clearly never gone to begin with, made Ricker grit his teeth in rage. It was a cruel trick—

"You have more things to be concerned about than my presence, dear Ricker."

Grinding his teeth, Ricker turned his attention back to the innkeeper's daughter. "How long am I stuck here?"

The girl shrugged nonchalantly. "You caused quite a ruckus. Papa still hasn't decided what he's going to have you do as punishment for your indecency. So, until he decides, you have to stay in here."

"And when do you think he'll come up with my punishment?"

"I don't know." The girl flopped down casually into a chair behind her, her hair bouncing at the action. She brushed it out of her face with a careless hand. "Papa can be pretty indecisive sometimes."

"Of course." Ricker sighed.

"I brought you some breakfast."

Ricker glanced up slowly, fighting back the surprise that wanted to manifest on his face. On the small table next to where the girl was sitting was a tray of food. There wasn't an overabundance of food, but finding himself awake in a jail cell with a hangover that turned his stomach and ripped at his skull, Ricker found that he wasn't overly hungry, at any rate.

He wasn't quite sure what he should say to the girl.

"'Thank you' would be appropriate."

"Thank you." Ricker stumbled slightly over the words, sending them too quickly past his lips. He heard Shadow laughing in his head and scowled heavily.

The jangling of keys drew his attention back to the girl and he found that she had stood, the tray of food in her hand, a set of keys fit into the cell door. Ricker turned his head to the side and watched

73

as she pushed the door open and took a step into the cell, before stopping suddenly, her eyes on him.

Smart, but too slow, he thought, catching the glimmer of trepidation in her gaze as she studied him. She was a slight girl, and while she was clearly used to farm work, she didn't have the strength to stop him if he chose to muscle past her, through the open door. If she was here by herself, which he thought likely, then it wouldn't take him long to leave the village behind, and no one would be able to catch him once he moved beyond the pastures that they knew and into the wood beyond, and none would follow him into the Undeadlands.

Ricker blinked slowly as he studied the girl before him. Her eyes, despite the uncertainty within them, showed a curiosity, as well, and she did not step back. Rather, she stood firmly in her position, waiting for him to make his move, so she could make her next one.

He frowned softly and, not knowing quite *why* he did it, took a step back and leaned against the far wall. He crossed his arms over his chest. With his eyes focused thoughtfully on the ground, he did not see the girl's soft smile.

She stepped further into the cell and laid the tray on a small table. Ricker glanced up as the girl stopped before she had stepped back through the cell door and gave him a curious look. He watched as her eyes lowered from his face to his neck, where he knew his Mark was bared for all to see.

"Does it... does it feel good?" She met his eyes again, innocent and curious. "When you breathe death?"

Ricker felt his fists clench of their own accord, knew his jaw had tightened. Part of him wanted to rage at the girl for asking such a question, but he knew there was no way that she could know how truly personal that question was. He could see her throat and she did not bear a likened Mark. In fact, he had noticed that all those in the village wore clothing in such a way that they were bared for all to see that they were not Marked. This was a place completely devoid of PlagueCursed, and he found it left him feeling even more alone than before, despite the fact that he had never expected to run into one during his time here.

His fists loosened as he wondered on how to answer the girl's question. How could he tell someone that he did not breathe the death from someone so much as he ate it? How could he describe the taste of the very soul that was bared before him as it was unbound from the blackness that sought to consume it? Was it possible to effectively describe in words the way he could tell the very essence of the person in front of him by how their death tasted as it slipped past metaphorical lips? The bitterness of a man who died unhappy; the sweet taste of a man who died deservedly; the spiciness of a life well-lived to its fullest.

The sharp taste, like a knife on the tongue, like a food too salty or tears licked from a sobbing man's cheek, at the too short life of a child, ended in unfair abruptity.

Does it feel good?

Ricker closed his eyes against the pain that wanted an outlet he wouldn't give it.

"Only when it works."

There was silence in the prison for a long time. Ricker's eyes closed gently as he willed the world around him to slip on by. There was a heavy click, as the wooden door to the jail shut behind the

75

girl as she left him to his thoughts. Ricker slid to the floor of his cell, ignoring Shadow and the tray of food.

And so the day passed.

When the girl returned at midday, she brought with her another tray of food. The scent of chicken, cooked slowly in a thick pumpkin sauce, filled the small building. Ricker hadn't moved since the morning, and when the girl entered the cell without hesitation this time, he didn't lift his head. He heard her steps as she moved to the table and replaced the untouched tray of breakfast food she had brought him hours before. She paused before leaving the cell and Ricker could feel her eyes on him.

"Is there something I can bring you, sir? Something that would be better?"

Lost somewhere half in thought, Ricker had to take a moment to digest her words.

Something better. Had he asked someone else, anyone else, they might have been able to write her a list of all the things they desired that would make their stay more comfortable, their life worth living. He'd once had these things, what seemed so long ago, but they had been lost and could not be retrieved. No matter how much he wished or begged the world, they were gone from him.

The cell door squeaked loudly as the girl exited and pushed it closed, locking it again. "If you need anything, sir, you can ask. I'll be happy to bring it to you." He heard the tinkle of keys as she replaced them in her pocket. "You should eat, though, or at least drink. It gets warm here, come afternoon."

Her voice held the innocence he had perceived upon first seeing her – the gentleness he had seen in her eyes that he knew would be stolen from her only painfully. He was not consciously aware of this observation, however. He was thinking about a sword, a basiliard, the metal gleaming, the hilt messily wrapped. He was choking on his pain as the thoughts flashed through his mind, but he didn't dare spit it out or swallow it, lest he lose the memory.

The door to the jail creaked open.

He'd lost so much, and he'd thrown more away. In the end, he'd had nothing at all left, save memories. And trinkets.

"Where are my clothes?"

There was silence for a moment, and though Ricker didn't look up, neither did the door click shut. He didn't know it, speaking as he was half-trapped in a memory, but his voice held a hollowness that sucked at the world. The girl had paused at the door not out of contemplation or suspicion, but in order to compose herself, as the sound of his voice was a window to the wounds he bore, festering beneath the mask he had shown all of them upon entering the village. He would probably still be wearing it, if he had been concentrating hard enough to realize it had fallen off.

"In the stables." He voice was quiet, controlled. The lie was undetectable.

"May I have them?" A mere whisper.

He could not see her nod, but she had forgotten this, and she slipped out of the jail before she could remember.

She was crying by the time she made it home.

"Eleanor?" A small woman came out of the house, her long, brown hair pulled up into a bun that had begun to frizz in the dry weather. She wore an apron liberally coated in pumpkin guts and she was wiping her filthy hands on a towel.

"Mama!" the girl cried, and flew into her mother's arms, sobbing.

"Hush, Eleanor, shhh..." the woman soothed, running a hand gently over her daughter's golden hair. "What is it, my little one?"

"Mama, you have to talk to Papa! Make him let the DeathBreather go. Please, Mama!"

"You been to see that Breather?" Eleanor flinched at her father's furious growl. The door to the house banged open and he came storming out to where Eleanor was being held by her mother. "Eleanor Miller, I told you to keep away from that monster!"

"You can't starve him, Papa!"

"The hell I can't. You were there, at the inn and Mass. The man's a bastard creature better off not gracing our good village—"

"Jacob!"

The man quelled slightly at his wife's firm reprimand. "Emily, you know what they're like. They've got abilities we haven't so they think they're better than us. Well, I won't have it. Not in this town! They were told to keep out!"

Eleanor, who still had tears running down her cheeks, looked more furious now than anything. Her hair was curled toward her face, frizzing slightly from the weather and her run toward her house. Her eyes, lime green and glistening with tears, were narrowed slightly and sparked with her father's same temper. "You can't judge everyone like that!"

"I've seen what they can do, Eleanor, and you'd be wise to listen to me! They're different from us – they can do things we can't. That means they're dangerous."

"Then what does that mean about *ME*?" Eleanor shoved away from her mother and took off toward the barn, ignoring her father's shouts and everything that she knew her mother was feeling. She couldn't deal with it right now, and she didn't want to know her father's answer to her question.

Emily Miller looked at her husband with a pitying expression. "I had wondered when you'd manage to ostracize her like that. I was hoping you'd wait until she was married so she'd have somewhere safe to run to when you drove her off. Fool man."

"Fool man? Fool man *what*? You know perfectly well that I meant the PlagueCursed and not her, and Eleanor'd know that just the same, if she'd stop her bawlin' long enough to think a little."

"What else can she possibly do? You won't let her care for the horses, she's not allowed to drive cattle, you don't want her near the jail—"

"Yeah, and I see how well forbiddin' her *that* worked out."

"She's not allowed to cook," Emily went on, ignoring her husband's interruption, "and she's not allowed to spend any time with Peter. What would you have her do to vent her frustration? Wait tables with more force than she does already? No, I suppose you'd forbid her that, too."

"Those men in that inn are not to be trusted."

"*Those men* consist of Paul Cobbler, James Carpenter, and their sons, all of whom Eleanor grew up with and you know very well wouldn't hurt a hair on her head."

"It's not the hair on her *head* I'm worried about."

"Yes, and I hear you accused our resident DeathBreather of wanting to force himself on her last night, as well, after attempting to back out of a bargain you know he had fulfilled." Her husband made to interrupt and she gave him a stern look, her voice getting louder. "And don't you *dare* attempt to lie to me, Miller. Your daughter told me precisely what happened and I've learned over the years to get an exaggerated, biased account from you, and then go to her for the real story. Don't you try to turn me against a poor drunken man half out of his wits, who you've thrown in jail and planned to starve to death."

"I wasn't going to starve him to *death*."

"What, then? Leave him to suffer hunger and thirst for two or three days before kicking him out of the village and letting him die on his own in the wilderness. The man's clearly a drifter and has no one to watch out for him. I suggest you take the night at the inn to think of what life like that would be, and then when you realized you're damn lucky to have your wife and your daughter, you go apologize to Eleanor for being the asshole you are. You can even tell her you can't help it, you're simply dysfunctional. I'll back you up on *that*."

Without waiting for a reply that would more than likely be another complaint, Emily turned and stormed back into the house to finish dissecting her pumpkins for the evening meal. She left her husband standing alone in the yard with his rage slowing simmering back down into a manageable level, and a desire to go kick the DeathBreather in the balls for being the cause of all this trouble. Instead, he went to the inn to make up a room for a night. Apparently, he was barred from bedding with his wife, which, lucky for the resident DeathBreather, would be why he would be allowed to escape.

~*~

"It would be like you, to shun the actions of the one decent person in this village."

Ricker hadn't yet moved from where he had slid down to the floor of the cell and leaned against the wall. Shadow's words penetrated the haze of his thoughts and he glanced up vaguely. "What?"

"That girl. She has the decency to bring you a meal for breakfast and you let the food go to waste. Now you're doing the same to lunch. Typical of you, being as you're so ungrateful to anyone *who offers you aid."*

"Are we talking about the girl, or you?"

"Who are you *talking about?"* Shadow's voice was teasing. Distantly, Ricker watched the ghost dance from shadow to shadow throughout the small cell. Strange that there was room for another ghost in here.

"I'm not talking," Ricker grumbled, slightly later than an actual response should have been spoken. He tried to ignore Shadow's condescending laugh.

"You really are *an asshole. I hope she realizes she's wasting her time, and her precious food, before one or the other proves to be a finite resource. Can't be an easy life here, and yet she's spending so much of her time pandering to your needs. Idiot child."* The word "idiot" was spoken

81

with such a tone of pity that Ricker felt a growl rumbling up from his throat.

"She is *not* an idiot, and that's more obvious than your intentions with your damn picking."

"Oh, my intentions. And what would they be, pray tell?"

Ricker snorted. "You'd like it if I stuck it out here, paid my time."

"More than anything."

"Locked in a jail cell, unable to chase after that kid and do away with him as he ought to be done away with."

"You've caught me, Ricker. You're a genius. How could I have ever thought to get anything past you?"

"Cut the sarcasm, Shadow. I'm getting out of here."

"Of course."

"Tonight."

"Yes, why wait? Don't give the villagers any time to think you might be plotting something. Or that girl. Smart one, that. You don't want to do anything to make her feel suspicious."

Ricker eyed the tray of food, only half-listening to Shadow. He couldn't let the girl think he planned on starving himself to make a point. She might try to keep a better eye on him that evening when she brought a meal, and that would definitely hinder his escape plans.

Grunting, Ricker pushed himself to his feet and shuffled over to the small table, taking the tray and collapsing onto his bed. Once he'd eyed the chicken, still steaming, his stomach gave a sharp growl, voicing its opinion that taking *this long* to finally eat was unacceptable. Firmly agreeing with this opinion, Ricker wolfed down his meal.

"So you're breaking out tonight, from a jail cell, with no tools and none of your weapons. You're an idiot, Ricker."

Licking pumpkin sauce from his fingers, Ricker grunted in reply. "I have a job to do, and you're not going to stop me from hunting the DeathSpeaker down. I'm not falling for any of your tricks, Shadow."

"Of course not," Shadow said, watching as Ricker stood and placed the empty tray back on the table. *"You're far too smart for that."*

~*~

Much later in the evening, after the sun had set below the horizon and only the last glimmers of colored light struck up from where it had slipped beyond view, the door to the jail opened for the last time.

Ricker was lying on his back, on the cot, feigning sleep. There had been no evening meal brought earlier, even though Ricker had been able to smell freshly-cooked food as it wafted from the inn. It had made him all the more glad that he'd eaten the chicken when it was warm.

He'd listened as the quiet descended on the village, the night sweeping in. As people began to head inside their homes or returning to the inn, the loudest sounds were those of doors shutting or the clop-clop of a cow's hooves as it pulled a cart behind it. He thought he heard one stop somewhere near the jail but didn't take the time to look. It was probably just waiting to load up the wagon for the next journey to a trading town.

As he listened, the door to the cell squeaked open. The girl's footsteps were becoming more familiar and he could recognize them now. She had lost her hesitation and her purposeful stride announced that she was coming nearer. He heard the empty tray slide off of the table, and something else get plunked down. It didn't sound like a tray of food. It was much heavier than that.

Something touched him on the shoulder, making Ricker, who had planned to feign sleep until the girl left, twitch away in surprise, his eyes flying open.

"Sorry, sir." The girl took a step backward, though there was no fear on her face. Frowning slightly, Ricker sat up. He caught movement out of the corner of his eye and turned his head.

Outside of the cell, standing calmly next to the small table, was a short woman with a serious expression on her face. She had thick brown hair pulled up into a bun that had probably been tightly-formed that morning but was beginning to fall down now. Her skin, like the girl's, was pale with a shimmering glow to it, but her eyes were dark brown, instead of green. Ricker found that her eyes were more like the girl's than her father's, however, in that they held a flicker of that same innocence – deeper-set and more refined with age, but still undoubtedly there.

"What's your name, DeathBreather?" The woman's voice was steady, calm, but held a deep authority that assured Ricker that while the innkeeper was a man of blunt words and strength, it was this woman that ran the show. Much to his surprise, he found he liked her.

"Ricker."

"Have you a trade name?"

A trade name. Ricker hadn't heard that term in some years, but he remembered it distinctly.

Those of a few centuries prior would equate them with their surnames, but trade names were very similar to centuries even before that, when the same rules applied. A person's surname, or their family name, was directly related to the job that they performed. A family who raised sheep would eventually be called Shepherd, the family that owned a mill would eventually be called Miller, and so on and so forth.

"Not for a long time." Ricker thought for a moment. "It would be Hunter, now, I suppose."

"Instead of Smith?"

The name made Ricker wince slightly, closing his eyes. Swallowing thickly, he nodded without looking at the woman. Oh, how that name called his memories forth…

"Shall I call you Hunter, then? My husband insists on calling you Breather, now, instead of Weaponsmith."

"Your husband's the innkeeper."

The woman smiled, almost feral. "Not for long if he continues acting the way he's been." Ricker grunted, a sound to stem a laugh, but he did not see the girl's smile and her mother's bright eyes. "But yes. I am Emily Miller. You've met my daughter, Eleanor."

Ricker glanced at the girl, who gave him a bright, happy smile. His lips twitched slightly in response and he nodded his head slightly to her, before turning back to Emily.

"Seeing as your husband's got such an opinion about me, why are you here, exactly?"

"My daughter wanted to return your clothes to you, as you'd asked." Ricker glanced back at the girl, to find his cloak had been draped haphazardly over the small table. "Because of my husband's very opinionated manner, I thought it best to accompany her." She grinned teasingly. "Besides that, I was very interested to meet the man that has so drawn my daughter's attention."

"Mama!" Eleanor's face had gone beet-red. "It's not like that," she mumbled. "Papa was being an asshole."

Ricker's eyebrows lifted in surprise, but Emily only laughed. "Unless you need something else, Hunter, we'll be leaving you. I believe Eleanor brought something for you to eat tonight."

Eleanor came to stand in front of him, a lidded bowl he hadn't noticed before held safely in her grasp. Ricker took it carefully, warming his hands on the hot wood. "Thank you."

Eleanor smiled and left the cell, slipping under her mother's arm. Emily turned back after Eleanor had slipped out of the door and gave him a fond, indulgent smile. "Eat well, Hunter, and have a safe journey."

Ricker bowed his head in silent thanks, thinking it was good she didn't intend to return before her husband was due to let him out of the cell. As the door to the jail shut behind her, Ricker moved over and picked up his cloak. He was surprised when the material pulled away from the table, revealing his satchel beneath it, as well as the rest of his clothes.

He changed, slipping on the familiar garments with a sense of relief, before throwing the cloak over his shoulders. He fingered the clasp gently, before snapping it into place, and settled down on the cot.

Spooning the smooth pumpkin soup into his mouth, he thought about his luck. He hadn't thought he'd have any of his equipment to help him escape, and here they had brought him everything he would need.

Ricker smiled like a shark. He was getting out tonight.

VII

The problem with having a jail in a building made of wood was that the walls didn't have the same level of strength as the metal bars which confined prisoners to their cells. More weight was put on the bars because they were better able to sustain it, and were expected to stand longer than the building itself. Normally, they would, unless something jeopardized their position.

Which was precisely what Ricker intended to do.

When Eleanor had brought his things back to him, she had brought him everything that had been taken from him upon his stay in the jail. This included, he was glad to discover, the large leather satchel he carried by a strap across his chest. Days ago, when Ricker had been at a monastery seeking information on the DeathSpeaker, Annabel had assumed that the pouch contained a weapon. She was right.

Ricker had made the crossbow himself, as he made all of his own weapons. Unless one lived near a trade city, specific parts for weapons were hard to find, and so Ricker, as a drifter moving across the world randomly, used whatever he could find to fashion himself weapons for his trade.

The base of the crossbow was an old exhaust pipe from a car, coppered and sharp on the outside with rust and pinched tight on one end where something heavy had been dropped on it, bending the one round end together and breaking it off from the muffler it had been connected to.

On one of his hunts for parts, Ricker had found an old toy rifle that someone had made from a strong wood. The trigger, when pulled back, causing the gun to click as two pieces of wood snapped against each other. To a child, the gun would have seemed real enough to use in a game of Soldiers and Drifters. When Ricker had found the toy rifle, it'd had a great crack in the wooden barrel and was sure to fall apart in that flaw. Ricker had put the rifle out of its misery, breaking it at the great crack and later sawing it down further, keeping the butt of the rifle, the toy trigger, and a part of the barrel. The barrel ended in a long, sharp point, which he'd jammed into the hollow, open end of the exhaust pipe until the sharp edges of the pipe had sliced into the wood of the toy gun, and he'd found an old can of black tar-like liquid and smeared it all over the area where the barrel and the pipe met, so they wouldn't fall apart.

Finding something with enough give for him to make a bow to set on top of the base had proved to be slightly difficult. Most of the things he had found, like a tire iron or a piece of copper wire, didn't have the give he required, while others, like a piece of wood or plastic, had the give he required but broke after a time, or if he pulled back on them too far. Eventually, Ricker had found an inch-thick piece of white, plastic pipe, about eight feet long, and had cut it into two and half or so feet increments, used one as the bow bar of his crossbow, and put the others in his satchel to replace the original when it would undoubtedly break. The only thing that Ricker had known from the beginning what he was using for it was the bowstring.

The wires that bound a DeathSpeaker's lips were unbreakable. A DeathSpeaker was born with their mouth already bound by wires that could not be severed by any means. Only the arrival of a DeathSpeaker's tenth year would have the wires leave their lips, disappearing back into the earth from whence they had come.

Ricker had met many DeathSpeakers during his self-made mission to destroy them all, and he had discovered how very useful the wires could be, both at binding a DeathSpeaker's lips together so that they could not attempt to speak, and as a bowstring. Unbreakable, the string would never lose its taut form and would remain in pristine condition, so long as he did not drop his crossbow and let the wires taste the earth. He had made that mistake once before, and the wire had disappeared into the ground more quickly than he was able to comprehend their action. Since then, he had been careful to keep his crossbow wrapped when he wasn't using it, and the extra wires he kept around for various means were locked away where they could not taste the earth.

Ricker dropped the large pouch onto the cot and hefted the crossbow up, digging an arrow from his pack. The arrows were made of sticks of metal, thin but cylindrical, with stiff feathers attached at one end to help guide the bolt through the air. The other end of the arrow was sharpened to a dull point. Like the crossbow itself, the arrows were heavier than they appeared, but Ricker paid no mind to this. He had been using the crossbow for years now, had built it himself, and knew well how it worked and how to make it work.

Fitting the arrow into the crossbow, Ricker pulled back hard on the bowstring and attached it to the locking mechanism with a quiet *click*. Then, placing the cocked weapon on the table, he pulled out a small tin case, half and inch thick and no longer than his hand, and opened it. Inside were over two dozen wires that had been taken from the lips of DeathSpeakers. Ricker carefully picked one up in each hand.

He held them close together, pinching the end of the one in his left hand and dangling the wire in his right hand over that. The two ends, almost as though they detected each other, were drawn together. There was a flash of silver, like metal, even though the wires were made of something quite different from metal, and the two wires had become one.

Picking up another, Ricker repeated the process, until all of the wires had joined into one long strip. Ricker had the silvery-black wire wrapped around his hand to keep it from touching the floor and he marveled at how it flashed silver like metal, but against his hand had the softness of a piece of thread. Ricker knew it was neither or those things, and something completely different – something he could never define.

"An interesting use for such an object," Shadow said, watching as Ricker removed the feathers from the arrow and slid the wire through the thin holes left behind, tying it tightly. Taking the other end and doing the same with another arrow, Ricker hefted the crossbow, aimed through one of the cracks in the wall.

With a sharp *snack*, Ricker pulled the trigger and the bowstring was released from the locking mechanism, springing forward and unleashing the arrow. The wires rippled behind the fierce bolt, settling only when the bolt buried itself in the wooden back of the wagon.

Sliding the second arrow into the crossbow, Ricker moved a little to the right, to another crack in the wooden wall that he had found, and aimed again. Pulling the trigger, the arrow ripped out of the crossbow, wire flagging behind, and slammed again into the back of the trailer. The cow harnessed to the wagon turned its head and let out a loud, low moo, dull eyes studying the wagon behind it.

Taking a third arrow, Ricker fit it into the crossbow and aimed once more. With one final glance at the wire, hanging loosely around six or seven thick boards that formed the walls, Ricker pulled the trigger.

The arrow tore from the bow and flew true to where it had been aimed. The tip skimmed the cow's back, tearing through hair and flesh. With a loud cry, the beast threw its massive bulk forward, taking the whole of the wagon with it.

There was a loud crack as the wires caught taut against the walls and ripped through them easily, ripping the boards away and tearing the wall out completely. The cow paid no mind to what went on behind it, other than to flee whatever had caused it such pain. The thundering of hooves on the hard dirt road echoed through the night, along with the beast's cries.

There was a creaking sound from above Ricker and he wasted no time, grabbing his pouch from off of the bed and throwing it over his shoulder as he leapt over scattered boards and wood chips. Crossbow still in hand, he slipped through the hole in the wall and out into the night.

Ricker heard a door open somewhere behind him to the left, and someone yelled after him, no doubt having heard all of the commotion. Further behind him, Ricker heard the jail crash to the ground, the weight of the ceiling too much for the compromised walls to handle. He didn't look back, at the jail, at the people coming out of their homes, even the yell from the familiar voice of the innkeeper. He raced past buildings and passed the town, the only thing on his heels an unwavering shadow. He did not slow until he had reached the wide pastures and was able to slip into the grasses and move among the cows that grazed or slept there.

Some of the great black and white beasts moved away from him, but others were so used to humans that they merely glanced his way and continued as they were, chewing grass with a slow, bored determination that was common for species of such intelligence. Ricker moved through the grass around them, taking the moment of mild cover to glance back toward the village to see if anyone had followed him.

Either no one was able to keep him in sight, or the villagers thought that he had already moved beyond their reach. Perhaps once they thought he was beyond their village, they wanted nothing more to do with him, not even to lock him in a cell for so disrupting their Mass. That was fine with him, if that was the case. He was more than happy to forget all about their village and continue toward his own ends.

"Oh, I doubt they'll completely forget about you. How could they?"

"I don't need a lecture right now, Shadow." Ricker scanned the pastures toward the village once more, but saw no one. Moving around a heifer, he headed opposite the town, toward the forest he knew lay beyond it.

"Most students believe they know all that they need to accomplish the tasks before them, but life rarely follows a path the living can see."

"And I suppose you can see where I am headed." Ricker didn't even bother to look over at the ghost, continuing his strong gait toward the wood.

"I, at least, do not walk through life wearing blinders."

"Perhaps that is because you're *dead*."

"... perhaps."

The loud silence before Shadow's quiet response caused Ricker to grimace at his own words. He shut his eyes for a moment, before looking down at the shade. "Shadow, I'm—"

"Now is not the time for apologies, Ricker." The ghost danced across the ground in agitation. *"What you do not see can hurt you."*

He had been slowing his pace to speak with the ghost, but at Shadow's words, kept up his light jog, brow furrowed. "Does that mean that I'm forgiven?" he asked, his voice quieter than he liked.

He didn't like to think that he was letting the shade see how much it meant to him that the ghost stuck around, that he was showing a vulnerable spot to the creature who already spied the weak points in his armor and seemed all too happy to poke them repeatedly with a sharp stick. If Ricker thought about it, however, which he tried to avoid doing, all of his secrets were bared for the ghost. However it was possible, Shadow remained existing past death and had the ability to read the deepest recesses of his mind. If he thought it, or felt it, then Shadow knew it, and no amount of pretending otherwise would trick the ghost out of the knowledge. And though he did not like it, in this small moment, Ricker could let himself slip... just a little.

"I see the things that you do not, Ricker. All that is behind you is clear to my eyes. You must keep moving forward."

Ricker wanted to ask why Shadow sounded so sad, saying that, as though there was an inevitability that he was privy to that Ricker could not see. The moment to ask was interrupted, however, by a scream that tore through the air behind him; the cry of a terrified woman confronted with something she could not bear.

The sound of it stopped Ricker cold. His feet ceased to move before his body was prepared, and he nearly lost himself to the ground, before regaining his equilibrium. His hands itched and he had the sudden urge to wash them, even though they bore nothing but scars and dirt. His fingers twitched as he turned on his heel, staring back toward the village, his mouth a desert of teeth and tongue.

"Ricker."

"That... Shadow?"

"You cannot go back there, Ricker."

"I know who screamed... don't I?" He was sure it was the Miller woman who had screamed; he was sure of it. But if he was so certain, why did his mind fill with the image of a pale-faced woman, years younger than Emily Miller, with charcoal hair and grey-green eyes overrun with tears?

"Ricker."

Who was that woman? Those eyes... he didn't know them, and yet... they seemed so familiar. That hair, black as midnight, tangled like his thoughts... he knew it. He knew... her name was...

A sharp flash of pain ripped across the left side of Ricker's head, making him grunt and bring his hand to his skull, his eyes squeezed shut. After a moment, the pain dulled to a shadowy sensation of memory and he was able to open his eyes.

"Shadow?"

"Ricker." He looked down to find that the shade was reflected on the ground, weight shifting from foot to foot, though the shadow did not separate from his own shoes. The hands, normally so calm, were in a constant, nervous motion. *"We must go."*

"But—" He wondered why he wanted so badly to go back to the village, to throw himself toward the people of the town. The cry of that woman – of Miller – had made him feel somehow responsible for what had happened to her daughter... to her.

Ricker shook his head. He had no knowledge to tell him that something had happened to Eleanor. It would do him no good to speculate.

"Please."

Ricker looked back down at the shade, who had stopped moving. Ricker could see, within those glowing white eyes, a pleading look that he had never seen before.

"You cannot go back, Ricker."

The wind blew gently at Ricker's back as he faced the town, but the world around him had gone silent. The woman did not scream again.

"Ricker."

"I'm coming, Shadow."

Ricker turned and headed into the wind, his eyes briefly glimpsing two glowing eyes as they closed softly, leaving the ground before him in shadow.

Ricker stepped into the darkness.

~*~

"You regret leaving."

The fire crackled angrily at the cold night air, leaping toward the sky as though to chase away the atmospheric haze that so chilled the nights. Ricker held a long stick in his hand and was poking the glowing coals, causing the fire to twitch into different shapes as the coals and wood were shifted.

Ricker stared into the flames, his forehead wrinkled in a scowl of epic proportions and he seemed content to completely ignore Shadow's question.

It made sense, however, that someone who had thwarted the eternal summons of death would be stubborn.

"Do you wish we had gone back?"

Ricker stabbed the stick more viciously into the coals until they gripped it and he let go of his end so that the stick was stuck at an angle. Grabbing at his belt, Ricker extracted a sharp knife from a hidden sheath and gripped the stick with one hand. With the other, he began to carefully cut away thin strips from the wood.

Patient as only those he hadn't life to live could be, Shadow flickered inconsistently against the dark earth, the tree roots and various vegetation in the clearing where Ricker had made camp caused the shade to take a slightly warped appearance, body twisted in a position only afforded to two-dimensional creatures and those who had passed beyond the stage of rigor mortis.

Ricker collected his careful shavings onto a piece of cloth, piling them in the center of the round, black fabric. While traveling over the years, Ricker had learned many things. The most important, however, was to be prepared, at all times, to face Death's tender mercies. The world was a cruel and unforgiving place. If Ricker had wandered too many times into a desert devoid of trees and had no fuel with which to create a protective fire, and had learned from that, then life's hard lessons had taught him well. Others had not been so fortunate, but they were gone, and Ricker was not.

"Ricker."

"What would you like me to say, Shadow?" Ricker asked wearily. He continued to shave the stick with cautious precision, the pile of shavings growing larger.

"What you think, precisely."

"Who was that woman?" He could feel his own tension in his back, building between his shoulder blades like rocks, and in the air, as thick as soup: rock soup, a recipe for discomfort.

Shadow was quiet for a while, and then, *"You determined yourself that it was the Miller woman."*

"You know that's not who I mean. She didn't look like the woman I was thinking of."

"Do you suppose I listen to your thoughts at all times, Ricker? How am I to know whom you are or are not thinking of? You assumed it was the Miller woman screaming, and it was. Why add more to it?"

Ricker paused in his movements, staring down at the flickering shade. "You are always so very happy to comment on my thoughts, and I've little doubt that you know exactly who I am speaking about. Who is she, Shadow? Why were you so determined to keep me from going back?"

"You wanted to find the DeathSpeaker. If you go back, he'll be out of your rea—"

"We both know you don't want to me to catch him, Shadow, because you know I intend to kill him. Who was the woman?"

"I can't answer that, Ricker."

"Who was she, Shadow?"

"I won't tell you, Ricker. Ask me all you like, but I won't tell you. You can't know, yet, and I won't say anything."

Ricker snarled at him and kept asking, badgering the ghost for an answer, but no matter how he worded it and how he snarled, Shadow would tell him nothing.

~*~

When they started walking the next morning, it was in silence. Ricker had spent the night angry at Shadow for not telling him what he felt he needed to know, and Shadow had remained stubborn and silent. Ricker kicked dirt over the glowing coals that had burned all night, and shouldered his pack. The cloth he had piled his wood shavings into the night before was folded up and tied into a pouch, tucked into his pack.

Ricker couldn't help but glance back the way they had come the previous night, but the temptation to go back to the village was less than it had been, and it caused him no pain to resist it. He headed off in the same direction that he had been walking. He was resolved not to speak to Shadow, still angry that the ghost was so unhelpful – like a parasite, the shade was happy to read his thoughts, but unwilling to offer any assistance when Ricker needed it. He knew that, if he ended up going the wrong direction, the ghost would correct him. Despite not wanting Ricker to kill the boy, for whatever reason, Shadow wanted him to find the boy. And Ricker would.

Ricker grimaced as he stepped over a large tree root that was arching out of the ground. While he knew that he was safer in the forest than he was in the open from other people, the forest itself was not a place that he could relax in. Last night, he had let his fire burn the night through, and he had made certain to stack it heavily enough with wood that it would not falter during the darkest hours before dawn. It was not merely the cold that Ricker had hoped to drive off, and he wasn't even all that concerned about the animals that dwelled within the wood. No, the truest danger of all was the wood itself.

It wasn't merely the humans and animals that had been altered by the Dark Plague. The land itself had changed, and not just by losing its sleek grasses in most of the areas, turning into a barren, dusty wasteland. The forests that had once bloomed green and flowered beautifully appeared dead at a glance, often with barren, dry, husky branches. Rarely, however, had Ricker wandered into a forest that was truly dead.

The very plant-life had gained a sentience, it often seemed, and Ricker could feel as though eyes were watching him as he walked through the forest. He had never encountered a plant that appeared to have eyes, and he didn't imagine that he would, but he had seen many hints that the vegetation was not as stagnant as many preferred to believe. Even now, walking quietly through the woods, Ricker could catch glimpses of the mobility of the forest. A tree to his left swayed lightly as he walked past it, in a manner that had nothing to do with the wind that gently blew through the branches. He watched idly as it tilted away from him, and he wondered at the possibility of the trees being able to scent the smoke from his fire on him.

The ground beneath him, covered in a mulch formed from the decomposing pieces of bark and branches that had fallen from the trees around him, shifted lightly. Ricker watched a long, thin vine, muddy brown and covered in soft nubs that would likely grow into thorns, slither past him through the mulch like a snake.

He paid little mind to the snake vine, other than to note that it was apparently very long, because it continued to move past him and he saw no end to it.

Shadow, he noted, seemed interested in the vine, flitting around the ground where the snake vine was slithering on. He seemed curious for a moment, his movements focused on that area, before he danced lightly away, in and out of the shadows of trees.

"Left here, Ricker."

Ricker said nothing to Shadow, glancing to his left, through the trees. He had been following something of a path – the trees, despite their clear wildness, had apparently been originally planted in something of an order. Ricker had been walking down one of the rows between two lines of trees, and as he paused and glanced to the left, he saw that the line rows continued on that way, too.

He stepped over the snaking vine and moved to the left, settling himself to walk down the new row. He didn't know how long he would travel this direction before Shadow corrected him again, but his eyes traversed the row of trees, watching as these moved and danced around him lightly, as well. He briefly considered that, if the trees were sentient and possibly feared him for his use of wood for fuel, walking through a forest surrounded by trees was probably not the safest place for him.

Most creatures will run when confronted, but backed into a corner, terrified and trapped, they attack.

He eyed the trees warily for a moment, his mouth a thoughtful grimace of concern, before he snorted loudly. Eyeing the tall, strong trunk of a tree, he laughed outright. How in the world could he possibly think that a tree, stiff and immobile as they were, could prove to be a danger to him?

He knocked his fist lightly against the trunk of the nearest one and grinned. "I'm a damn fool if I think a plant is going to get the best of me." Shoving off from the tree, he moved onward down the row, ignoring the way the branches moved lightly against the wind, quivering angrily at him.

Behind him, Shadow flickered from one shadow to the next on the ground, but said nothing.

The forest was much larger than Ricker had originally thought. He thought that it might be nearing midday, but the branches of the trees in this part of the wood were thick and he couldn't see the sky beyond them. His judgments of time were never too far off their mark and he thought it might be time soon to stop for a break.

Behind him, Shadow made a sound, like a low grunt of surprise in the back of his throat. Ricker's eyebrows drew down in the confusion mere moments before he glanced ahead of him and caught sight of the boy.

He was dressed in a simple brown robe that hung loose on his body, low to the ground but not quite low enough to cover his dirty, bare feet. The boy was faced away from Ricker, but he could see that the sleeves of his robe were wide, sagging down low as they were from his arms, his hands up at his face. The boy's head was bare of hair, and Ricker was sure, from that and his dress, that the boy had come from a monastery. .

Even as Ricker quietly reached back and grabbed his crossbow from the pouch on his back, he knew he couldn't be sure this was the boy he was looking for. Not until he saw his face, and the kid was facing the wrong direction.

His arm bringing the heavy weapon down to chest level, Ricker grabbed one his bolts and fit it into the crossbow and pulling the bowstring back until it clicked loudly in place. In the silence of the strangely-quiet wood, he knew the boy had heard it.

Hefting the crossbow, he finger on the trigger, Ricker's eyes narrowed. If this was the boy he was looking for, then his job would be done with a simple twitch of his hand...

"Boy, what're you doing so far from home?"

The kid turned to face him, as Ricker knew he would, and something in his chest clenched hard at the sight of the boy's eyes – a deep blue that haunted his every waking moment and tormented him in his dreams.

And there were wires that bound the boy's lips, black and shining.

They were unraveling.

VIII

Ricker had never seen the wires of the DeathSpeaker unravel before, and he wished he wasn't seeing it happen now. It was not because he was watching one of these creatures reach their maturity, knowing that it would know *how* to speak and that it *would* speak in order to destroy. It was not *just* because he was watching a force of destruction be released from bonds that should never have had a termination point.

It was because he was afraid.

His fear was not logical, not sensible. It was completely irrational and he knew that. Ricker knew there was no point to this fear, this blind terror that built up inside of him and began to spill over like a flood overtaking a river. A DeathSpeaker had no power over a DeathBreather. As he breathed, he stole the very force of a DeathSpeaker's power into his lungs. He could still hear their tongues. He could hear them speak, but their words – their voices – would bring him none of the death that they brought to others. He was immune to their power, and so there was no reason for him to fear this child.

But the fear that writhed in his heart was not a force that could think. It was not a logical emotion or a rational reaction. It was primal. It was the single-minded knowledge that the force of nature that stood before him was a greater force than himself. The DeathSpeaker was danger and danger must be known and fled from; as an antelope would flee a lion, as a mouse would flee a cat, so should all living things flee a DeathSpeaker.

Ricker was a man, however, or greater still than a man – he was a DeathBreather. He was not an animal and so he resisted the need to flee, and the adrenaline that raced through his blood turned down another path, raced through another riverbed of action in his veins, and the need to fight came alive.

Hand gripping the handle of his crossbow, Ricker pulled his index finger tight as he took a step closer to the boy, his aim steady. His eyes were focused sharply on the boy's unbinding lips, avoiding his wide blue eyes. He was not watching where his steps fell and so he did not see the slithering vine twitch as his booted heel came down on top of it, or how it writhed angrily as he moved on.

Ricker watched as the boy's fingers touched his lips uncertainly, and his eyes were sharp as the DeathSpeaker tensed, frightened. And he did not miss when the boy's self preservation skills kicked in and he took a step back.

Ricker's aim had never faltered and the crossbow was steady in his hands. In the same instant that the boy retreated, Ricker pulled the trigger.

There was a sharp clicking sound as the trigger fell, the *sassass!* of the bowstring sliding forward, its momentum stopped abruptly, only for the bolt to continue on, flung forward by the force of the crossbow's release.

It would have sliced through the boy's throat and left him choking on his own blood, if not for one simple fact.

Snaking vines did not like to be stepped on.

The feeling of something thin and strong wrapping around his calf was the only warning

Ricker got before his feet were literally yanked out from underneath him. He threw his arms wide on instinct, trying to move in order to catch himself, and the crossbow was thrown off its aim, the bolt flying off into the forest. Ricker landed heavily on his back, the force of his weight pressed against the ground knocking his breath clear from his lungs. As he struggled to regain control of his breathing, he had a moment's peace, before he felt the vine slither inside his boot, curling around his ankle. Ricker had but a moment to contemplate how utterly bad this was about to get, before the vine jerked sharply on his leg, and he was suddenly moving through the forest faster than he would have thought the vine could carry him.

His right hand banged hard against something and the crossbow was torn from his grasp. His fingers ached from where the triggering mechanism had snagged against his fingers before being ripped free, but Ricker ignored that in favor of trying to kick the vine free of his leg. This proved impossible; the vine was dragging him along with too much force and didn't offer the slack he would need to kick with his bound leg. He tried to use his other leg to force his boot off, but the vine had wrapped around his foot tightly and then curled viciously around the outside of his boot. Attempting to beat it off proved to cause him pain and do nothing to stall the vine.

A sudden jerk at the back of his ankle and the bending of his knee was all the warning Ricker had before the vine's direction changed and his body twisted to accommodate the movement down a row perpendicular to the one they had been going down. Ricker snarled out a few choice swear words as he was slammed roughly against the side of a tree, the harsh bark against his back letting him know that his coat and shirt had both ridden up from his dragging, and the feeling of the forest floor against his bare back was not a mental exaggeration on his part. He thought he felt the skin of his back torn open by the tree's rough surface, before the vine's continued force sent him rolling across the uneven ground, before he managed to stop his sideways movement. He was on his back again, and the vine had never slowed.

Fingers fumbling at his waist, Ricker was glad to note that his belt hadn't been torn off. The rough leather was familiar under his fingers and his hands quickly found the eight inch-long knife he kept there. Steadying himself as best he could, he drew a deep breath and then forced himself to sit up, bending at the waist as far as he could until he had grabbed hold of his own boot. The vine continued to drag him and Ricker grunted as his butt was forced to take the majority of his weight and hit quite a number of painful knots and stones in the ground. Ricker didn't release hold of his boot even as his position caused him to lose his balance and he toppled over, until his entire left side was dragging on the ground.

Keeping his head above the ground with a tilting position that made his neck ache kept his left eye and ear relatively safe. Ricker clutched the hilt of his knife tightly and began attacking the vine with fervor.

The blade didn't slice cleanly through the vine, which was much sturdier than Ricker had originally thought. The vine was not made of mostly water, like the stem of a flower, as he had anticipated. It proved to be difficult to cut through, like the growing trunk of a yearling tree, even though it clearly had the flexibility of a willow vine. But it couldn't stand up to Ricker's sheer determination. Bumping along the forest floor, grunting and grimacing, Ricker finally sliced through the vine on the outside of his boot.

The vine jerked away from him violently and continued through the forest at an even faster past than Ricker had been traveling behind it. There was a shriek in the distance, echoing through the trees, and Ricker wondered what less-troublesome prey the vine had chosen to go after.

Slumping to the ground with a relieved sigh, Ricker rolled over onto his back and drew in a deep breath, cherishing the stillness around him as he wasn't dragged over rock and root. His left side hurt from the most recent part of the dragging, though his back stung, and he was sure he had some cuts and scratches that would need to be washed thoroughly to keep from getting an infection from all the dirt that he had been dragged through.

The snap of a twig caused Ricker to twist his neck violently to see who was coming upon him. He was startled to see the flash of a brown robe, and he knew it had to be the DeathSpeaker.

Surging to his feet, he faltered in his movements slightly when the flicker of an unnatural movement danced through the shadows of the trees.

"You may want to lay back down, Ricker."

"Why?"

That distant shriek he'd heard before came again, seconds before he felt something wrap tightly around each foot. Both of his legs were jerked out from underneath him, and Ricker slammed face-first into the ground, sparing himself a broken nose only by the instinctive movement of his hands to catch himself.

"What is going—" The vines surged together and Ricker found himself being dragged backward through the forest. "Shadow!"

"Really, Ricker, did you expect that vine to not run home and tell its mother that some big bully sliced its end off? Of course two of its elders were going to come after you."

Ricker didn't get a chance to reply, as he was very quickly dragged out of sight of Shadow. He kept his head up as best his could, not fancying the idea of slamming his chin against anything, or breaking his teeth. It was far more unpleasant to be dragged along the ground on his stomach than on his back. His knees bent in the other direction and he knew that if he caught his foot on anything, it was entirely likely that he would break his kneecap. The very thought of that happening made him shudder as a chill raced up his spine, and Ricker dearly hoped that these vines kept to the bare aisle between the trees.

He would have liked to think that he was just unlucky enough to have wandered into an area with a number of snaking vines, but thinking about what Shadow had said, he knew the ghost was right. That shriek he'd heard after the retreat of the original vine should have been enough warning for him to get the hell away, but he'd been too relieved at being free to think clearly about it. He knew, like most people, however, that the forests were full of sentient plants, and he should have known enough not to stick around after first being attacked. Now, he'd been accosted by two more of the snaking vines, with an even less-likely chance of getting away. Not to mention that his grip had slacked on the knife when he'd been catching his breath after escaping the first vine, and some time between then and being dragged off by these two, he'd lost his hold on it. Admittedly, that was probably a good thing, as he had the distinct feeling that if he had retained his grip on it, he probably would have stabbed himself in the head on accident when he'd been tripped.

Still, that left him weaponless and at the mercies of two very angry snake vines, and no idea where he was being dragged off to. Although, he had his ideas…

Snaking vines that traveled a great distance, multiple vines that interacted and worked with each other, and actions toward a flesh and blood creature that were decidedly not like those of a creature prone to being prey to another: Ricker was pretty sure that he had been accosted by a plant that leaned toward the carnivorous spectrum.

This meant his day was about to get infinitely *worse*.

"So you do know how to think on your feet. And on the ground, as it were."

Ricker twisted his head and found that Shadow was keeping pace with him, the ghost flitting from each dark patch on the ground around him. Ricker cursed as a sharp stone snagged his right ear. He attempted to curl up to hide his head from being further struck, but the force of the vines pulling him wouldn't allow it, and he was left doing his best to keep his head above the ground. .

"You know where they're taking you, of course." Ricker frowned. *"The snaking vines, as they're known, all connect in one place. As ants carry food back to their queen, so do the vines for theirs."*

"The bulb," Ricker groaned, remembering hearing about such a thing once, but never having had to see it for himself.

"It seems you'll get your chance." The ghost flickered out of view and Ricker's eyes searched for him but could find no hint that the shade remained anywhere near him. He opened his mouth to call out for the shadow.

His feet were jerked upward. Ricker let out a yell as his knees bent and his body was lifted from the ground. He was pulled up rapidly, and while it kept him from dragging across the ground, the movement swung him like a pendulum. He hit the side of a tree near him across his already aching left side and grimaced. The tree itself quivered at the strike, and he was sure that it would have taken a swing at him if trees weren't known to be quite immobile due to their armor-like bark.

He was left swinging the other way as one vine released him, leaving him twisting dizzily, upside down. His body ached from being dragged along the forest floor, and he could feel the blood rushing to his head. His arms hung down past his face in an uncomfortable position that required less energy than folding them against the force of gravity. He huffed angrily at the three foot space between himself and the ground, and kicked his loose leg at the vine still holding him. His teeth clenched when the vine only tightened in response to his kicking, and he instead fought to steady his leg so it stood straight up like the other, instead of bending to try and futilely place him feet-first back on the ground.

"That looks uncomfortable, doesn't it?"

"Shadow?" Ricker turned his head this way and that, looking for the ghost.

111

"We're behind you, Ricker."

"We?" Ricker shifted his body weight abruptly, trying to make himself turn so that he could see the ghost and his companion. He caught a brief glimpse of the shade reflected against a thick tree bearing apples, and the DeathSpeaker, before the two spun out of sight again.

"Damnit!" Ricker struggled to stop himself from twisting in the air, though his struggles only made it worse. "Shadow, what the hell is that boy still doing here?"

"It seems he's having a bit of a bad day, Ricker. You see, today is his birthday, and an hour ago, his mouth started hurting, and it hasn't stopped."

"Really? No shit." Ricker glared at the boy as they spun past his vision. "I can see from here his wires are loosening. Happy birthday, kid. I'm gonna shoot you when I get down from here. Might want to start runnin'."

To Ricker's disgust, the boy actually looked at Shadow for advice.

"I'd be less concerned about Mortimer and more worried about your own predicament, at the moment." The ghost flickered away from the boy and danced on the ground inside Ricker's own shadow. *"Or did you not notice that you're the main course in the vines' delivery of breakfast in bed?"*

Ricker had looked down when the ghost moved into his own shadow, warping it, and as he watched now, the ghost circled an area on the ground that Ricker had noticed was raised up. He had glimpsed it only briefly and thought it was a decomposing tree stump, but as he studied it closer now, he realized that its edges were not rotted, but

112

simply curved, and soft. The ground lifted upward into a hemispherical shape, like the crown of a mushroom, dark brown and patterned like tree bark. Upon closer inspection, however, it looked as though the crown would actually be quite smooth to the touch.

Looking as closely as he could, Ricker saw that the top of this crown had four flaps, visible only barely because of the X-shaped lips that would allow the flaps to pull back, revealing the interior of the crown. As he watched, the lips began to secrete a pinkish liquid that made Ricker's stomach churn.

"Is that blood?"

"No. You're not lucky enough to be dangling above a bulb that has recently eaten. And I'm afraid you don't have the lung capacity to hold your breath as long as it would take to stand against the pheromones."

"Pheromones?" Ricker gave the shade a blank look. It was not a word he had heard before. He didn't know it, but the word had lost meaning to almost the entire world after the nuclear war centuries ago wiped out nearly all scientists and recorded information. What few understood the meaning of the word didn't pass it on to their successors, as it lacked relevancy or importance at the time.

"Aggression inhibitors... the bulb, oh nevermind. You're not willing to learn any other time. You're about to be eaten by a plant, Ricker, and allow me to give you a little background information on this particular species. It's a hybrid, of course. I don't think any of the original plants survived the Plague without breeding with something else, but this one is a particularly fun plant."

"Shadow!" The folds of the plant had begun to roll back slowly, as someone waking up in the morning will stretch their arms above their head for a comfortably long time, yawning at the morning. As the lips of the plant folded backward, Ricker was able to see into the bulb's gullet – and it could be described as nothing else – which was a deep crimson color, as though the sides of the plant's throat were drenched liberally in a thick coating of fresh blood. A third of the way to the crest of the plant's crown, there was a circle row of teeth-shaped thorns all around the inside of the gullet. The thorns were black and gleamed, reflective the meager light in the forest like liquid.

Though, that was beginning not to matter.

"Don't interrupt, Ricker. You have time. Now, this plant doesn't have a name, of course, since no one's cared to offer one, but it was born a hybrid of the genus Taraxacum, *and the genus* Cuscuta. *That is, a plant once known as a dandelion, and a parasitic plant called a dodder. Interesting that the two evolved together into a hybrid such as this, but I imagine the sentience allowed for the vines to be so helpful."*

Ricker was still very much afraid, and very worried about his position above the plant, but there was a sweet scent in the air that was tingling just out of reach. He licked his lips and was sure that he could taste sugar in the air. He breathed in deeply, but saw the gleaming black thorns inside that great throat and shook himself.

"The bulb secretes a pheromone – a scent – that attracts prey and makes them complacent, until the point where it is able to begin feeding upon you. Those thorns are not black from color. They're translucent and filled with a toxin that will be

injected into your bloodstream at a single scratch. It is a paralytic agent. It won't inhibit your body's ability to register pain, or put you to sleep, but it will keep you still for the three days it will take for the bulb to digest you to a point where you will likely lose too much blood to remain alive. Very effective and, I must admit, pretty intriguing from a scientific standpoint."

Ricker, who had begun to drift off into the sweet scent around him, was jerked back into reality abruptly when the vine holding his leg untwisted around his heel and he dropped a foot closer to the bulb beneath him. The bulb's crown had rolled back completely, revealing that its depths sank at least two feet further than it appeared to at first glance. Apparently, the majority of the bulb's mass existed beneath the ground, which made sense, in an effort to keep from being harmed.

Ricker felt at once relaxed and nauseous. The second sensation overruled the first, and Ricker barely noticed the dream-like effects of the pheromones leaving him.

"Shadow!"

"I'm afraid there's little I can do to help you, Ricker. I am, after all, quite insubstantial. If it makes you feel any better, though, death really isn't as bad as they say. Take it from someone who knows."

"Shadow, this plant has *teeth*."

"Yes, I saw that. A rather ingenious evolution, though I do wonder how that came about."

"SHADOW!"

"I have no hands to help you with, dear. However, if you're really interested in escaping your current predicament, I imagine Mortimer

115

might be willing to help you." Ricker's eyes moved from the gullet beneath him to Shadow in surprise. *"For a price, of course."*

Ricker stared at Shadow a moment that was too much offered considering his present state. "You planned this, didn't you?"

"I did not. I couldn't have done it better myself, had I, though."

"I think I hate you, Shadow."

"The question only remains, then: will you take your hate with you into the gullet and the grave, or make a deal so you can go on hating me for... however long you manage not to drive someone to kill you?" Ricker's narrowed eyes stayed focused on Shadow as he tried to think of what to say. *"Each second of glaring steals from your precious life, Ricker. Do you really have a better idea?"*

"He's a *DeathSpeaker!*"

"I didn't say you had to keep him as a pet. You can take him back to the monastery, make sure he takes a vow of silence, and then we'll be on our way again. Of course, if you'd rather hold your current position in the food chain..."

Ricker let out a low sound, like a growl. Shadow's laughing didn't prompt a more pleasant response from him.

"Mortimer will help you if you promise not to kill him."

Ricker had gathered that aspect already from what Shadow had said. Glancing at the boy briefly, he could see the uncertainty in the DeathSpeaker's gaze. He was glancing back and forth between Shadow and Ricker, no doubt trying to decide if it would just be safer to run now. It would have been, of course, but Ricker wasn't about to tell the boy that now and have him leave Ricker to his fate.

He grumbled darkly, but said, "Get me down, boy and I'll take you back to the damn monastery." He narrowed his eyes as the DeathSpeaker looked at him. "Mark me, though, boy. If you Speak, I'll kill you without a thought. You have my word on that."

The boy glanced at Shadow, his thin brows scrunched over his eyes in confusion and fear. His hands were still clasped over his lips, the wires no doubt causing him pain as they crawled out of the position they have remained in for ten years.

"Ricker never goes against his word, Mortimer. If he says he'll take you back to the monastery, then you can count on that."

Ricker let out a yell, his attention stolen by the vine unraveling some more and dropping him almost straight into the bulb's thorn-fanged throat. Struggling against gravity, he managed to swing and pull himself upward until his hands were wrapped around the vine unraveling from where it had wrapped thickly around his leg.

He twisted his hands in the vine, clinging tightly to keep himself pulled up and away from the bulb, which had begun to make great convulsive movements, its crown quivering, while the lower innards of the gullet bulged in rhythm, as though it were swallowing in excitement.

"Shadow!" Ricker called, as the vine slipped away from the upper part of his leg. "We haven't the time for pandering to childish fears."

"But a moment, Ricker," Shadow said distractedly. *"Down its hatch, Mortimer. And don't pinch your fingers."*

Ricker turned his head from where he dangled by the strength of his hands and the vines precarious grip on his leg. The boy had lowered his hands from his mouth. They were preoccupied by holding up the heavy weight of Ricker's crossbow. The DeathSpeaker must have retrieved it from where it had been knocked from Ricker's hand, and now he held it up with his right hand under the base, his left curled around the trigger, and his eyes narrowed at the tip of the arrow, trying to aim it properly. Ricker glanced down at the bulb before him, pulsing and convulsing even more rapidly now. The boy was aiming to shoot an arrow right down the bulb's crimson gullet.

The very distinguishable sound of the crossbow being activated caused Ricker to twitch, the weapon not being in his hands. The bolt ripped from the bowstring – he had a brief moment to wonder how the boy managed to pull the tight string back to lock it – and tore through the opening in the top of the bulb. From where the boy was standing, he had a view of the plant's insides, and so he was able to aim it right. The crossbow bolt ripped through the bulb's pulsing insides, tearing a hole through the quivering red mass. Viscous yellowish liquid oozed out of the hole in the throbbing walls of the bulb's insides, which had taken on an uneven rhythm of movement. Quivering erratically, the bulb spurted pus from its gullet and began to collapse in on itself, as a river finding a new channel, the liquid that made up its mass discovered a new exit to follow.

The vine wrapped around Ricker's leg slackened completely. He held tightly to it, but the vine pulled easily from the body of the bulb with a wet, sucking sound. Ricker scrabbled comically for a second at the surrounding vegetation, but gravity won again. He landed top of the sunken bulb, the yellow pus soaking quickly into the back of his pants. Ricker groaned in annoyance, even as the vine tumbled out of the trees where it had loosely wrapped itself and pattered down over Ricker's chest, like a dead serpent he had previously charmed.

Ricker felt the back of his legs, wet from the liquid oozing still from the bulb, begin to tingle oddly. He threw his hands over his face, grumbling into his palms, before running his hands up his face and brushing his hair back away from his forehead with splayed fingers.

"Shadow."

"Yes, Ricker?" The ghost, who had been dancing around the DeathSpeaker's legs, no doubt speaking to him telepathically, flitted over to where Ricker was lying on the ground. The ghost made a big production of avoiding the puddles and small rivers of pus.

"The liquid causes a paralytic effect, too, doesn't it?"

"Why, yes, Ricker, it does, though not in any separate means than the other. This is merely the reservoir of the toxin, intermixed with the nutrients the plant needed in order to survive, which Mortimer ingeniously removed from the bulb's digestive chamber. I'm really rather impressed with him. Clever boy."

"I hate you, Shadow."

"We have previously deduced as much. Regardless of your feelings about anyone, you have probably five minutes before you won't be able to feel your bladder relax, so you may want to make yourself a tad bit more comfortable, and find the

119

means to create a fire. Despite his apparent skill, that little trick may be beyond Mortimer for the time being."

Ricker grimaced deeply at the thought of being paralyzed and at the mercy of the DeathSpeaker, whether it be his help or his harm. The fact that the boy's voice could do nothing to him was little comfort. He held Ricker's crossbow, and that was a weapon he couldn't Breathe and defend against.

"Do not think so little of me."

Ricker glanced over at the ghost, who had stopped flitting about and was sitting down in Ricker's shadow, as though sitting side by side with him. The close proximity, despite the distance between their states of existence, and Shadow's slightly hurt tone, was much different from the way the two of them usually interacted. Ricker's surprise stilled his tongue.

"I may disagree with you on many fronts, but I will not let any harm come to you. Not from the paths you insist on walking, not from the enemies you pit yourself against, and not from this young boy, even if you have greatly misunderstood him." The ghost's white eyes gleamed in the darkness of his form. *"Whatever your future holds, Ricker, I will not abandon you."*

Staring at the shade, Ricker swallowed, but found that there was nothing he could say.

~*~

Thirty minutes later and Ricker had no feeling below his ribcage. He had moved, with much grumbling and some difficulty, away from the dead plant, and directed the boy to find some dry

120

wood nearby. Ricker had struggled with weakening limbs to sit in a position that wouldn't have him collapsing when the toxins fully kicked in fully. That left him now leaning up against the trunk of a tree that, thankfully, didn't seem to mind too much. The boy had gathered a little wood at first and left again to find some more, with Shadow's help. While they did that, Ricker gathered a pinch of the shavings he had gathered from a tree branch the day before and settled them under the small pile of timber he had positioned into a kind of wooden tent.

He had learned the hard way to always carry a decent-sized piece of flint with him. Using sticks, especially with his bowstring available, to light a fire was possible, but much more difficult. Not to mention that finding two sticks of a usable size was not always an option. With the flint stone and one of his steel knives (and he had a decent few with him), he was able to create a few sparks. A couple landed on the shavings and smoldered lightly. Blowing very lightly, Ricker was relieved when a small flame appeared and began to consume the small, shriveling pieces of bark. He took a few of the smaller sticks the boy had gathered and placed them in the small flame so they would catch quickly.

It was one thing to walk through a forest, knowing you were in the midst of sentient vegetation, while armed, and quite another to be sitting, half-paralyzed, in the middle of a sentient forest that knew you had just killed one of its more prominent creatures. Or, he hoped one of the more prominent. He didn't feel much like getting into a fight with something more dangerous than the snake vine and its bulb.

The boy had left the crossbow with Ricker, and he leaned over and grabbed it. He pulled the bowstring back with some difficulty. The toxin, despite having left him capable of movement above his ribs, had weakened the strength in his arms. It made Ricker wonder again how the boy would have been able to pull the bowstring back, since Ricker distinctly remembered firing the bolt into the forest when he missed hitting the boy. He frowned as it clicked into the locking position, and he fitted an arrow into the firing slot.

There was no way that the boy was strong enough to pull back and lock the bowstring himself. Shadow was insubstantial, and Ricker hadn't done it, so someone else must have.

But who could possibly have helped the boy, and where were they?

Had the plant—

No, no, that was just ridiculous. Although the vines were quite happy to show their animosity toward Ricker, and even with acknowledging their sentience, he couldn't believe one would have stopped to help Mortimer cock the crossbow. Plants didn't use tools like humans did; they didn't need to.

So then, who?

Ricker leaned back against the tree and shut his eyes, listening. The forest was thick in this area, forbidding the wind to breeze through except at the highest part of the canopy. Without the interference of the wind against his ears, the forest held an eerie silence. There were no birds to sing tunes from one leaf to the next, and the predatory plants that clearly were present would keep any mammalian predators at bay. More than likely, the unnatural sentience of the forest itself is what kept the birds and other animals from making their home amidst the trees.

With his eyes closed and his attention focused on his hearing, the sound of dirt shifting nearby came to Ricker's ears. It was not too close, and it might have been nothing more than dirt cascading naturally down a small incline, but Ricker hoped that any plants holding animosity toward him would think twice about approaching due to the fire.

The crack of a stick underfoot came from Ricker's left, though when he glanced that way briefly, he couldn't see who it was. Closing his eyes again, he listened longer, and after a moment, heard the familiar sound of Shadow's voice speaking gently. So the boy was to his left, accompanied by the shade.

Ricker listened for a long time, blocking out the sounds of Shadow's voice and the boy's steps as best he could. He kept his eyes closed and his ears open as the world around him stirred in the quiet life that only plants could manage. By the time that Shadow and the boy returned ten minutes later, Ricker was no closer to discovering who had helped the boy, or who else was in the forest with them. As the boy dropped his small armload of wood on the ground where Shadow was swirling and, of all things, making insulting expressions, Ricker decided to take the direct route.

"Boy, who helped you in the forest earlier?"

Pausing in the act of brushing dust and bark from his robes, the boy glanced up at Ricker, the wires of his mouth wiggling like worms on a hook. His eyebrows were drawn down and his mouth twisted into as much of a confused grimace as the wires would allow.

"You're not strong enough to use the crossbow on your own. Who pulled the bowstring back for you?"

The boy cocked his head to the side, his confused expression morphing slightly. He glanced at Shadow for a moment with his forehead scrunched up, then looked back at Ricker. As though it had been an obvious answer, the boy pointed at the ghost.

Ricker rolled his eyes. "Did you tell him to lie to me, Shadow?"

"A boy as clever as this doesn't need someone to make up answers for him. He can do it all on his own." The ghost sounded amused and smug at once.

Grumbling, Ricker folded his arms over his chest. "It doesn't matter. If they're around and they show themselves, I'm not unarmed." He raised his voice sharply. "You hear that? I'm armed to the teeth, so don't think about trying anything!" His voice echoed through the forest, dancing around him from tree to tree.

"To the teeth just means," Shadow explained patiently to the boy, *"that if it comes down to a battle of wits, Ricker will cheat and try to chew his opponent's arm off."*

"Shut up, Shadow."

"At once, your majesty."

Ignoring the ghost's jibe, Ricker looked sharply at the boy and pointed a finger at him. "Sit."

The boy sat.

"I bet he can lie down and roll over, too."

Ricker glanced at Shadow in confusion. "What?"

Shadow sighed. *"Nevermind. Sometimes I forget things have changed so much."*

Ricker snorted. "And yet you don't have blinders." He studied the boy, who had gone back to picking at his lips with his fingers. "Quit that."

Glancing at him in trepidation, the boy lowered his hands, folding them together in his lap. Ricker scowled at him. Of all the things to happen... he hadn't spent a great deal of time thinking about it before, as he'd been busy dealing with preparing to be paralyzed for a while, and figuring out who else was in the forest, but now that he had a moment, he was feeling properly irked at his predicament. He knew things happened to alter plans, and mistakes often occurred, but to get saddled with the creature he had been hunting? He scoffed at himself mentally. And to give his word to take the boy back to the monastery... he was a fool; a fool who'd had no better choice at the moment, yes, but no less a fool.

So the fool found himself sitting in the company of both his prey and his ultimate fate: a DeathSpeaker and a ghost. He was already forced to bear the presence of a creature who got his deadly kicks from sarcastic responses to Ricker's every word, broken by infrequent and disturbing moments of kindness and understanding. Now, he was left half-paralyzed and trapped against a tree, at once terrified and enthralled, as he watched the wires remove themselves from the boy's lips.

And they did remove *themselves*. Like living things, the wires writhed where they were trapped within the boy's skin. They squirmed and twisted and slithered from the holes in his lips where the skin had grown around them snugly. Blood drizzled down the boy's mouth, droplets rolling over his lips, as the wires peeled away from his face, tearing skin with them as they went.

125

Ricker ignored how the boy shifted his weight in discomfort, his fingers twitching and arms lifting halfway to his face before he replaced them on his lap. Ricker's eyes were only for the boy's mouth, as the gleaming black wires slithered out of his mouth, leaving tiny black holes behind. As Ricker watched, one of the wires released itself completely from the boy's skin and tumbled down his robe. The boy jerked his hand away instinctively and the wire hit the ground. It burrowed into the dirt like an erratic snake seeking refuge, and a moment later, another wire followed.

They fell, one by one, six wires in all. They dripped small droplets of blood and trailed skin behind them, but none of them remained behind. When the last one had burrowed into the earth, leaving no trace of itself behind, Ricker bothered to glance at the boy.

His legs were partially pulled to his chest and his hands were clenching the material of his robes. Blood dribbled from his chin, running down his face from the eight holes around his mouth – three above his upper lip, three below, and one on each side. The boy's eyes were shut tightly, tears beading like jewels on his lashes, and his face was screwed up in what Ricker knew to be pain. The fact that the boy did not cry – did not make a sound – made no sense to Ricker, unless the boy was remembering Ricker's promise to kill him if he ever uttered a word. It was smart of him to keep his silence, even his cries, but Ricker couldn't deny he was disappointed. It would have been so much easier to kill the boy now.

Sniffling through his nose, the boy opened his eyes, releasing a few small tears down his cheeks. Ricker gritted his teeth at those eyes – the deepest of blues, a color that haunted his dreams and was clearly determined to burden his waking moments, as well. The boy looked at him, not pleadingly, but there was a quiet request in that gaze.

Ricker leaned back against the tree and shut his eyes. The child had no right to ask that of him.

He remained awake for some time, thoughts drifting in and out aimlessly, as he listened to the boy move around, sniffling and shifting until he had gained a comfortable enough position that sleep could claim him. And then Ricker began to drift away, as well. Just before sleep took him, a thought came to his mind suddenly, as the best thoughts are wont to come.

Ricker had promised to return the boy to the monastery, but beyond that, he had sworn nothing. So he would take the boy to the monastery, and after his word had been kept, he would kill the boy.

And that would be the end of it.

IX

There were bodies everywhere.

It had occurred too suddenly for them to be afraid. They had received no warning; they had no idea they were in danger. The dirt road Ricker followed was lined with corpses displaying a mockery of life. Here and there, lips were pulled back in a smile. One man's mouth was open wide, his head thrown back in a laugh. Two women had fallen to the ground together and lay with their arms still tangled around the other – a hug they would be trapped in even as the scavengers plucked out their eyes.

Ricker walked on past them. He ignored the eyes that gazed at him emptily, glazed with the fog of death, openly staring into eternity. Hands that had tumbled into gravity reached for him endlessly, but he overstepped their immobile reach and walked on, kicking dust around his long gait.

He was not interested in the dead, and in their death and final peace, they would have no interest in him. His eyes, unglazed, his fingers, twitching, were for the living that still dwelled within the dead town he saw ahead of him. There would be only one, and Ricker had a bolt waiting to meet his throat.

Ricker waded through streets of pale flesh, the town a busy place of refuge where people could escape the real world in a sea of bodies like themselves, finding an escape in the illusion that they were not alone and doomed.

He found the DeathSpeaker in the city's market. Merchants were slumped over carts filled with goods. One man had collapsed fallen forward

128

onto a display of weapons. His face was peaceful and he had clearly been dead before the iron dagger impaled him just under the chin. His lips were pulled back in a smile, displaying bloody teeth and the crimson dagger blade, which had sliced through half of his tongue, leaving it dangling by a thin piece of flesh.

The DeathSpeaker was crouched on the ground, a woman cradled in his lap. Unlike the others he had seen, her face was caught in a perpetual expression of fear, his eyes wide, white now in death. There were bodies piled nearby, having been standing close together when they died and fallen in a tangle of limbs and weaponry. Soldiers, or citizens taking up arms, no doubt having come to accost the creature who had killed them all.

Even as all the town lay dead, the DeathSpeaker still spoke.

Ricker pulled the bowstring back, locking it into place and fitting the bolt into its chamber. The DeathSpeaker didn't look up at him. His eyes were for the woman alone, and his fingers stroked her greying hairs. She was maybe thirty years older than the boy's ten years. From what Ricker could see, they had similar features. Ricker always pitied the rare few woman who survived giving birth to a DeathSpeaker. The realization, when those ten years were up, of what their child had become did little else but break their hearts.

He raised the crossbow, pointing it at the boy. His eyes narrowed, his voice was soft, but his tone cold.

"You'll not end me the same way you did them, boy. You never should have Spoke to begin with."

The boy looked up, surprise in his eyes, as though he had not realized that there was someone else there. There were tears in his eyes, magnifying the dark brown irises.

He opened his mouth to ask a question.

The bolt slid through his throat like a needle through fabric, severing his vocal chords in an instant. The boy slumped forward, mouth working to try and say something. There was silence but for the sound of his choking breaths as blood rushed from the hole in his throat, staining his clothes and painting his mother's face red. Eventually, even that sound stopped.

Then, there was only silence.

When Mortimer blinked his eyes open the next morning, the fire has been reduced to a few dimly-glowing coals and his face felt like the man had been stabbing it all night long. He reached up and touched his fingers gingerly to his lips. The skin had been peeled off in places and was very sore, and the blood had dried on his face and came off in flakes, sometimes pulling skin with it. Mortimer brushed half-heartedly at his skin, resisting the immediate urge to moan. He knew what Ricker would do if he heard a sound come from him, but more than that, he remembered Father Fabula's words to him. DeathSpeakers mustn't speak, ever, unless they wanted everyone around them to die.

Mortimer didn't want that. Even if Ricker was a jerk, like the ghost had said, Mortimer didn't get to decide whether his life was worth keeping or not. He didn't deserve to make that kind of choice, and he wouldn't want to if he could.

Opening his mouth proved to stretch the skin and break up the dried blood, but hurt a lot!

Mortimer couldn't help it, though, and sucked in a great breath in a yawn. His tongue darted out and licked his lips, causing Mortimer to spend some minutes examining his tongue with his fingers. It was so strange! He had seen Father Fabula's tongue many times as the man spoke – it moved around in his mouth differently at each word. Mortimer had never expected his tongue to be so squishy, though, while also being firm, and very wet.

Mortimer grinned at the feeling of his tongue darting out between his closed mouth and smearing spit across the dry, cracked lips. He ran his tongue over his teeth next, and then spent a lot of time touching the inside of his mouth with his fingers. Some of his teeth were flat, with bumpy ridges and an indent in the center, while others were sharp. His front top teeth were very large and flat, but didn't have the ridges like his other flat teeth. He also discovered that some of his sharp teeth were *very* sharp, when he scraped his tongue too hard over a tooth on the top of his mouth and a strange taste filled his mouth – sweet and bitter at once. He swallowed an odd liquid, and licked his lips again, leaving a smear of blood behind.

Ricker leaned against the tree with his arms crossed, his hands tightened into fists. He had woken with a gasp as the present had returned to him in a rush of consciousness, his legs tingling painfully but mobile once again. The recollection of his dream only caused him to sigh and look forlornly at the boy who sat a few feet away, clearly fascinated by the insides of his own mouth.

It never failed that every time he came upon a new DeathSpeaker, he would have that dream again. It had been one of the few times that he hadn't regretted his decision to destroy the DeathSpeakers he found.

No... no, that wasn't true. He never regretted the actions he took against them. They were dangerous creatures, not fit to live in a world they were so willing to destroy. That was what the dream, which was merely a memory so often replayed, meant: the DeathSpeakers needed to be destroyed. They were too dangerous to be left to their own devices. When the wires unbound their lips, they would speak. Whether it was an actual desire to do harm or merely a compulsion to use their voice didn't matter to him. It was the results that counted, in the end. When they spoke, those who heard died. They couldn't be allowed to speak.

And since they wouldn't resist speaking, they couldn't be allowed to live.

Ricker's finger found the trigger of the crossbow. The bowstring was locked and a bolt already fitted into place. He lifted the weapon into his lap and rested it on his knee, turning it so it pointed at the boy.

He was facing away from Ricker, attention too focused on investigating his lips and tongue and teeth to notice Ricker was awake. From the back, it would be easy to kill him. A bolt at this close of range would rip through his throat just as easily. Or he could fire the bolt into the boy's spine, severing it. He would be unable to run while Ricker ended his life, and then he would go on and find the next DeathSpeaker, until he had ended them all.

Ricker's finger tightened on the trigger.

Ricker never goes against his word, Mortimer.

Dangling from the snake vine, Shadow had told the boy that to convince him to help Ricker escape. And it was true; when Ricker swore to do something, he never went back on it. He had failed to keep his promise once, and had lost... everything. Since, he had never failed to keep his word. He had never gone back on what he had sworn to do.

Ricker sighed and set the crossbow on the ground next to him, before running a hand over his face. He had promised to take the boy back to the monastery, so he would. It would take him days, though, to go back over his steps, and if possible, he wanted to avoid the town that he had escaped from. No doubt they would have words about him breaking down their jail.

The sound of a woman's scream echoed around in his memory and Ricker closed his eyes. He could retrace his steps and go back and see what the problem was. It didn't mean he would let himself be caught...

"You're forgetting one crucial detail."

Huffing a soft sigh, Ricker reached down and plucked the crossbow bolt out of the chamber. He pulled the trigger and let the unloaded bowstring *thunnnt!* back into place.

Shadow laughed and, as Ricker glanced around, swarmed into view through the many layers of shade offered by the trees. Within the countless shadows of the forest, the ghost appeared yet darker as his eyes glowed brightly, and had almost free reign to move among them.

"Not what I meant, but not displeasing, either."

Ricker frowned at the ghost. "What did you mean?"

"You wish to return to the monastery empty-handed?" The shade seemed to clasp his chin in a

hand and Ricker saw those glowing eyes narrow thoughtfully at him, as though he were something to be studied. *"Father Thomas asked something else of you, if you'll recall."*

Ricker did recall. Father Thomas had used another of the monks in the monastery to inform him of the DeathSpeaker, so he need not be the one to directly call for the boy's death. But when Ricker had arrived, it had been Father Thomas who had told him of the second thing he desired.

And while Ricker was not in the habit of doing favors for people, the priest had made him an offer that he would be foolish to ignore. There were more DeathSpeakers that the man knew the whereabouts of. Killing them would be Ricker's next job, after he had dealt with Mortimer. But unless he learned where they were from Father Thomas, he would have to spend precious time looking for them himself.

Ricker glanced at the boy with narrowed eyes. There was a problem in timing. He had promised to return the boy to the monastery, and only after he had kept his promise could he deal with the DeathSpeaker. But he couldn't return to the monastery without the gem if he wanted Father Thomas to keep his side of the bargain.

Groaning, Ricker buried his face in a hand. "I'm going to have to bring the boy with me." Shadow laughed brightly.

"You're enjoying this, aren't you?"

"Eh, perhaps a little, but I think it will be good for you to spend some time with Mortimer. He may be able to help you develop your deplorable social skills."

"My social skills might not be so *deplorable* if you were a better conversationalist."

"Tsk, tsk, Ricker. You'll never get any answers that way. You have to actually ask the questions."

Gritting his teeth, Ricker blew a breath of air out of his nose in agitation. He truly hated it when Shadow called him on things he'd been attempting to subvert.

"The boy—"

"Has a name," Shadow interrupted in a casual tone. *"But he does not have the pendant. It was stolen from him."*

"I suppose you know that from reading his mind?"

"In part. I was polite enough to ask first, and he was kind enough to think on the answer at a level I did not have to look too hard to read. Mortimer is actually very cooperative, and he has manners, unlike some people I know."

"Subtle."

"I don't want to insult you in ways you're too ignorant to comprehend." He ignored Ricker's scowl. *"As for where you might find the pendant now that it's gone rogue from its guardian, you've thought the answer for that yourself."*

"There are a lot of places I've thought of recently, Shadow," Ricker grumbled. Why the shade insisted on bringing this up *now*, instead of mentioning it before, was far beyond him. The jewel-that-wasn't had been pushed to the back of his mind since he'd left the monastery behind, but Shadow rarely let thoughts he saw important lay dead for long, especially when Ricker's focus lay on murdering another DeathSpeaker child.

"When Father Thomas initially told you about the pendant, you were thinking about how rubies can still be sold for prices to people who

deem them worthy of the cost, regardless of the wealth of the current world and the necessity for things that don't fall under the category of 'pretty.'"

"So instead of traipsing back through wastelands and farmlands, you'd rather I go toward the cities?"

"What you do *is your own choice, as I've no control over you."*

"Right," Ricker muttered.

"But if you wish to find the pendant, if only for what you will gain in the end, then your best choice of action would be to follow those instincts you've honed so well after years of being a killing machine."

Ricker's expression argued on whether to form a grimace or a scowl and ended up somewhere in between. He was very practiced at killing, and despite the fact that he believed that those he hunted were right to be ended, that did not mean that he didn't find the necessity of murder to be distasteful. He did not enjoy the act of taking the life of a creature that appeared to be human, and more often than not one that had not yet reached adulthood.

Shadow bringing the subject and his views on it up as often as he did was not helpful toward Ricker's personal regard for himself, nor toward any chance of his stopping in his actions. It annoyed him deeply, even while, secretly, he found himself even more disgusted with his place in life, wondering, and remembering, how he had managed to get here.

Whenever he had a chance to think about it, or had the thought stalk up slowly and attack him like a great cat, Ricker would realize that he had managed to spend however long without actively thinking about his son. And then, as the relief rolled in that he had forgotten for that long, and the despair fell in upon him at having remembered at all, the shame would roll in like a tide, tossing him about senselessly, until he wanted nothing more than to lie down and die.

Ricker's entire existence seemed to be made up of contradiction after contradiction. He was an assassin who hated killing, a weaponsmith who left the forge behind him, a living man with a ghost's shadow, and a father without a family.

He might have been able to survive dealing with one of the contradictions tormenting his life, but he had not deserved that form of mercy, it seemed. He had lost his son first, and the others had simply followed after that.

True, it was he who had chosen to leave his forge behind, and he who had decided to become an assassin and destroy the DeathSpeakers, but he had not chosen to wander through life with a ghost tailing him like some sort of lost sheep – only a talking one, with more advice than a room of royal advisors.

His leaving his forge behind had become a necessity when he chose to become an assassin. Becoming an assassin had been necessary when he chose to avenge his son. And he *would* avenge him. He would destroy all of the DeathSpeakers, if it took him his whole life.

And that would be the end of it.

~*~

"What does the pendant do?"

They had walked from morning until just after the sun had passed beyond the peak of its ascent in the sky. Now, Ricker was settled down by a large rock, searching through his satchel for something to eat. Preparing food took fresh ingredients, which were impossible to keep on hand when traveling on foot, so Ricker often settled for simple dried foods. They weren't the greatest, but he wouldn't starve.

"What does it do?*"* Ricker asked. The shade was cast against the rock, so it appeared he was sitting up next to Ricker. His legs were crossed beneath him and he was sipping tea from the shadow of a teacup he had formed himself. Mortimer, for his part, had become completely fascinated by the fact that the ghost could form random objects out of darkness, and was watching the ghost "drink tea."

"Father Thomas didn't seem inclined to tell me anything about it. It can't possibly be just a jewel. In fact, he said it wasn't."

"And you believed him."

Ricker glared at the ghost. He earned a tilted head in response and, though he could not see it, he presumed a wide, mocking smile.

There was a loud sound, like the growl of an animal, and Mortimer sucked in a breath. He jumped to his feet and ran over to Ricker, ducking down beside him and wrapping his arm fearfully around Ricker's chest.

"Get off!" Ricker shoved the boy away from him and stood up quickly, walking a few feet away until he had put a more comfortable distance between himself and the boy.

"Was that really necessary?"

I'm not going to cuddle him, Ricker thought loudly. *I ought to kill him for that gasp.*

Shadow tsked loudly, letting go of his teacup. The shadowy form disappeared suddenly in a wisp, sucked back into the darkness from which it had been birthed.

"You know as well as I – perhaps better, even – that DeathSpeakers have no need to eat so long as their wires remain intact, binding their lips. They are lucky to be so sustained by their Marks. Now, of course, his wires are gone. He is dealing with something he has never had to deal with before, Ricker. Hunger."

The ghost moved closer to Mortimer, so the boy could better see him, and took off his top hat.

"You're the one who found it necessary to bring the child with you. He's your responsibility now."

Shadow ignored Ricker's growl, flipping his hat upside down and reaching in. His hand scrambled around inside it for a moment, before he pulled it back out.

The shadow of a black rabbit dangled from his fist by the ears.

Mortimer grinned.

X

    The city was Ricker's least favorite place to go. Out in the rural areas, things were spread out, due to the farmlands stretching across acres of land, or because of the wastelands, in which there was nothing *to* spread out. In the urban areas, however, everything was pushed together to accommodate as much as possible into the smallest manageable area. People lived on top of each other – literally, in some cases, when the buildings that had begun to fall down ages ago were claimed and people attempted to make them livable. They never looked at all as good as they once had, and were not nearly as safe, but the people living in them didn't know that, and didn't care.

    And the *smell*.

    Contrary to the way he preferred to live, some people had managed to figure out how to work the mechanics that had made up the previous world. These people tended to live in the urban areas, partly because that was where most of the mechanics had ended up, and because a lot of farmers were descended from farmers, and in the centuries since the Great War, tradition had picked up again, as it always did.

    But the cities often held mechanical creations, either ones salvaged from the old, or bits and pieces thrown together in a Frankenstein's monster mesh of churning metal and burning fuel. They were loud and filled the air with no small amount of exhaust, and Ricker despised being anywhere near them. So when he saw the Trade City in the distance, his lips twisted into a grimace and he growled under his breath. Behind him,

Mortimer walked with Shadow flickering around within his dark reflection, a curious and slightly disgusted look on his face, as he smelled something foul in the air.

"Seems Mortimer doesn't like it, either."

"Hm," Ricker grumbled. "He's not as stupid as I would have thought, then." He ignored the swat he saw the ghost give his shadow's head and continued walking. "Come, boy, and don't get lost. I won't go hunting for you."

"That, I doubt."

Ricker ignored him.

To be honest, Ricker had no idea how many cities there were spread throughout their world, but he had been to three (and three too many, as far as he was concerned). The Trade City, where he found himself, was an area stuffed full of people who didn't want to live outside of a place of luxury.

The city was built in a circular formation, with the main roads that went through it traveling north to south, and east to west through the center of the city. The central area was made up of the buildings of government; the home of whoever was ruling the city at the time and the barracks, which were filled with soldiers who roamed the city and made sure those who lived there did as they were told. That the soldiers and the city's ruler were corrupt was a given.

Surrounding the governmental area was a large ring of shops overtop which those who worked them lived, food carts and merchant stands crowding the streets. The Merchant District of the city was very large and formed into a ring that was still crowded despite the mass amount of room it took up.

Surrounding the Merchant District were the homes of all who lived there. Broken down buildings had been made into places for three or four families to live together, and people squashed in on each other in an attempt to fit as many as they could within the city. Being so close to the main trade allowed them access to safe food and water, although it meant that they, themselves, honing no talent beyond their ability to live close to so many other people, had nothing to trade. This made for a great deal of crime.

People who lived there hounded the merchants during opening hours, loitering about and begging, avoiding the soldiers whenever they came near. The soldiers themselves, while beating off people they caught stealing or begging for the wares, would often help themselves to whatever they wanted, and the merchants could do nothing to stop them.

Ricker felt a tug on the back of his cloak and glared down at the boy, who had clutched his fingers around the material and was holding on fearfully, while looking around at the dilapidated outskirts of the city still a mile away. Ricker opened his mouth to snarl, but Shadow spoke first.

"Leave him alone on this, I think, Ricker."

The faint echoing tenor to the ghost's voice gave away that he was speaking solely to Ricker's ears. Narrowing his eyes, Ricker responded with a thought. *You think?*

"Do you really wish for him to be swept away by the packs of people who flood through here? He is too small to fight them off. That, of course, on top of the fact that he has not been outside of a monastery before this adventure of his began. He is frightened, Ricker."

And why do I care about that?

"Because you are not nearly as heartless as you would like yourself to believe, never mind anyone else." He saw the shade flicker into view before him, briefly, glowing eyes narrowed. *"He is a child, whether you choose to acknowledge that or not. And regardless of your opinions on the matter, he did not choose his fate. You're doing that for him."*

Ricker reached back and grabbed hold of the boy's arm, pulling him forward roughly. He felt the boy resist and grit his teeth, glaring backward.

The frightened look on the child's face was half-hidden by his other arm, which he had brought up to shield his face. Ricker's teeth tightened until he thought his jaw would break. He had never been the kind of person to hurt a child. He hunted DeathSpeakers, yes, and most of them were children whom he was forced to kill, yes. However, Ricker's means were always swift, and as painless as he could make them with what weapons he had. He didn't chase down DeathSpeakers in an attempt to cause them suffering.

One would think he had beaten the boy earlier that day, not made the mistake of giving him something to eat. If Ricker was honest with himself, he should have known better. The boy had only just lost his wires and he had never eaten before. Unused to food, he should have been given something with a bland flavor that would help him to grow accustomed to food and eating it.

Ricker wasn't in the habit of carrying bowls of porridge in his satchel. He'd had some dried fruit and nuts he'd traded for at a village before he went to the monastery, and some dried jerky.

Of course, he'd given the boy the jerky.

Salted in order to draw out the moisture, jerky had an incredible flavor to it – such a flavor, in fact, that even he sometimes found his mouth ached if he had a particularly sapid piece. Of course, to someone who had never eaten before, that savory pleasurable-pain that eating jerky could be was just pain.

Ricker snarled at the guilt that threatened to overcome him, even now. It was the boy's own fault for shoving so much of the jerky in his mouth at once. And when Ricker had offered him some water to wash away the flavor, the boy should have taken it, instead of flinching away from him and crying until Shadow had convinced him to take a drink.

It wasn't Ricker's fault the boy had been so foolish.

He loosened his grasp and allowed the child to pull away. The boy took a few steps back and looked at him fearfully.

It wasn't his fault.

"Death to those who are different, Ricker," Shadow whispered viciously into his ear, and Ricker shut his eyes against the words.

That's not—

"That's exactly *what you think,"* Shadow snarled. *"You've just decided to pick which ones are too different to live."* Ricker clenched his hand into a fist around his cloak's clasp. *"Mortimer knows what the pendant looks like. You do not. And I refuse to help you. You want the gem, ask him for help."*

Ricker swallowed. Shadow did not like what he did, that much had always been clear. He was rarely so cruel, however, in his tone, even if his words were biting and cut deeply. The change was not as frightening as it was painful. Ricker didn't like the thought that, despite his lingering presence, the shade had begun to hate him.

There was a soft sigh, whispering on a brush of wind. *"I do not hate you, Ricker, but you refuse to listen. Each DeathSpeaker you kill, you further destroy yourself."*

"That makes no sense," Ricker murmured, and ignored the curious look the boy gave him.

"It won't be long before you realize what I mean, but I cannot tell you. You'll discover it on your own, and I fear what will happen when you do." The viciousness in Shadow's voice had gone, replaced by that sorrow that Ricker had heard at times before. *"The boy's name is Mortimer. Please use it. You're frightening him, and the only thing he ever did to wrong you was be born."*

Ricker opened his eyes and looked at the boy, who was giving him a hybrid look of curiosity and fear. He stared for a long moment, thinking, trying to put things into perspective.

He hated DeathSpeakers.

He hated DeathSpeakers, because he remembered coming home to find his son's body, bright blue eyes glazed and staring. And it hurt him to remember, even as it shamed him that he had ever forgotten. But he remembered how he'd wandered, looking for the killer, and how he'd hunted DeathSpeakers down for even daring to live, and how could he give that up when his son remained dead?

Not that killing them would bring Lucas back.

Letting them live wouldn't avenge his son.

Ricker's head *screamed*. It felt like there was pressure building up behind his eyes, trying to force his skull apart, and he could barely stand it. Some part of him knew he wasn't looking at this fully; he wasn't seeing all that he needed to see to make a decision. And without all of the information, any decision he made would be seriously lacking. But he couldn't just decide *not* to go after DeathSpeakers anymore, just because of something Shadow had said. He couldn't change his entire life based on a few words, but how could he keep going as he was?

He wasn't planning on killing the boy now, though. He had made a promise not to, and while he'd planned on using a loophole in that promise to kill the boy later, for now, the boy wasn't at the end of his crossbow. Considering that he had sworn to return the boy to the monastery, Mortimer was then under Ricker's protection.

And if he concentrated on the moment... on getting the pendant and returning to the monastery, then he could deal with things that would happen after that when their time came up.

The pressure behind his eyes eased and Ricker sighed in relief, realizing only then that he had brought his one hand up and was pinching the bridge of his nose tightly. Opening his eyes and lowering his hand, he found the boy still standing in front of him, looking frightened and concerned at once.

The existence of that concern, however overrun by fear, allowed Ricker to fully place himself in the here and now. He would figure out what to do about the boy another time.

"Mortimer, right?"

The boy's shoulders twitched, startled, but he nodded slowly, his eyes wide. Ricker thrust out his hand for the boy to take.

Mortimer stared at his hand for some time, before looking up into Ricker's face, not with a question, but uncertainty. Ricker bit back his impatience at the child's hesitation, though his lips still twisted in a silent snarl. He jerked his hand, calling the boy's attention back to it without a word, and only then did Mortimer step forward and slip his much smaller hand into Ricker's.

With a sharp nod, Ricker started walking and the boy was forced to follow him lest the grip on his hand pull him along regardless. Ricker's shoulders were tense as he walked, and he hated that he found himself cherishing the feeling of that small hand clutched within his own. It had been years... how many, he wasn't sure. He hadn't held the hand of a child since his son had died.

But he knew what the boy was, and that this was wrong. This was not a child whose hand he grasped. This was a monster; a creature born to destroy all around it with his voice alone. This was a burden on the world, and one it only had to carry because of the past mistakes of man and the apathy of a false god. It was foolish of his heart to let him find peace in this moment of betrayal to his cause, but even knowing that, Ricker couldn't bring himself to tear his hand away from the boy's.

If he had to bear the presence of this child until they reached the monastery, then he should be permitted, at least, to bear it in such a way that it did not crush him.

Ricker tried to ignore the feeling of his own resolve crumbling beneath him. Even as he felt the weight of his crossbow on his back, he knew that the weight of this boy's existence was heavier still, and too much for him to bear.

Ricker closed his eyes and tried to swallow the heaviness in his heart. He couldn't allow his emotions to interfere with what he needed to do. The boy was a *DeathSpeaker*, he couldn't forget that.

But he's also just a boy.

Why did this argument sound so old in his head? Had he needed to fight himself so viciously during every kill? No... no, he'd never given himself time to doubt his decisions, and even afterward, he'd known his choices were the right ones. Even with the nightmares...

He had to see him as a DeathSpeaker and nothing more. Not a child, not a boy, not the charge of the priests of the Northern Monastery.

A DeathSpeaker.

Ricker drew a silent breath that shook all the way down into his lungs. His teeth chattered lightly, but he stilled his jaw and walked on, pulling the DeathSpeaker behind him. One step... two steps... three steps closer to finding the gem, and to putting everything behind him.

He held the boy's small hand in his like a lifeline as thin as a piece of string.

~*~

There were two colors that were so prominent in the city that their existence anywhere else made whatever they covered seem as false as everything in the smog-filled ruins. The ground in the city was asphalt, or macadam, depending upon the dialect of your residence, although the people who lived in the cities in Ricker's time didn't recall either of these names for it. It was the ground in the city area, chopped up and broken by time, great cracks running through it. Like all stone that covered the ground in what had once been a wide area, it was called "concrete," because that was a word that had been commonly written and left for people over the years to find.

The concrete in the Trade City was predominantly black, though it often turned a dark grey as it lost its luster. The buildings scrunched together like the bent wires of an old slinky crumbled, dropping dust and stones and revealing their innards beyond walls that had once been colored. They, too, were grey; light grey, just a little darker than pale – the color flesh turns when blood stops running through veins.

Filth lined the streets, junked up the rare small spaces between buildings, and filled unlivable areas (those unlivable by people who had anywhere else to stay, that is). The streets smelled of vomit, blood, and piss. Some places had scorch marks where experiments with old technology went wrong, or where people got out of line and the Trade City Soldiers got creative in getting rid of the problem. Beyond the main road, there were cracks and coves abound filled with shadows that reached mockingly outward, pretending places of security.

They were anything but.

Ricker's eyes were narrowed as he moved down the main road, stepping carefully over the wide, uneven breaks in the concrete and keeping a firm hand around Mortimer's. People who saw him coming the other way stepped clear of his path, and even those in front of him who couldn't see him coming moved aside. The shadows in the dark spaces where buildings had rotted, or in the alleys that quivered with the scent of dirt and death, reached for the boy but didn't dare touch him.

149

Ricker's name had traveled far, but even those that didn't recognize who he was had enough inclination about what he was to stay clear. His eyes tracked the area, scanning the crowds like an eagle studies the blades of grass beneath him, searching for the mouse that stands out. Ricker was looking for a thief, or someone who had traded something *with* a thief. He was looking, perhaps, for another hunter like himself. Someone who would have, at one point, touched an artifact he was determined to find.

"All right... Mortimer," Ricker said quietly, struggling on the boy's name. "What does this pendant look like?"

He caught movement in the corner of his eye and turned his head slightly. The boy was looking at him with a look of fear and revulsion on his face. It took Ricker a moment to realize why.

"You're not explaining anything, are you, Shadow?"

"You're on your own in that, Ricker."

The ghost's smug tone was grating, but he did his best to ignore it. Turning back to the boy, he snapped his words out on the tail of a growl. "I'm not telling you to speak. You wore the pendant, correct?" The boy nodded, still studying his face. "Think about what it looked like. I only know it masks itself as a ruby."

The boy squinted his eyes and cocked his head to the side curiously.

"He wants to know what a ruby is," Shadow explained helpfully, but didn't bother to provide an answer.

"It's a glass rock, the color of blood. Is that what the pendant looked like?" Another nod. "How big?"

Mortimer looked at his left hand briefly, raising it almost to chin level. He fisted it and opened it again, before turning it over to gaze thoughtfully at his palm. Cupping his hand, his fingers curling, he held it out to Ricker as though to hand him something.

"You can fit it in the palm of your hand," Shadow murmured, bemused. *"It seems smaller than I remember."*

Ricker gave the ghost a sharp look at he was cast at his feet. "You've *seen* the stone?"

"It's not a stone, Ricker, and yes, I've seen it. Held it, in fact. I was commissioned to study it, to find out what it was made from, how it worked." His glaring white eyes flashed to Ricker's. *"All studies that failed to come up with any information that made sense to a mortal mind. It is beyond us to comprehend, and should not remain in our hands."*

"And you want *me* to find it?" he asked, and then thought for a moment. "You want me to return it to the *monastery?*"

"Truthfully? No. But I'll take what I can get. Anything is better than where it is now." His eyes moved to Mortimer, who had turned to look at him, his right hand still clutched in Ricker's. Absently, Ricker had moved them off to the shoulder of the main road, close to one of the dark alleys. There was a scuttling sound within, but a sharp look from Ricker silenced the scuttler.

"I didn't say anything because parts of what I know might no longer be viable. It's been almost two hundred years since I held the amulet. Anything about it could have changed within that time period, whereas you had it around your neck not three days ago."

Ricker realized Mortimer must have silently asked the question which prompted Shadow's speech. The fact that the shade was willing to explain things for Mortimer's benefit, but not his, was telling. *"Ricker has a better source of information in what he's looking for in you than he does in me."*

Ricker grumbled in annoyance. "He has a point." Mortimer glanced up at him, but Ricker turned a glare on Shadow. "It still would have been nice if you'd've shared that bit of information. What does the stone do?"

"It's not a stone."

"Rock, then."

The ghost sighed. *"What did the priests tell you at the monastery, Mortimer?"*

The silence lasted for a few minutes, interrupted only by Shadow's suggestion that Ricker keep walking. With the shade surreptitiously in the lead, to any passersby, it appeared that a man was walking through the city holding the hand of a young child. Luckily, in areas as heavily populated as the Trade City, it was not uncommon to see PlagueCursed about, so other than a few people who stared, and one or two who moved quickly to the other side of the street, no one made a big fuss over the obvious Mark on Mortimer's face.

The three reached the Merchant District and turned to walk among the shops and carts, dodging merchants and consumers and beggars alike. Ricker scanned each face they passed but saw no pendants bleeding like rubies, and no faces that showed him any manner of theft other than what usually went on in a market. They had just passed a soldier bearing a sword that Ricker recognized as a paltry attempt at weaponsmithing when Shadow finally spoke.

"They didn't tell him much," the ghost informed Ricker, speaking solely to him due to the number of people about. *"Father Thomas was not merely opposed to the idea of Mortimer being given the amulet; he was opposed to the amulet existing at all. It was in the care of Mortimer's guardian, Father Fabula, and apparently, Father Thomas had no love of him for this very reason, as well as the fact that Fabula was of the lesser-loved priests who held no dominant belief system."*

Ricker made a surprised sound in the back of his throat. *That's unexpected.*

"Quite. It was one of the reasons, apparently, that he was so willing to take Mortimer in. From what Mortimer has gleaned from his years at the monastery, many of the other priests, Father Thomas included, believe that the PlagueCursed are the first arrivals of the Devil's army against mankind."

Groaning, Ricker rubbed his forehead. "You can't be serious." Mortimer was watching him curiously as they walked.

"I wonder, actually, what the man would attempt to do to you, should you return to his presence with the gem in hand."

Ricker raised an eyebrow and watched the shade give a shrug. *"It is an unknown, but you yourself considered him to be a man one should not wish to cross. Your instincts, while occasionally warped, are not often incorrect. That the man is on the verge of death himself does not mean that he won't attempt to take you down into the bowels of Hell with him. Especially if he has convinced himself that you're a walking demon."*

Ricker grunted in agreement, his mouth twisted into a frown. It wasn't the first time he'd heard of that particular belief system, though he'd never met a priest before who held it.

Had Ricker been aware of the belief systems that predominated the world two hundred years prior, he would have been able to list how they had been altered over time, as all religions are wont to be. Once, a thousand years ago, paintings had shown Jesus of Nazareth crucified on the Cross, holding himself up by his own inner strength, in his power, ignoring the pain of the stakes through his wrists and feet. The populace had once been made up of a people who were strong. They lived hard lives, and warrior's lives, and so the mortal Son they worshipped mirrored that strength.

By the end of the second millennia since the birth of Christ, humankind relied predominantly upon technology and their strength was nowhere near what it had once been; the world had guns and bombs and there was less of a need for physical prowess. As the people became a weaker version of themselves, the victims of the crises that rose around them, so their view of their savior changed, and Jesus Christ was depicted in images as a victim of Roman ministrations. He hung limply on the Cross, held up only by the strength of the stakes through his wrists, as he had no strength of his own to give.

In the two centuries since the Dark Plague had ravished the earth and stolen away lives and history and most of what the world had once been defined by, that view of the Lord had changed again. The strength of armies was little known in this world, where the population was so depleted and what people remained were often weak from lack of proper nutrition. The idea of someone captured by soldiers and hung on a cross to die was something the people couldn't relate to. Everyone knew of the Dark Plague, however, which still ravaged the world when let loose, but was nothing in comparison to the vast wave of death that it had once been. People could see how God would have shown mercy by sending down his only son to take the Dark Plague for the people, so its force would not follow them into the world beyond death.

But that dark prince of a world beneath humankind's feet was strong, and they knew that it must be he who ravaged the unborn children as they were trapped in the womb, turning them into his minions, and allowing them to enter the world as PlagueCursed.

Ricker scoffed, jerking his head to the side. "It's nothing but a children's tale."

"Much the same can be said for all beliefs, of gods and gems alike."

Ricker eyed him sharply. "You *do* know what the stone does."

"I know what legends say the artifact is capable of. Whether or not they are true is something that could only be discovered via an experience I hope we do not achieve."

"Shadow," Ricker murmured. He stared down at the ghost, noting out of the corner of his eye that Mortimer's gaze, too, was locked upon the shade. "You called it an artifact. What is it, exactly? What does it do?"

The ghost was silent for a long time. Ricker and Mortimer kept walking, the shade mirroring Ricker's steps as he walked. Ricker scanned the crowd as they walked, searching for danger and blood-red-not-jewels alike.

"What would you ask for, if you could have one wish?"

A pair of eyes flashed before Ricker's memory, so bright they were like twin blue stars. His heart clenched in his chest and he felt the sudden rebelling of his stomach, but fought down the nausea. He'd halted in the middle of the street, drawing a shaking breath as he pinched the bridge of his nose, eyes shut tightly.

"You know the answer to that," he whispered.

"Yes."

The silence returned, during which time he'd felt the boy pull on his hand. He followed the direction blindly, too busy trying to compose himself to worry that he was allow the DeathSpeaker to lead him, even briefly. Mortimer merely led them over to the side of the path, away from the main traffic of people.

When Ricker had calmed himself, he looked first at Shadow. The ghost was watching the boy, who had released Ricker's hand and was watching people walk by. Perhaps the ghost had done it out of curiosity, or maybe he had meant to give Ricker a few moments of privacy. Regardless, Ricker was grateful for the chance to clear his face.

Shadow shifted back around until he was gazing at Ricker with those glowing white eyes. *"Legends tell of a blood red jewel that is no such thing, crafted by the hands of a deity."* He continued speaking, not giving Ricker a chance to interject, though that could do nothing to stop the man's scowl of disgust. *"Some legends tell that the gem grants one wish,* any *wish, no matter how large. Other myths tell a different tale – that the gem cannot be equated with a genie, but is greater still than that. That it is, in fact, the piece of a god."*

Ricker raised an eyebrow at Shadow. "A piece of a god?" Shadow gave a noncommittal shrug. "So... what? Break the stone and you kill the god?"

"I would have my doubts, as it seems a foolish item to let lie around if it is, in fact, a means to an end. The end, as it were.

"It's up to interpretation, as no two works I have ever read agree on every point. Some people believe that merely holding the artifact gives them the status and power of a god. Others hold to the fact that is it an unanswered prayer – a single wish waiting to be granted. There are some who believe it is a way to attain immortality – the fabled Philosopher's Stone, if you will."

"The what?"

Shadow sighed. *"Nevermind. The one theory that has always seemed the least popular, perhaps because the idea is so very disturbing, is the idea that the stone, being directly connected to the deity that created it, can be used to summon the deity."*

"Which means, basically, all of the theories were correct."

"Precisely. If the artifact allows for the summoning of a deity, it would grant the bearer with the power of a god in their hands, to do whatever they wished. And, of course, then there's the question of whether the gem is a servant of the deity, or a leash that would bind them."

"And which," Ricker muttered.

"Yes. And perhaps that is the true reason it is such a desired artifact. Immortality, absolute control, and wishes aside, there is one question that has always haunted mankind's mind, seeking an

157

answer with desperation enough to destroy all until the answer is found."

Ricker blew a derisive snort out of his nose. "Does God give a shit?"

"Less a question about God, I think, than a question about life, about everything. One question that would hold all the answers. If it is a stone to grant one wish, Ricker, what one question would you wish to be answered?"

Ricker looked hopelessly at the ghost. After a moment, he shook his head with a shrug.

"Why?"

Why. A simple word. A simple question, so easily understood, but the answers... yes, the answers would be endless. That one question would answer them all. Why? Why was the sky hazy? Why is there no more grass? Why do humans exist? Why did a god let them destroy so much? Why is the world ending? *Why did you let my son die?*

Ricker swallowed thickly.

"There are legends aplenty, Ricker. Given more time, I could have found more still, I'm certain. I don't know what *the stone does. I only know it shouldn't be in the hands of those who would use it for harm if they could."*

Ricker nodded slowly. *You trust me with it?*

"I trust you, *Ricker. It bothers me that you do not trust yourself. That you think you would take the stone and use it to—"*

"I know what I would use it for. If I could." *If I gave in.*

"You won't. Not if you find something worth fighting for; something more than death and envy. There has to be something you want more than that."

158

Ricker felt like he was trying to swallow a sob and choke out a laugh. "You sound concerned, Shadow. Are you worried about me?"

"I always worry for you, you madman."

Ricker couldn't help the laugh that ruptured past his lips, frothing with hysteria. He felt Mortimer's hand tighten around his.

A moment later, a scream shattered the marketplace, and people began to die.

XI

A red-haired woman looking at a merchant's stand collapsed, dead, on top of a cart of fruit. Melons burst beneath her weight, dripping crimson juices down through the cracks in the boards of the wagon.

A man standing behind a counter ruined the rich-colored fabrics he was selling when he was thrown forward by the force of his death, spitting blood across the cloth.

It wasn't until an older woman looking at the wares on a stand to Ricker's left was thrown backward and to the ground that he realized people were being picked out and shot down. The woman lay on her back, her arms thrown outward as though to keep her afloat on the ground, with a long, shining black arrow protruding from her chest.

Ricker recognized the barest hint of comprehension peeking through the masses – an understanding that would ultimately lead to all-out panic. People shuffled around each other like a herd of cattle who hear the call of a predator. Instinct tells them that they are doomed, but like unintelligent kowtowers, they wait for someone else to make the decision to flee.

So they wait, and they wait, and they wait.

And meanwhile, they continue to be shot down.

But Ricker could see that ignorance slowly giving way to fear. He didn't wait for the tide to change as people's brains clicked on. He sought out the closest building with his eyes and made a beeline for it. Even crumbling from disuse and age, the heavy steel and stone of a large building would withstand the onslaught of fear and death better than the wooden crates and carts that permeated the street.

Dragging Mortimer behind him, Ricker was almost to the crooked steel door of the building when a woman's fight or flight response kicked in.

It was probably her scream, rather than the fact that she was running, that drew the attention of those around her. And with all eyes on her, it made a much larger impact when the shining black arrow struck her in the back and sent her crashing into the grave.

Panic erupted like a mountain.

Screams shattered the air and people began running. There was no actual route of escape, no destination for them to move to. They simply ran, and when someone fell, others continued to run, trampling their comrades. Eyes wide and rolling like a stampede of flighty horses, their attackers had only to fire an arrow. With the crowd of people as large as it was, there was no way they could miss.

Ricker wasn't alone in viewing the building as a safe house. His movement toward the door alerted others that it was there. He had only reached for the handle when people began to slam into his back, pressing him up against the steel, as though with enough force, they could push him through it. The door opened outward, and with people shoving against him, there was no way for him to move it. An elbow slammed into his ribs, someone stepped on his foot, and bodies pressed up close against his. Mortimer, hand as tight as the boy could hold it around his, was pressed up against Ricker, looking beyond frightened at this point. It was when his face was shoved up against the door and pain rocketed through the bridge of his nose that Ricker had had enough.

He let go of Mortimer's hand and reached back with both hands to grab his crossbow. His hands fumbled as he was jostled from behind, but he loaded a bolt in the chamber quickly enough and turned around, his elbow forcefully pushing aside anyone in the way of his movement. Staring now at the crowd gathered around him, still pressing against him, he lowered the crossbow from where it pointed at the sky, the sharp edge of the bolt thrust out into the crowd.

The sound of the bowstring could barely be heard beyond the roar of people, but the dull *thunk* it made when it impacted human flesh, and the sound of the man dropping dead to the ground, was the only thing that could be heard in the shocked silence of the people who realized what had happened.

Ricker didn't bother reloading the crossbow. Holding it up where everyone could see it was enough. He bared his teeth in a soundless snarl at the crowd, and spoke very quietly.

He couldn't have made a bigger impression had he painted his words across the faces of the onlookers in the dead man's blood.

"Get the hell away from me."

The crowd fled, trampling over the man Ricker had shot without a moment's hesitation. Huffing darkly, he replaced the crossbow in the satchel on his back and turned back around. The door creaked a rusty iron sound when he opened it, and rang like a gong against the stone outside the building. Ricker did his best not to cringe and stepped into the dark hall beyond.

He tried not to show his surprise when he felt Mortimer grab his hand.

"This is ominous," Shadow commented dryly. He had moved ahead of them into the building, for which Ricker was grateful. The light of his glowing eyes gave some manner of direction. *"By the way, I should perhaps commend you on your aim."*

"Oh?" Ricker asked distractedly, squinting to try and see through the gloom. From what he could tell, there wasn't much to see. The hallway was filled with all manner of garbage; torn bags, old boxes with their sides torn, innards spilling out, and pieces of junk piled hither and thither. From the heavy layer of dust or dirt that covered everything, it looked like the building hadn't been used in a long time.

"You had a whole crowd of people to choose from to make your point, but you chose to take out the one attacking them all from behind. Not an easy shot, I saw. You had those three merchants crowding in front of him, blocking your view."

"Maybe I just like a challenge."

"Or maybe you're a more decent guy than you'd like others to believe. Rather nasty weapon he was carrying, too. Not something you'd make, I wager."

"Not likely." Ricker had gotten an ugly view of the weapon the ragged man had been wielding when he'd shoved it through the back of a young girl. That the people in front of her hadn't reacted to being coating in her blood was proof that they were trapped in panic. The weapon itself was a blade, but not one that had been crafted. Rather, the blade was little more than a bunch of scrap metal molded

163

together and every edge sharpened. It was an ugly piece of work, if effective.

Ricker understood what Shadow was saying: praise for being a good boy and protecting those who required protection, slaying someone who deserved it. Instead of his usual means of going after children – DeathSpeakers, yes, but still children. He would rather Shadow not bring up his good deeds, though. It made him feel ridiculous, being praised like he was a child in need of positive reinforcement, and not a grown man who'd chosen his own path.

And then chosen another when the first one was ripped from him.

"There are stairs here."

Ricker swallowed his thoughts on the past and turned toward Shadow's glowing eyes, glad for the distraction. They were far enough away from the door that the light from outside did little to aid him, so he moved slowly toward Shadow's glowing eyes. As he neared the ghost, he pulled Mortimer in front of him. Ricker was forced to let go of Mortimer's hand so the both of them could steady themselves at the stairs, one hand gripping the rotted railing on the wall.

Ricker moved cautiously, kicking the stair ahead of the one he was on each time so he knew where to place his foot before he put his full weight down. He kept a firm grip on the railing with his left hand, his right trailing over the wall on the other side. With Mortimer in front of him, he moved slowly enough so as to not push into the boy from behind.

The stairs were wooden and old. Ricker could feel them bend slightly beneath his weight, which was not a pleasant sensation in the least. He was somewhat glad for the darkness, because it kept him from seeing the rotted state he was certain the boards were in, which would have made his journey up them even more disconcerting.

"Are we close to the top, Shadow?" he asked, hearing an irregular few steps from Mortimer and bumping into him. The boy must have tripped.

"Just a few more steps," Shadow assured him. Ricker listened as Mortimer continued to climb up the stairs, and heard the sound beneath his feet changed from a muffled thump to a louder, higher-pitched tapping. Stone again.

The strange cool feeling of the railing beneath his hands when he took another step made him wrinkle his nose. The wood was wet and grimy beneath his fingers. He could feel tiny pieces of it coming off against his palm. He grimaced and took the next few steps more quickly, not liking the idea of standing on stairs that were being subjected to water damage.

In retrospect, slower and lighter steps would have been safer.

There wasn't a loud crack or snapping sound. The silence was eerie as the step disintegrated underneath his foot and Ricker felt his leg plunge right through the hole that formed where his foothold had been. He let out a surprised yell, his hand slipping on the wet railing as he tried to catch himself, and his right knee slammed down on the soggy wooden step in front of him. His hands flew out, trying to catch something he could hold on to.

The slap of skin on skin rang in his ears. The skin of his palm stung as something struck it sharply, but his downward momentum was halted by long fingers that curled around his hand. His own calloused hand tightened over the one that grabbed him, and his left hand fought his blindness until he was able to grab hold of the railing in a tight fist and draw a deep breath of relief.

His knee, which ached from slamming against the step, was still there and he used that position to drag his other leg out from where it had fallen through the stairs. Once both of his knees were positioned on stairs and better able to hold his weight, he loosened his death grip on the hand that had caught his and felt the other release him. He breathed a few deep breaths as he felt his heart racing in his chest. Nodding, despite the fact that no one could see him in the darkness, he gasped out, "Thank you."

"Are you all right, Ricker?" Shadow asked, and he caught sight of the ghost's glowing eyes in the darkness.

"Fine," he said, finding his footing on the stairs and pulling himself upright. "Who else is here, Shadow?"

He glanced up to see the eyes narrow again from a widened position. That was... odd. *"No one is here."*

"Who caught my hand?" he asked, shaking his right hand for Shadow to see, even while he kept his left tightly wrapped around the railing.

"Ricker, no one is here but for you, Mortimer, and myself."

Ricker didn't believe him, of course. The hand that had grabbed his had been as substantial as stone (and far more substantial than the rotting stairs beneath him), and it had certainly been larger than one of Mortimer's hands. The fingers had not been thick, though, or rough like his, but thin and smooth, with slightly large knuckles. More than likely the hand of a woman.

There *had* to be someone else there, and briefly, he was reminded of when he had first met Mortimer and how the boy had somehow armed his crossbow despite not having the strength to do so.

So you do *have someone helping you.*

"For a god's sake, Ricker, must all your thoughts consistently return to conspiracy theories? Can you not simply be grateful?"

"And who am I to be grateful *to*?"

"You could be grateful to me for putting up with your crap for so long."

Ricker rolled his eyes, expelling a sigh. "Fine. *Thank you*, Shadow, for burdening me with your presence for so many years."

"You're quite welcome, of course."

Ricker huffed and steadied himself with a hand on the landing. He didn't trust the slippery, rotting railing to hold his weight should he attempt to hold it too tightly, and so he moved carefully up the few remaining stairs, bent over to catch himself in case they crumbled again.

He had just stepped to the left on the landing, putting the wall behind him, when he heard the muffled *tap-tap* of shoes on cement, as someone tried to move quietly within the dark hall. Ricker's eyes narrowed at the sound and he turned his head, searching the darkness futilely with his eyes for whoever else was there.

"Just you and the boy, Shadow?"

"... No." Ricker rolled his eyes at the uncertainty in Shadow's voice. He whipped around, his mouth open to tell the ghost exactly what he thought about him trying to keep secrets from him.

The person that came bursting out of the shadows took him completely by surprise.

Ricker's arm swung up to grab his crossbow, but there wasn't enough time for him to even flip open his satchel. In the darkness of the landing, with the only light being what filtered through a filthy windowpane, the face of his attacker was as pale as death's sun-spurned bones. Hair a tangled mass of greasy tendrils flapping like snakes about her head, the woman was a wraith of a human being, teeth bared for Ricker's throat.

She let loose a scream of fury at something beyond his understanding, her body crashing into his and knocking him from his feet. He landed with a loud crack as some part of his crossbow snapped beneath his weight. The metal pipe that made up the weapon's barrel crushed itself against his spine and Ricker gasped for breath between a throb of pain at the sharp edges of the bow digging into his back.

The woman landed on top of him, hair flying every which way, but not as fast as her hands. With fingers splayed, she raked raggedly broken nails at his collar, her lips pulled back. Saliva oozed between crooked teeth blackened with rot, but she seemed not to notice, as she tore senselessly at his throat.

Ricker grabbed her by the shoulders and shoved her away from him, but her fingers had found a place on his collar and she jerked it sharply. There was a ripping sound as something small was torn loose, and then the clatter of metal on stone. Even with her heavy breathing, amplified in the darkness of the landing as she heaved in his face, he heard the sound sharply, as though amidst the deepest silence. His fingers reached up, grasping his collar and finding it empty.

The clasp was gone.

He couldn't have named the feeling that gripped him had someone asked. The slow revelation of loss, the burning rush of rage, the deep, foaming sensation of regret churned within his soul like acid. Even as he desperately scanned the hall for the clasp, he knew it was beyond his reach. He had lost it, as he'd lost so many things before that.

Claws raked at his throat. His collar torn away, the woman's ragged fingernails tore flesh, blurring the black skin of his Mark with crimson tears. He felt the tickling sensation of liquid running down the sides of his neck even as he shoved her back by the shoulders and raised a leg between them, pushing her further away with a heel to her stomach.

He scrambled to his feet, the darkened room a perfect match to his mood, as he heard more footsteps join the stumbled gait of the woman's.

"Ricker." The echoing tone of Shadow's voice in his head foretold of his presence lingering only within his mind. He nearly made a grab for the invisible shade, his soul begging for comfort for the reminder of a loss too deep to escape. *"I've taken Mortimer elsewhere. There are three, and I am not here."*

Ricker's eyes narrowed. *I understand.* He was alone in this.

And so were his attackers.

The human mind is a truly amazing thing. As the world turns on an average day, only the most meager of dissimilarities cause people to appear different. It is when life thrusts forth an injustice with the ugliness of Caliban that the true measure of a person's strengths are seen – when men and women jump further than they were ever able, lift objects too heavy from someone thrice their strength, and become something they never would have thought themselves capable.

This is what happened to Ricker, trapped in an unstable, alien realm with three people who clearly meant him harm. He felt Shadow's presence slip from his mind and heard, in the darkness, the heavy breathing of three adults waiting for the moment to strike. He heard them, their lungs expanding with each inhalation, their bodies shifting, shoes tapping on the ground. And his eyes, all but blind, pilfered the darkness from around him until he could see, almost as though the sun had risen within the building.

The stairs he had fallen to were just ahead of him on his right, and beyond them, the hall went on for ten feet before the collapsed ceiling blocked any further travel. The woman who had attacked him stood there on bent knees, her eyes scanning for him in the shadows, long stringy drippings of hair hanging in her face, her mouth opened as she breathed. Her face, he saw, had not been pale from the lack of light, but jaundiced by plague, her eyes shadowed by black bags. Her skin was thin and hung off her too-visible bones. She truly *was* a wraith.

Ricker moved silently, turning to look behind him. Two men blocked his path, one a tall creature stretching two inches beyond Ricker's height, his head bare, eyes hidden by hard wrinkles. His face had a glow to it from the hazy sunlight, and his arms and legs were punched full of muscle from a life of physical labor.

The other man was not nearly as strong as he companion, but he needn't have been. His mouth was open, like the woman's, only instead of simply breathing through it, his tongue hung down from between his lips. A black tongue.

The Mark of a SoulSiren.

His hair was red and hung to his shoulders in a weaving tide. His eyes were brown, light in color, and locked firmly upon Ricker's.

And in his ears, already, Ricker could hear the deep thrumming of a song to match his heart, his soul, and his Mark.

All Ricker wanted to do, as he felt the song, a soundless tune of feeling, trickle through his bones, was give up. Lie down on the ground and let his power go. He wanted nothing more than for the SoulSiren to taste of his deepest secrets and tear his breath away, and with it, his existence.

Let him be a DeathBreather no longer.

Let him simply be nothing at all.

The man's lips were dark – grey imposing upon red flesh. The tongue, long and black, descended, twitching and slapping at the air as though it could taste his power from inches away, like a serpent flicking its tongue. Ricker watched with vague comprehension as those lips parted further, floodgates opening, to sing a summon to his power and breathe in his breath and—

The song stopped with an "uff" of breath from the SoulSiren. Ricker drew a shaky gasp and felt himself sway in a loss of equilibrium. His chest ached from not breathing and his head spun every which way but right. The world was pitch and he realized his eyes were closed.

He opened them and stared into the wide, brown eyes of the man in front of him. He watched as those irises bloomed with a death-glaze, moments before the man collapsed to the ground, Ricker's dagger sticking up out of his chest.

And suddenly, the world was in motion again.

The woman behind him let out a scream and Ricker was sure he'd heard her feet pounding on the floor, but above the beating of his own heart, he couldn't be certain. The muscled bald man in front of him lunged forward, but Ricker was smaller than he, and faster. He dodged to the right, just barely out of reach of the man, but not out of reach of the woman behind him.

Ragged nails slashed at the back of his neck, but he was already moving. One hand reached back and grabbed for a crossbow bolt, forgoing his bow, as he dodged around the man and ran past him, toward the door lit up like a beacon in the hall. He swiped his arm behind him as he heard the woman's desperate panting close in. She shrieked as the sharp tip of the bolt sliced across her flesh and jerked away from the attack, leaving Ricker free to run full-tilt into the crash bar, sending the heavy iron door swinging open.

He bolted through the entryway into a stairwell made of stone. There were a series of windows along the stairs that let in light. His heart pounded in his chest as he leapt up the stairs, skipping every other step to get ahead.

He knew the other two were still following him. He heard the crash bar slam against the door again, and then the sound of feet on stone. In the sunlit stairwell, he never noticed that his abrupt ability to see in the dark faded. It was as though he had been bound, for a moment, to the very darkness around him, lending him a kinship with them that shuffled them to the side, but it had been a temporary bond, and one not meant to last long or be overly obvious.

But Ricker realized none of this, and those behind him were too far away to see the shadows disperse back into the darkness. He ran on, up two flights of stairs, past closed doors, his cloak flapping against his legs.

The stairs finally came to an end at a broken door half-hanging from its hinges and not fully latched. He could see sunlight through the cracks where the door didn't close and pushed it open, rushing through.

He shoes clapped across the roof.

He raced to the edge of the building, peering over. Three stories below, the ground looked incredibly solid.

He could hear the feet of his pursuers *tap-tap-clapping* on the steps and he ran around the edge of the building, looking for a way off that didn't include death—

There!

Another building, half a story shorter than the one he was on. It would have been too far to jump had it been the same height, but shorter as it was, he might just be able to make it. Ricker backed up to get a running start.

The door to the roof made a clattering sound as it struck the wall.

Ricker raced across the roof, and threw himself over the edge.

He missed the next roof by a foot.

~*~

Mortimer swept a hand across his face, wiping away tears of fright and peering through a blurred vision at the destruction surrounding him.

The world had gone mad.

Or perhaps the world had already been mad, and within the confines of the monastery, he had simply been protected from it.

He didn't know. All he knew was that people were lying on the ground, floating in pools of their own blood, while others ran around with various weapons, killing those that fled before them.

He didn't know where Ricker was. Shadow had led him away and out of the building when the three people had attacked. The ghost had moved through the streets and, afraid of being left behind, Mortimer had swiftly followed.

They'd used falling-down buildings as throughways to avoid sight of the city's attackers, and when they'd had to run through the main areas, they'd moved quickly. Right now, Mortimer didn't know where he was in regards to anything else. Shadow had finally led them to a long, narrow alley between two tall buildings. There was a large wooden fence in the back of the alley far too tall for anyone to scale, the boards old and worn and broken in some places. Mortimer crouched in a dark corner beside that fence, his body hidden from the front of the alley by the shadows and the half-collapsed wall he was positioned behind.

Shadow had led him there and told him to not move unless someone had come all the way to the back of the alley and found him. Mortimer had done as he was told and crouched there in the shadows, watching fearfully as people ran past the alley's entrance.

One or two people had paused at the entrance, looking back the alley as though considering whether it would be a good hiding spot. In these moments, Mortimer would tense up, preparing to run, but each time, the people would reconsider and move on quickly, seeking refuge elsewhere. He didn't know what it was that drove the people off, but he was grateful.

When someone wasn't standing at the entrance of the alley, Mortimer had a full view of the destruction going on beyond it. People ran, panic-stricken, in senseless circles, trying to escape death that came from all directions. Arrows came ripping down from the sky, sending people flying to the ground in a violent leap into death. Other men and women were less secretive about their attacks, tackling people to the ground and digging into their flesh with ragged fingernails, or sinking their teeth into their limbs. Mortimer shuddered as he watched a man scream and thrash as his attacker began to eat him.

But even the brusquest case of cannibalism wasn't the worst thing to watch. People fell to the ground dead with an arrow in their backs, and trampled over a child who had tripped during their flight, but it was nothing to the SoulSiren.

Mortimer didn't know what they were seeing or hearing that drew them, but people would stop in the middle of running and turn to face the man standing not far from the alleyway. His hair was grey, cut so short that it simply stuck up from his head, and his pale face held the wrinkles of age. His eyes, however, glittered with a dark lust, and his black tongue hung down from between jaws gaping with a raucous grin.

He saw nothing, but his tongue flapped at the air like a happily-waved hand, and people would stop fleeing and move toward him, as though nothing around them was going wrong at all. Even when one of the people moving toward the man would get shot down, the others didn't hesitate, so deeply were they entranced.

Then they would reach the SoulSiren, and he would lean over with flapping tongue and lusting eyes. Their lips would purse, as though for a kiss, and then he would *smile.*

And they would fall to the ground, dead.

The chaotic destruction from arrows flying and cannibals attacking amidst the screams of fleeing men and women was distressing, but it was the placid willingness of those who walked right into death's arms that was truly terrifying.

Mortimer watched as a man, forty years old, with messy blonde hair collapsed before that flapping tongue; he was the last person surrounding the SoulSiren to fall.

Shivering in the back of the alley, Mortimer desperately wished that Shadow was with him. The ghost had disappeared right after telling him to stay in the back of the alley, and he had been alone ever since. He didn't know where the ghost had gone, but he wished he hadn't been left behind. He was frightened, and he didn't want to be here anymore.

He didn't want to stay in the back of the alley.

He didn't want to hide from the people looking for him.

He wanted to come out... to come out, to show himself.

He wanted to go with the people looking so desperately for him.

He wanted to be found.

The dark eyes of the SoulSiren gleamed.

~*~

Hester was very pleased.

Things were going accordingly. Master had allowed her the privilege of leading his army in a march of destruction. He didn't call them an army, of course, for alone, each was weaker than the weakest trained soldier. They were PlagueCursed or they were plagued; either a carrier altered by that stream of death, or one dying from it. But together, en mass, they were a truly powerful force. Hester was more than happy to lead them from the starving hills and to the slaughter, where they might be the wolves and hunt the sheep.

And feast. Oh, how they feasted.

The soldiers of the Trade City attempted to fight back, but from the moment she had stepped through the city gates, they were doomed.

A man screamed. It was not the high-pitched scream movie-makers would tempt you to think were made, if for no other reason than a paltry chuckle. Nor was it the baritone cry of a man whose masculinity would not falter come fear or fury or pain. No.

This cry was an old one – a sound grown from ancient times, long before speech. Long before men thought of anything but how to slay their dinner and take it home; before men felt anything but physical pain or the rumble of hunger. It was a cry that existed before men believed they were separate from the beasts that roamed the world, and before, even, men thought to believe anything at all.

This was the sound of Life itself crying out as it was smothered. The first sound Existence had ever uttered – a howl that stretched from birth until now, the very moment of its demise.

It was a sound that she lived for.

And that other people died for.

Hester watched with passive pleasure as the soldier was dragged to the ground by the weight of the two chasing him. Fingernails like claws tore into his flesh, while crooked, blackened teeth sank into the smooth skin of his throat. There was a sharp sound, a growl of hunger, and then a great plume of blood that was stifled a moment later by the suckling of a hungry mouth.

The man let out a wail of agony as they tore into him. It merged together in Hester's mind with the constant shriek of existence, and she watched his body writhe in death, until his scream had become a gurgle and he stilled under his attackers' ministrations.

Hester watched for a moment longer, but the man's form was growing paler still with blood loss. She could imagine being near enough to him to feel how his skin was cooling, and she found that with the life gone from him, the fight gone from him, her interest was lost.

Turning her attention elsewhere, she saw a familiar head of short, grey hair sauntering through the masses, the lazy confidence of a lion rolling off his shoulders. Hester recognized him immediately as Marcus, one of the PlagueCursed she had brought with her when entering the city. She watched as he walked across the bloodstained ground, his normally lengthy stride shortened due to the burden he was pulling behind him.

Hester's expression didn't change, but her eyes focused firmly upon that burden.

She ignored the look of vain pleasure that fluttered across Marcus' face as he slurped at the excess liquid running down his mouth from where his tongue dangled and flapped. She kept her eyes on Mortimer as she spoke.

"Where did you find him?"

"Came to me." The corners of the SoulSiren's lips turned up around his tongue as he whispered the words like they were a secret wish that had been granted. "He was in an alley, frightened, alone." He hissed a sound of pleasure and Mortimer stepped closer to him, expression blank and eyes glazed. "May I keep him?"

"He belongs to Master." Hester raised one of her gloved hands and pressed two of her fingers against the boy's forehead, pressing only lightly enough that his head tilted vaguely backward. "Master has claimed his tongue."

She saw Marcus beginning to pout. "Perhaps when Master has finished with him, you may be allowed to keep him."

"Do you think so?" Marcus slurped again, sucking saliva back into his mouth.

"Perhaps."

Hester rather doubted it, to be honest, but Marcus didn't need to know he only had a few days left to live.

Shuddering in pleasure at the thought, Marcus flicked and flapped his tongue excitedly. Mortimer moved with a lethargic disinterest, coming to a halt only when Hester put her hand on his sleeve. The boy didn't meet her gaze, just continued staring blankly off into the distance, as though searching for his soul.

Considering he was wrapped in Marcus' song, that wasn't an unlikely theory.

"Shall I return to our master?"

Hester paused in thought, looking up from the boy. If she sent Marcus back to Master, he would return to his death and afterwards be of no use to her. She had the pendant, and now she had the boy, but there was still one potential obstacle she needed to make certain would not step in her way.

"Has the DeathBreather been finished?"

Marcus grimaced around his tongue, which was the only answer she needed.

"George is dead." He shuffled uncomfortably from foot to foot. "Rebecca said he was Singing when the 'Breather stabbed him."

Hester made no motion to express her disappointment, but Marcus flinched violently anyway. Perhaps he had learned to read her.

"Meaning you are useless to me."

Marcus looked desperately at the still-hypnotized Mortimer, as though he wished he hadn't handed the boy over until *after* he'd revealed all of the bad news.

"*Mar*cus."

The SoulSiren twitched. So rarely did Hester emphasize any part of her speech that most people thought she simply didn't. Those who were fooled into thinking thusly were lucky. They never heard her emphasize and know fear. They never heard her utter their name in such a way that they *knew* they were about to die.

"What good are you to me, Marcus?"

His lips quivered but he could make no sound appear. He swallowed and withdrew his tongue into his mouth, wiping the sheen of drool from his lips with a nervous palm.

Behind Hester, Mortimer blinked and shook his head, as though shaking off the remnants of a dream.

"What use, Marcus, could I possibly have for you if the DeathBreather is untouched by your song?"

"I…" Marcus stumbled backward, glancing left to right, searching for an escape. His breathing had sped up, his eyes widening. "I… I can Sing for the boy. M-Make 'im stay."

"Mortimer will not run. He is a smart boy. Are you a smart boy, Marcus?"

The SoulSiren gave a shudder that shook his whole body. Hester raised a hand and crooked a finger at him. It was a testament to how much he feared her that he obeyed immediately, even ascertained of the consequences.

Hester ran a gloved hand tenderly down the side of his face, the other hand cupping his jaw. Marcus shivered steadily in her grasp but made no move to escape.

"Good boy, Marcus," she whispered, patting his cheek with mock fondness. "Perhaps you can still be useful."

Marcus felt a cool chill rush through him – relief, and fear.

"The DeathBreather needs to die. He must not follow us."

"What do you want me to do?"

"*Mar*cus." He flinched. "I want you to Sing."

XII

Ricker's mouth twisted into a grimace as he regained consciousness. He was on his back, arms partially twisted around the iron bars of the rusty fire escape. His head ached dully and his vision swam when he blinked. Ricker groaned and swallowed thickly.

Clearly, of all the things he was, an acrobat was not one of them.

He gasped as he tried to untangle his arm. Pain, hot and sudden as a brand, sliced through his forearm. He froze, sucking in a breath, as he tried desperately to reverse his movements and stop the pain. His chest heaved erratically with pained breaths that sent throbbing waves through his arm.

He didn't think it was broken. If it was broken, it wouldn't hurt this damn much.

Shuddering, he grit his teeth and tried again to move. He shrugged and lifted his shoulder, his forearm dangling limply, and rotated his arm. His shoulder cracked loudly, sending a fast jolt of pain through his bones that made Ricker grunt. The pain was brushed away seconds later with a sense of relief and he sagged against the fire escape, his shoulder quivering lightly as it began to relax. He let his arm lay across his chest, and sighed deeply as he wished fervently that he had found some other escape than to jump off the side of the roof.

His body ached from his unexpected crash. He had planned on landing on the roof, so missing and falling a good five feet before the sudden stop threw his balance off. His legs hadn't been prepared to land at such an angle, though despite his aches and pains, he was glad the fire escape had been there to break his fall. He wouldn't have been faring nearly as well had he continued on to the ground many feet below.

The back of his head ached with a strange burning sensation and he knew he'd struck it upon falling. That would certainly explain his lack of consciousness, but the wet, warm sensation on the back of his neck was worrisome. He refrained from brushing his palm across the back of his skull. It would undoubtedly hurt, and frankly, he didn't want to know.

"Ricker."

Ricker opened his eyes, surprised more by the fact that they had been closed than by the ghost's presence.

"Sha'w?"

"You're being hunted, Ricker. Get up."

"Thaw-chu wer'with'a boy." His eyelids slipped downward of their own accord and he felt himself falter in consciousness. His head felt heavy – *all of him* felt heavy – and he just wanted to lie here—

"Get up, *Ricker."* Something hit him hard on the underside of his boot. Ricker groaned loudly and he turned his head away from the nagging voice. *"There is a SoulSiren singing for you and I doubt your luck shall hold again."*

His eyes blinked open slowly. His every sense was dashing in and out of his conscious control and he rolled his eyes around, searching for the ghost.

Odd, that he was above Ricker, wasn't it?

"SoulSiren?" he tried to ask, but it came out so slurred and broken on his tongue, he wondered if even he would have understood it, had he heard himself speak.

183

"Yes, you know, tall, gleaming eyes, drooling black tongue that makes people do whatever they say. They don't tend to be the friendly sort, absolute power and all that."

Again, something struck the sole of his boot and Ricker grunted, eyes opening. *"Get up. I can't drag your ugly ass all of the way out of the town. You're going to have to fight."*

"Crossbow's... busted," he murmured, rolling over until he had flopped onto his stomach. He rested his forehead on the grate beneath him.

"Are you a weaponsmith or not?"

"'mahunter."

"Hunter, then. Best to take up your name and act it, before they start calling you Dead." Ricker snorted a sound like a laugh. *"They're already calling you Prey, Ricker."*

"S'why you—you—" He scowled a moment. "Yousssstanding 'bove me?"

The shade flickered at the edge of his peripheral vision and Ricker lifted his head. The ghost danced in the shadows across the grate just in front of him and Ricker frowned. He had been sure...

He must have hit his head very hard.

"You did. Now please, get up. You must get moving. I can lead you the safest way I know, but it won't be safe enough. You must be able to fight."

Putting his hands underneath him proved the easy part of getting himself to his feet. Ricker had not lifted his head an inch off the ground when the entire world swam to his left, tilted sideways, and left him retching.

He didn't remember what he had eaten that day, but all of it came up, spilling through the holes in the grate. He felt someone kick him hard across his right side and swore loudly in between heaves, his head feeling as though it were splitting in two.

Eventually, the retching stopped and Ricker lay on his right side in his own vomit, shivering from a chill that swept through him continuously. The scent of his own puke made his stomach churn, but he didn't think he had the energy to be sick again.

"Ricker."

"Go'way," he murmured.

He thought he felt something soft touch his side, just below his ribs, but it might have been his clothes settling. The wind danced over his forehead, cool, with a tender touch, and he breathed a sigh of relief as the pain in his head eased. He swallowed and cracked open his eyes, searching for Shadow. He found the ghost beneath him, avoiding the vomit that lingered on the tracks of the grate by twisting into an odd position that warped Ricker's shadow.

He pushed himself up again, and this time made it into a sitting position without losing control of all of his faculties. He swiped the filth from his face and wiped his hands on his pants, before forcing himself to his feet. His head still pounded, but nowhere near as badly as it had before. He managed to stay standing even as a sharp pain tore through his skull, behind his eyes. He moaned softly, shutting his eyes for a time, until he felt the wind soothe it again.

"Ricker."

"Whey..." He cleared his throat. "Where are we... going?"

"Down first." Shadow flitted near a ladder to make his point. *"And then west, the fastest way to the edge of town."*

"The boy?" he murmured, taking the rungs of the ladder slowly. Rust came off against his hands, smearing orange over his palms, but he focused on keeping his feet on the ladder and not letting himself tilt sideways like his head was trying. A few times, he had to stop and rest a few moments, breathing deeply and swallowing down bile. He felt like the ache in his head had been pushed back but was waiting just out of sight to ambush him. It wasn't a pleasant feeling.

"We will meet him at the edge of town."

The ground met his feet with a kiss, and then his face with a slap. Ricker grunted, the wind knocked out of him. He heard Shadow laugh, but the sound seemed strained. He spat dirt and pushed himself to his feet, staggering a few steps before catching his balance.

He raised his time in time enough to duck the blow to his face.

A clenched first severed the air above his head, Ricker having moved just fast enough to avoid being struck. The momentum from the failed strike threw his attacker off balance and Ricker used that to move out of reach.

A few feet away, he got a good look at the man attacking him. Had that fist actually impacted with his skull, he was pretty sure he wouldn't have gotten up again; not on top of the concussion he clearly already had. Just moving around in the jerky motions he had made to avoid being hit was making his head ache.

The man was taller than Ricker by a few inches, and broader-shouldered, his muscles thick and straining his gleaming skin. If Ricker had to guess from his strength and clothing, the man was in the Trade City delivering supplies. Either he was

186

one of the men paid to unload product, or he pulled the damn cart himself, perhaps both. The man's hands were large, his fists like flesh-colored bricks. His eyes held none of the fury to be expected from someone swinging a cinderblock fist at your face. They were dull and glazed, and his face was lax.

The work of a SoulSiren.

The man moved quickly, turning and lunging for him again, swinging a fist. Ricker hesitated, leg-muscles tensed, watching the man come at him with his left shoulder facing the man, his teeth clenched. At the last moment, he ducked and retreated backward, letting the man lumber past him in his miss.

And Ricker struck. He moved forward with the speed and silence of a jungle cat, pulling a blade from his belt and twisting it in his hand as his arm arched through the air. The wooden hilt of the knife struck the man behind the ear and he went down without a whimper, crashing heavily to the ground.

Sighing, he replaced the blade on his belt and looked around to see if anyone else was attempting to ambush him. For the moment, the world around him was clear of people, and his lips twisted into a grimace as he turned his attention to the ground. "A little warning would have been nice."

His shadow didn't move as he waited, and he realized that the top hat and tailcoat were missing, and the hair of his shadow was ridiculously tame. Frowning, he glanced around but caught no sight of a twitching shade.

"Shadow?"

Ricker touched the aching back of his head and waited, but if the ghost had been there before, he wasn't there now. Wincing as his fingers brushed the bare wound in his skull, Ricker wondered when the ghost had left. Maybe Shadow had never been there to start with.

There was a sound, close but far in the distance, like a thousand whispers brushing against his eardrums. Ricker shook his head to ward off the call of the SoulSiren and started moving again. Whether Shadow had truly been there or not, it was clear he was being hunted. If the SoulSiren was singing, it had the whole supply of what people remained alive in the village as its disposal. He needed to move quickly to keep ahead of the mass surely coming for him, and find Shadow and the boy.

Or just the boy. Shadow would find him, he always did.

Ricker moved with a cautious pace, his footsteps measured and quiet. He couldn't see anyone around, but that didn't mean anything. Every dark alleyway he passed, even cracked door into a crumbling building, was a threshold for disaster. His own footsteps were as silent as he could make them so that he could hear everything else that went on around him. He didn't want to be caught off guard by someone attacking from behind, and even the quietest of exhalations from the shadows would give him an edge that may well save his life.

In the distance, beyond the whispered murmurs of the SoulSiren's call, he could hear the screams of those dying. He could only imagine what all manner of monsters had been unleashed on the city if he was hearing the call of his second SoulSiren. With the SoulSiren's call loud enough for him to hear from such a distance, he was sure it must be audible to most of the vicinity, as well. If those people were still screaming despite the call, they were in such pain that the sound of the song did nothing to entrance them.

He pitied them for that. The trance would have been a merciful release from the pain, even if the ending was the same.

He restrained his initial reaction at the soft hiss of breath that met his ears and kept his pace steady. His natural inclination was to tilt his head for a better position for hearing, but he didn't dare give off his knowledge that someone was there, and he kept his eyes straight. His ears were primed for sound, however, and so he could hear the soft breathing of someone other than himself, not far behind him. Actually, it sounded now as though they were closer than they had been previously, and were getting even close—

The clang of metal on metal ached in his ears, but more painful still was the quiver that raced up Ricker's arm as the large wrench swung down atop his blade. The hilt bit into the palm of his hand, but Ricker held on to it. His eyes took in the woman who had attacked him.

Her hair and nails weren't nearly as unkempt as the last woman he had dealt with, but the reason why was clear from her blank expression. Another victim of the SoulSiren, attacking him from the trance.

He gritted his teeth and swung his leg up between their two bodies, planting his boot against the woman's stomach and kicking her back. She staggered backward but regained her balance quickly and flicked her auburn hair out of her eyes with a toss of her head. She gripped the monkey wrench tightly in her fist and rushed at him without a sound, swinging her arm in an upward arc.

Ricker jerked backward, the wrench barely missing ripping his nose off. He brought the blade up to block her downward swing, but this time, the wrench struck the blade too hard and it went flying out of his hand. He felt a sharp pain on the left side of his neck and the feeling of something wet trickling down his skin.

The wrench made a whooshing sound as it cut through the air where his head had been a moment before he ducked down low. The woman grunted, the air knocked out of her, as Ricker lunged forward and ran his shoulder into her stomach. He knocked her backward to the ground, catching himself on his knees to keep from landing on her, and tore the wrench out of her hands as it swung down at his head.

She threw herself upward in an attempt to bite him and Ricker grabbed her shoulders, forcing her back against the ground. It amazed him how much fury could be in her attacks when her eyes were so dulled, but he was more concerned with what to do. Were she willingly attacking him, taking her out would cause him no remorse, but she wasn't.

The crunch of stones underfoot at his back made Ricker twitch in expectation, but a blow didn't come. Instead, a warm breath brushed against the back of his neck and the murmuring song that lingered just beyond his range of hearing suddenly intensified. He tried to shut his ears off to it, but it was all he could do to not—

Kill her.

It would be easy.

He should kill her.

So much of the problem could be dealt with simply by ending her life.

So kill her.

Snap her neck.

Slit her throat.

Disembowel her.

Dismember her.

End her.

Ricker slammed his head backward with all the force he could manage. He could feel the bones break against his skull and heard the loud crack, and the scream of pain that took its place. He glanced down quickly to find the woman blinking rapidly, a confused look on her face.

Pushing himself quickly to his feet, Ricker spun to face the SoulSiren.

He stopped moving, but the world didn't. It kept on spinning, the back of his head aching suddenly as though demanding to know why he did something so stupid as to use his skull as a weapon. He swayed slightly but kept his legs, closing his eyes until the world settled.

When he opened his eyes, the SoulSiren was watching him, one hand clasped over his broken nose. He had drawn his tongue back into his mouth and was wiping his arm across his chin, trying to clean his face off and only managing to smear blood across his face and arm.

"Never had no one block my song before." The SoulSiren's voice was nasally from his nose being broken. Ricker grimaced as he watched blood run down from behind his hand and seep between his lips.

Ricker wondered how long it was that he had been unconscious on that fire escape. "I dealt with another of your kind earlier today." The SoulSiren didn't look surprised. "You came after me anyway?"

He glanced behind him, hand still clutching his nose as his eyes scanned the area for... something. After a moment, he looked back at Ricker. "Rather face you one on one than disobey her."

At Ricker's confused look, the SoulSiren revealed a bloody smile. "She's the one who's got your boy. She's gonna take the DeathSpeaker back to our master, and with the gem..." He trailed off, tilting his head slightly to the side. "Well, you won't have to worry about that."

Ricker grinned at him. "You're not going to kill me."

"No? And what makes you say—aurgh!"

"Because you're dead."

Blood ran down from the SoulSiren's throat, where the blade protruded from his esophagus. Ricker watched dispassionately as the man fell forward, the hilt of his blade sticking out the back of his neck.

He glanced up to find the woman he had been fighting before standing there. She was glaring in a fury at the SoulSiren, but her face had gone ash white. Her one hand was touching the skin of her throat, as though in an attempt to protect it from the same treatment she had just subjected the SoulSiren to.

She realized she was being watched and looked up. Her lips quivered and she folded her hands together, looking down at them, before returning her attention to the SoulSiren.

It occurred to Ricker that, now that he was dead, the SoulSiren was no different from any other human. Killing someone in self-defense hadn't been a problem for Ricker in years. He'd stopped really being bothered about shedding people's blood a long time ago. He'd certainly had a lot of practice.

That didn't mean that everyone else was so... cold.

"You did what you had to," Ricker murmured, keeping his voice soft. He grabbed one of the woman's hands in his own and squeezed it in a gesture meant to offer comfort. "What's your name?"

The woman looked up at him, startled by his actions. He watched the stricken expression on her face relax minorly. "Helen."

For a moment, it was like he was holding someone else's hand. The smooth skin and long fingers of another woman from years ago made his heart flutter, and he felt his lips turn up in a smile. How long had it been since he'd held her hand? Since he'd held the hand of any woman?

"Stop."

Ricker blinked, his mind returning to him as he felt the woman pull her hand out of his. She took a few steps backward and was giving him a wary look. Ricker watched her for a moment, tightening his empty hand into a fist. She looked so much like Lottie, it had been easy, for a moment, to think...

"You should probably find a place to hide until things settle down." The words surprised Ricker even as he spoke them. Helen was giving him a confused, cautious look, but Ricker shook his head and took a step away from her. "Find somewhere to hide until this is all over."

As he turned around and headed off in the other direction, he briefly wondered how she would tell when it *was* all over. Maybe it would never be over, not until the people attacking the city had found everyone, Helen included, and killed them all.

He couldn't worry about it. It wasn't his place to save the world. It wasn't his place to save anyone. He was supposed to hunt DeathSpeakers and kill them. That was all he was good at. It was all he needed to be good at.

The SoulSiren dead, there were no entranced people who attacked him as he made his way westward. From what he could see, the majority of people in the city were dead. Whether they had banded together and fought back before falling or their attackers had been withdrawn, he didn't know, but he didn't pass by any living person who moved toward him. A few people here and there ran past him, their faces covered in blood or fear, or both.

The streets were splattered and smeared with blood, red footprints marking the trail of more than a few passersby. He stepped around bodies left lying in the street, skin turning grey as the heat of life's blood fled them. He averted his eyes from those who had been stripped of their clothing, or others whose death-pale skin was torn open, or missing.

He kept walking, the city seeming as dead as the people in whose blood he stepped. The sounds and smells that had been heavily present when they had entered the city had been replaced by the silence only equal with that found in tombs, and the smell of uncovered graves. Even the screams he had heard previously had gone silent, and the only sounds that met his ears were his own breaths, and the sound of his footsteps splashing through pools of blood that hadn't yet been soaked into the earth.

It was as he stepped around an overturned cart that he caught sight of the gem.

There was no way he could have avoided seeing it. It was uncovered and worn as a pendant around the pale neck of a woman he hadn't seen before. He knew who she was, however, from the words the SoulSiren had spoken to him, and the fact that she had Mortimer at her side.

Tearing his eyes away from the jewel was difficult, for it shone like a sun itself, redder than a flame. He could have spent days, weeks staring at it, but he forced his eyes away to the boy.

His eyes were focused on the ground, but wide with fear, his lips pressed tightly together. Ricker noticed that the woman didn't have a hand on him, but still the boy didn't move to get away from her. The woman wasn't a SoulSiren and clearly Mortimer wasn't held by the song of another, so was it merely fear that kept him from fleeing?

But what reason would he have to so fear her?

"You took your time."

Ricker glanced at his shadow to find it had warped again. The top hat had returned and he could see the tails of Shadow's coat waving lightly as he moved. "I was a little distracted by the people who kept trying to kill me."

"I did warn you."

"You left rather quickly." Ricker didn't say anything about not being sure that Shadow's warning hadn't been just a figment of his imagination. Whether the ghost was paying attention to his thoughts or not, he didn't seem inclined to bring it up.

"I wanted to be sure Mortimer was safe. Things were far more chaotic here than where you had found yourself. As it is, he was not able to

remain hidden as I had hoped." The ghost sounded incredibly unhappy with the present situation. Not having that tone of voice directed toward his actions was a nice change, but it didn't bode well for the state of things.

"Who is she? The SoulSiren mentioned her."

"She's a DeathHand."

Ricker swallowed. "Oh." He heard Shadow make an agreeable sound.

Although not the most dangerous type of PlagueCursed, in Ricker's opinion, DeathHand's were probably the most deadly. A DeathSpeaker could be stopped by keeping them from speaking, or a SoulSiren by keeping their tongues in their mouths. DeathHands could be stopped by clothing, but Ricker had yet to meet a person who kept every part of their body covered at all times.

A single part of their skin, no matter how small, would instantly kill whomever they touched. Ricker didn't know if any other PlagueCursed were immune to DeathHands, as he was to DeathSpeakers. He had never before come across one of their kind.

"Most of them don't manage to survive into adulthood. She must have had some sort of help."

"There aren't very many people who can help a DeathHand without dying."

"Death doesn't stop everyone, Ricker."

No, that was clearly true. More than once, Ricker had wondered what it was that kept Shadow here. The ghost wouldn't tell him, but it had to have been something important, for him to cling to life so desperately.

The two watched as the woman spoke with two people standing in front of her. It was clear that she was leading the lot of them. The two people before her were listening to her raptly, and with more than a little fear on their faces. If they knew she was a DeathHand, that made sense. One foolish move or too many screw-ups on their part could have her giving them a pat on the back that would end their lives.

The two people turned and headed back to the main group. Ricker watched as they presumably recited their orders to the larger group, and as one the majority of them turned and started walking northwest, out of the city. Ricker could see only three people stay behind, along with the DeathHand and Mortimer.

"That's rather convenient."

"What reason do they have to stay here? Everyone is dead."

"Not everyone. That woman is still alive because you stayed your hand." Ricker felt the ghost's eyes on him but refused to meet his gaze. *"It would have been much easier to kill her."*

"Physically."

"But that's just it, isn't it? Let me ask you something. Why are you so set on rescuing the boy?"

Ricker twisted his head in surprise, looking down at the ghost. "What?"

Shadow shrugged. *"You've been hunting DeathSpeakers for years now. You've killed every one you've come across, and the only reason you haven't killed Mortimer yet is because you made a deal with him, promising not to. This is an easy way out."*

"I'd be breaking my deal." Ricker looked sharply away from the ghost, but his eyes only found their way back to the boy.

"You promised to take him back to the monastery, but you're only human, Ricker. Despite being an assassin, despite being a DeathBreather, you can still fail. Easily."

He clamped his teeth together until his jaws cried from the pain, but he didn't respond to the ghost, didn't look at him.

"You know how easy it is for you to fail in protecting someone, so why are you trying so hard? You and I both know you don't want to succeed." The ghost waited for a moment, before adding, *"Or have you changed your mind? Are you, perhaps, trying to save him where you couldn't save a different child?"*

"Shadow," Ricker murmured, but shook his head, closing his eyes and running a hand down his face. In his mind, he could see a pair of deep blue eyes. He had stopped being able to tell if the eyes belonged to his son, or if they belonged to Mortimer. Was there even a line separating them anymore?

"Either he means something, or he means nothing, Ricker. Is he your prey or your protectee?"

Ricker sighed and opened his eyes, watching as Mortimer flinched when the DeathHand reached for him. "I don't know," he said quietly.

"Perhaps that's something you need to figure out. And soon."

She had removed the gloves that had previously been covering her hands, but she grabbed Mortimer's shoulder, where his robes covered him. She pulled on his shoulder until he moved to where she wanted and nudged him in the back to keep him moving. It was clear from the hunch of his shoulders and his ducked head that he feared her touch, but still he didn't run.

198

"It's going to be hard to get the gem from her when her gloves are off."

"I don't care about the gem. I just want to get Mortimer away from her."

"I don't suppose you have a weapon?"

Ricker reached his right hand to the left side of his waist and grabbed the katzbalger he kept hidden behind the folds of his cloak. The sword was not carried in a scabbard, but held to his belt with a thick band of leather that the blade slid through up to its s-shaped guard. It came free quietly and Ricker adjusted his grip carefully on the hilt, keeping the point of the blade pointed at the ground.

"Good to know you're not completely useless. Head northwest once you have Mortimer."

"What about you?"

"Don't worry for the dead, Ricker." The ghost's white eyes faded and he disappeared from sight. *"I'll keep Hester occupied."* Ricker's shadow returned to its normal shape as the ghost left his side. Ricker didn't look for him, but crouched low to the ground and began moving closer to the DeathHand.

Her back was to him as she urged Mortimer to keep walking, but Ricker kept his steps slow and even to be safe. The hilt of his sword was gripped tightly in his right hand, the blade ready, and he crept up on the woman, reaching his left arm out to grab hold of her cloak.

Either he'd made too much noise or she had somehow sensed his presence, but he hadn't yet reached her when she spun, arm thrust out to grab him.

Ricker brought the blade up, blocking her touch, and there was a splash of red on steel as the edge sliced easily through her palm. She didn't make a sound in response to the pain, but pulled away. She retreated quickly and reached out, grabbing Mortimer's arm around his robe sleeve and holding him tightly.

Ricker stood up, straightening his legs and pointed the sword at her. "I only want the boy."

"No."

Ricker ground his teeth. "Have it your way, then." He lunged at her, swinging the katzbalger in an upward arc from crotch to right shoulder. She was fast and retreated just far enough to avoid the tip of the blade, and moved forward the instant the sword had reached above her height.

Her hands were like snakes. Each one struck at him with the intent to bite, every finger a fang dripping with death. He ducked a swipe with her right hand, leapt back to avoid the left and swung the sword up. She had released Mortimer to allow her a better space to move in, but he hadn't run. It was becoming clear to Ricker why. As fast as she was, how could Mortimer hope to escape her? Even if he could, where did he have to run to?

And more fervently running through Ricker's mind, where was Shadow?

She sidestepped a downward swing of his sword and leapt upon him. He tried to swing his blade around to intercept her, but he wasn't fast enough. She hit him hard, in the chest, knocking him off his feet. His back hit the ground hard and the sword went flying from his hand. He heard it hit the ground too far away from him to reach, and then she moved to slap him.

He caught her clothed wrist in his left hand, her palm barely an inch from his face. This close he could easily see her Mark, staining her flesh like a drunken tattoo. His knuckles were white from gripping her arm so tightly, but she pressed against him, stronger than she looked.

Ricker grabbed her other arm before she could try and touch him, twisting his fingers in the cloth of her sleeve until it was tight around her forearm. She struggled against him, alternately trying to pull her arms away or push against his hold and grab his face.

He struggled to keep a firm grip on her as she moved wildly around, twisting away from him. In a sudden gesture, she freed her left arm, her sleeve untangling from his fingers, and the serpent lunged for his face.

He rolled. His left arm still holding her other arm, he twisted his body suddenly to the left, kicking his legs and hitting her hard across the side. He heard her gasp in surprise, their bodies tangling for a moment, only their combined clothes keeping him from dying a very quick death. And then he was beyond her, and he released her arm, catching his feet and standing quickly.

He spun, a hand at his belt, and turned in time to see she had already reached her own feet and had both hands up, fingers curled like claws as she attacked.

His own hands moved quickly. His left arm moved in an arc, the dagger tearing easily from the right side of his belt and slicing across her chest, leaving a line of blood from her stomach to her right shoulder. His right hand stabbed forward, catching her hand in a single motion. The long, thin sliver of metal slipped easily through her skin and cut through the muscles of her palm, squeezing between bones and ripping through the skin between two knuckles. He retreated quickly, abandoning the weapon.

She didn't even cry out when he struck her, but she stopped her advance, her fingers digging into the palm of her hand. Blood ran down her fingers and dripped to the ground, but she ignored the slippery metal and grasped the end of the long needle. She tore it out of her hand, merely grimacing at the sharpened hook on the end tore the inside of her hand upon its ejection. She tossed it away without looking at it, clenching her wounded hand into a fist. She narrowed her eyes at him, but her expression didn't change.

Ricker watched her guardedly, muscles tense. Where was Shadow?

Ricker gripped the dagger in his left hand, bending his knees. He glanced at Mortimer. The boy was standing a few feet behind the DeathHand, his arms folded over his chest, hands buried in the folds of his cloak. His eyes were wide, the pupils dilated but glazed. He looked completely petrified.

Ricker growled under his breath and returned his attention to the woman. She was watching him closely, blood dripping from her clenched fist, seeping out from between her fingers.

"I know who you are, DeathBreather." Her eyes flicked to his neck, where his Mark was bared for all to see, before meeting his eyes again. "Your name haunts the world, more feared than even my touch." She wagged the fingers of her uninjured hand. "Impressive. But not impressive enough for me to permit you the boy." She lowered her hand to her side. "He belongs to Master. He always has."

"I'm not *asking*."

"Ask or demand, it matters not. He is not yours to claim. Master has searched the world over for a DeathSpeaker, and here Mortimer is. He belongs to no one else, and you cannot have him."

Ricker gripped the dagger tight and advanced, but the woman retreated. "Ah-ah," she said, grabbed Mortimer's arm and pulling the startled boy against her chest. "I said that he belonged to Master, and he does. But Master would be displeased if I should allow him to fall into the hands of another." She raised her bloody hand and splayed her fingers, her skin a mere breath from Mortimer's bare cheek. "You shall not take him, *Rigor*." Ricker's eyes narrowed at the name. "Try, and neither you nor Master shall have the boy's breath."

"That's a desperate gamble."

Ricker clenched his teeth to avoid swearing in his surprise. His thoughts, unrestrained, swayed between *Where have you been* and *Why weren't you dealing with her?* He didn't dare speak them aloud in case his furious tone caused the woman to react strongly, but Shadow easily heard him.

"I was *dealing with her, or rather, I am, indirectly."*

What?

"Interesting fact, Ricker: the people of the Trade City are at least partway intelligent. Knowing that there are such creatures as DeathHands about, they have precautions against them. Observe."

The sound of the arrow striking soundly perfectly ended Shadow's statement. The woman let out a breath of surprise, if not pain, and staggered back. The arrow stuck out of her right shoulder, where it pinned her cloak to her skin. Ricker could see thick blood running down the material.

"Listen up!" someone shouted from behind Ricker. He turned, surprised to see a group of city guards standing twenty yards away. The one yelling held a shortbow in his hands, an arrow strung but the bowstring loose. As Ricker watched, however, the man beside him pulled an arrow from the quiver on his back and fitted it in his own shortbow, pulling the bowstring taut. He was clearly the one to have taken the shot, since none of the others were bearing bows.

"We know what you are, DeathHand, and we'll have no more of this. You've caused enough damage. Leave, or we'll be forced to kill you."

"Where do I fit in all this?" Ricker muttered to Shadow, his voice low.

He heard the ghost scoff. *"I hardly think you're the important one here."* Ricker rolled his eyes. *"I can't say, once Hester's dealt with, though I doubt it will be so easy for them."*

Ricker glanced back at the guards. There were seven of them. "You think they'll have *trouble?"*

"No, Ricker. I think they're all going to die. Get Mortimer."

"Leave the boy go, DeathHand, and we'll see about giving you safe passage!"

Hester's eyes moved from the guards to Ricker. Her fingers twitched.

The blade was out of his hands two seconds before he'd realized he had thrown it. He hadn't bothered aiming for her hands – the blade went straight for her face.

Hester jerked, flinging both hands up to defend against the thrown dagger. It nicked her fingers as she ducked out of the way of it, just as Ricker yelled, "Mortimer!"

The boy's wide eyes turned to him and he moved, leaping away from the woman. She reached out for him, catching him cloak in her one hand and pulling hard, the collar snagging against his throat.

Mortimer choked, but twisted, swinging his arm around to push her away. She reached out with blood-slicked fingers and grabbed his hand.

Mortimer dug his fingers into the wound in her palm and scratched through her hand in a swift moment. Hester jerked away from him in surprise and, freed, Mortimer bolted. He ran at Ricker, who grabbed the sleeve of his cloak and started running, not even bothering to see what the guards were doing.

Somewhere, behind them, a shade danced in the darkness of the guards' shadows, and they advanced on their prey.

Hester was regarding her hands curiously as the guards advanced. She supposed it was possibly that the boy had been able to touch her because her skin was so coated with her own blood that it worked as a shield against the touch of her flesh. It seemed so unlikely, though, and it had never happened before. The blood of her victims, no matter how liberally flowing, had never worked to keep her death-encrusted skin from stealing their life away. What would make this different?

How strange…

"DeathHand!"

Hester glanced up to find that she had been surrounded. Five guards stood close to her, various blades drawn, with the two archers some distance off, bowstrings pulled taut. She regarded them with a disinterested look.

"You're hereby under arrest for orchestrating an attack upon the Trade City. You will follow us to the city's prison, where you'll stay until it's been decided what to do with you."

She heard a few of the others murmur about appropriateness and death and not knowing who was currently in charge, but she didn't bother to listen too closely. Her hand still felt warm from where the boy had touched her and it had nothing to do with the fresh wave of blood flowing from the deepened wound.

One of the men stepped closer and reached for her.

Hester's eyes flicked to him. Her hands twitched.

Two of the guards dropped to the ground dead, their skin greying as they fell, swords clattering to the ground.

The muffled *thunt* of twin bowstrings sounded, but she hadn't stopped moving. The arrows flew by her head, one tearing through her hair but never touching her. A guard screamed, falling to the ground with an arrow sticking out of his knee. Hester ignored him.

She moved, hand striking upward to caress another guard from neck to chin. He fell, choking on his own death, even as she was moving again. The slice of steel through the air was expected and she avoided it with ease, twisting past the blade and pressing her body up against the guard's. He faltered, his adam's apple bobbing as he struggled to find a way to use the blade against her when she was so close. She leaned her face in until her lips were barely inches from his and studied his face. He had gone white with fear, his lips quivering.

She exhaled a soft breath against his mouth, her eyes latching onto his. She studied his fearful gaze for a long moment.

"I will refrain from ending your life," she murmured, "if you end theirs." She tilted her head just slightly, a curious motion, and pressed her hand against his chest, pushing herself back.

The boy gripped the handle of his sword tightly, and lunged.

He ran right past her, blade swinging.

"Damn it, Paul!" one of the guards yelled, ducking the swinging blade. It sliced through his bow, knocking the useless weapon out of the man's hand. He retreated out of reach of the blade, but the young guard advanced.

"Paul, stop this!"

"I'm sorry, but I won't die for you two!" Paul yelled. He swung his blade at the guard still holding his bow, but missed. The blade arched upward with the motion, giving his comrade an opening.

The arrow slammed into his chest. He staggered backward, gasping, arms wind milling wildly for balance. The unarmed guard had moved forward, arms splayed, looking concerned. Paul caught his feet and advanced, swinging the blade.

"Paul—"

The sword cut across the guard's shoulders first, splitting skin until the white of his collarbone was visible, and then slicing through the thin skin of his throat. The second arrow sliced clean through the spray of blood and sank into the flesh of Paul's stomach. He dropped the sword as he fell, gasping, his stomach burning. He tried to scream but only managed to spew blood over himself.

Hester stepped up behind the archer and grabbed his gloved hand as he was reaching for another arrow. She turned him to face her, watching his eyes go wide in surprise. Surely he hadn't so easily forgotten about her?

"That action will not be necessary." She lowered his arm down to his side and reached for the buttons on his shirt, undoing them one by one until she had bared his chest. All the while, he stood in silence, shivering slightly.

"Hm," she hummed softly, studying the scars on his skin closely. "You have been a soldier for a very long time."

The guard swallowed thickly but said nothing. She flicked her eyes to his face for a long moment, before taking a step closer, pushing his coat down his arms until his entire torso was bared. She traced her hands down his chest, a mere hair away from touching his skin.

"Perhaps it is time for you to retire."

Her fingers clutched his flesh and she felt him jerk in her grasp, his lungs drawing a sudden gasp of breath. Her hands smoothed his flesh with a careful caress and he shuddered beneath her touch. Brown eyes rolled upward in his skull, showing her only white. She felt his chest sink low as the breath eased from his lungs, and she breathed deeply as she heard it sigh from his lips. She could almost smell that spice of life tingling on his last breath.

The body fell to the ground with a loud sound and Hester sighed. She tilted her head when she heard the whimpering behind her and turned. She had already dealt with the guard who had been shot in the leg, easing him into death with a brush against his temple. It was Paul, alone, who remained alive.

He was lying on his back, blood soaking his clothes from his wounds, and something yellow trying to force its way beyond the arrow in his stomach. He was gasping for breath, his chest rising and falling erratically. Hester walked over and crouched down beside him. He turned his head and peered at her with dilated pupils.

"He-help?" he whispered, choking on the words and dribbling blood down the side of his mouth.

Hester studied him for a long moment, noting how the pain had given his eyes a slight glaze, and his forehead was covered in sweat, his brown hair slick with it. His face and chest were spattered with blood, not all of it his own. He was giving her a hopeful look and she met his gaze.

"You followed instructions very well, Paul. You did just as you were told." She patted his chest lightly with her hand. He coughed heavily, blood spraying from his mouth and painting his chin red. She ignored it. "I did make a deal with you. If you dealt with your fellows, I would refrain from killing you." She tapped his chest. "I will keep my end of the bargain, Paul."

She watched his eyes widen in realization. He tried to shake his head, but he started coughing heavily and she could hear the liquid in his throat. Blood ran from the sides of his mouth as he gasped between coughs, trying to breathe despite the blood running into his lungs.

Hester remained crouched beside him as the pool beneath him grew. She watched curiously as his breathing slowed, and as he seemed to forget to breathe for a few seconds, before drawing a sudden gasp that began his coughing anew. A dim fog had rolled into his eyes, but he still seemed to be able to see, and was periodically distracted from staring at her by something she couldn't catch sight of, no matter how hard she looked. A greenish-yellow pus had oozed out around the arrow shaft in his stomach and colored the blood that covered the ground.

She stayed beside him until he'd choked on his last breath, falling still with his eyes still open.

He laid just as he had when she'd first crouched beside him, and she frowned at the grey of his skin, the fog of his dead eyes. He looked just the same as any of the others she had ended the lives of, but he hadn't gone near so quickly. She found herself wishing his breath hadn't faltered because suddenly… suddenly she felt very much like she had been left behind.

She stood up suddenly, cold. The air had begun to chill as the sun sank toward the horizon. She had been here for hours, and she didn't want to be here any longer.

She looked down at the man's death-glazed eyes and wondered what he had seen that had distracted him.

She reached a hand down and pressed his eyelids closed. One sprang back up, as though, even in death, he was determined to stare at her with those wide eyes.

She turned and left the Trade City quickly. There was nothing left for her there.

XIII

They'd run until Mortimer couldn't run any longer, and then Ricker had picked him up and kept going at a fast walk. He didn't stop to eat or sleep throughout the day, even once Shadow arrived sometime around midday and made frequent suggestions toward resting. With the ghost's aid, Ricker kept walking throughout the night, until Shadow had finally put his foot down and refused to lead him anymore until he'd *slept*.

So they slept.

And in the morning, they walked. When they were hungry, they ate. But mostly, they walked, and walked, and walked, and the sun rose and it set and days passed. It became less about getting away from the Trade City and more about finding somewhere safe to stop, to breathe, to rest.

And then they were attacked.

It was unexpected because they were expecting an attack, at any moment, but from a PlagueCursed or a half-starved groups of cannibals or an armed guard who'd followed them from the Trade City.

Not from a farmer passing them on the road.

But the man had turned suddenly, a fist flying. Had Ricker been better-rested or had more to eat than dried jerky and plague-ridden fruit, he might have been alert enough to duck. Had he not still been fighting off a consistent headache from the concussion he'd suffered days before, he might have managed to remain conscious after the first strike. As it was, he'd had a moment of clarity – enough time to grab Mortimer by the arm and pull the boy behind him – before the space between the fist and his face was less than nothing, and all that met him was darkness.

For Ricker, having his workmanship so praised he was called far away to deliver weapons had never been a pleasant thing. At one time, he'd had a wife, and while he no longer had a wife, he now had a son. The trades he made from such long excursions was good, much better than the meager offerings he garnered from local work, but it never seemed to balance out the time he lost with his son.

He pushed the door to their home open and reminded himself to oil the hinges as the door creaked loudly in protest. Closing the door behind him, he lowered his heavy pack to the floor, looking around the kitchen.

The countertops were spotless, all the plates tucked away in a cupboard somewhere. It didn't look as though his son had taken the time to eat at all while he was gone, and Ricker marveled again at how much he took after his mother.

"Lucas!" he called, hefting the leather-wrapped parcel in his hands and heading toward the stairs. "I'm home! I brought you a gift!"

There was no answer, but the sun still hadn't fully crested the horizon. Shaking his head, Ricker took the stairs quickly in his excitement. Five days was the longest he ever wanted to be away from his son until the boy had reached his adulthood, and the way things were going, Lucas would take up his trade, anyway, and he'd keep him on as an apprentice. Lottie had grown up in a family of farmers and Ricker hadn't thought he would be lucky enough for the boy to follow in his footsteps, but by some grace, he had.

Ricker pushed open the door to his son's room and stepped inside, grinning. He could see the giant lump Lucas' body formed in the thick blankets, still curled up in bed. He moved over and grabbed the quilt.

"Time to get up, Luc—"

The sight would forever haunt Ricker's dreams. Lucas lay on his side as though sleeping, his arms limp as they stretched out in front of him. His skin had turned a pale blue-grey color, except for his lower right side, where Ricker could see the blood had pooled under his skin from lying in that same position. His neck was bruised, black and purple and blue, all around, where his neck had been broken. His head was twisted to be looking up at the ceiling, while the rest of his body faced the wall.

Ricker's lips quivered as his eyes found those of his son. They were staring right at him, glazed in death, but still they seemed just as bright to him as they always had; vibrant, unfairly full of life where the rest of him wasn't, and blue.

Those damn haunting blue eyes.

Ricker snapped awake with a cry, his head screaming in pain. He rolled over onto his stomach and vomited bile. His fingers clenched, searching for a purchase that would allow him to crawl away from this pain.

"You ain't hurt that bad, Breather. Grow a pair."

Ricker's shoulders shook and he struggled to catch his breath between the desperate rebelling of his stomach. He heard a low keening sound and thought, perhaps, it was coming from the back of his own throat. He couldn't seem to focus his mind between the desperate heaves of his stomach and the pain that was shooting through the left side of his skull.

"Shadow," he murmured. He could feel tears leaking down his cheeks, and he pressed his forehead against the dirt. His fingers sank into the earth and he choked on a breath. "Shadow."

The silence that met his ears beyond the sound of his own desperation, his attempts to calm himself, was more haunting even than the dream. He didn't care if he sounded desperate – he knew he did. He didn't care that he was on his hands and knees in the dry dirt and his own bile, begging for a response from the dead. He called out for the ghost, loud enough that the man could hear him.

"Shadow, please!"

There was no answer from the ghost. The shadows did not dance in such a way as to betray the shade's presence. The ghost had left him.

"Quit your whinin', boy." A boot nudged hard against his hips and Ricker fell over onto his side. He rolled over until he was staring up at the man above him through squinted eyes, his head and heart aching.

"Innkeeper," he muttered, upon seeing the man's face. The man sneered at him.

"So you do remember me, even through the drink." Ricker felt a sharp nudge against his ribs and hid his wince, his eyes tightening. "You remember tearing down my jail, too, I'll wager. An' pissing on Saint Francis."

"I remember pinning your fat face to the bar when you attacked me."

"The way you were looking at my daughter—"

"I would *never* touch a child!"

214

His yell echoed through the quiet air, silencing the innkeeper with its ferocity. When Ricker's rage at the accusation faded to a more manageable level, he was surprised to find himself standing, breathing heavily, his fists clenched tightly. There was an odd weight at his neck and he reached up, his fingers touching the cold edge of a metal collar. His eyes narrowing, his hand traced the sharp edge of the collar to around the back of his neck, where he felt the large links of a chain.

Spinning around, he was unsurprised to find the chain fell down from the back of the collar and trailed through the dirt for a few yards. He couldn't quite discern the means by which the chain was held, but it seemed to end in the ground at one point and he had a feeling if he followed it, he would find a spike of some sort keeping him locked within a limited space of movement.

Ricker turned back around to find the innkeeper watching him with a look of smug pride upon his face. He stalked forward with a snarl in his throat. "What do you think—" The collar snapped against this throat and he jerked to retreat a step, his hands at his throat instinctively.

"Not only did you disrupt Mass and defile our saint's shrine, but you didn't have the decency to remain imprisoned, as was your due. You destroyed my jail." He tossed something at him and, on instinct, Ricker reached out to catch it.

The thin blade of the skinning knife was still sharp and sliced easily through the skin of his palm. Ricker hissed, dropping the blade into the dirt. The wound burned, and blood began to run down his hand. He clenched his jaw and looked back up at the innkeeper.

"That's yours again, Breather. Now I want back what's mine." He jerked a hand at the crumbled remains of what had once been the jail. "Rebuild the jail. Then you can leave."

Ricker watched the innkeeper walk off. He wasn't awed by the man's ability to leave him chained and bleeding without concern. He was also unsurprised to find that his cloak and weapons were once again missing. He had been stripped while unconscious and left in nothing but his boots and pants, though considering the innkeeper's feelings toward him, he felt lucky he wasn't without those, as well.

The chain that bound him clinked loudly as he moved around the area in which he was chained. Most of the space he was confined to was consumed by rubble from the jail. The building had collapsed more thoroughly than he had predicted it would, though it was possible it had received help in that after he had managed to escape.

Ricker investigated the chain and collar that bound him. They were welded together firmly. Whoever had done the job was taking no chances that the two could be broken apart. The links of the chain were heavy and large, and Ricker trailed each one through his fingers carefully, looking for weaknesses. And when he reached the end of the chain, he inspected the metal stake that was firmly lodged into the ground.

It was two-pronged, with a large, flat top. The chain had been crafted and, perhaps, adjusted in such a way that the end of it was a series of links that connected back to one another, creating a kind of metal noose, though it couldn't be loosened or tightened. The two spiked ends of the stake straddled the noose, one inside of it and the other outside, to hold it firmly in place. Ricker couldn't tell how long the prongs were or how far they sank down into the ground, but he tried to pull the stake out of the ground to no avail. The thing wouldn't even budge, and without the proper tools, he couldn't hope to break the links of the chain.

It was the third time that he caught someone watching him out of the corner of his eye that Ricker finally gave in to the inevitable. Clearly, the innkeeper was determined that he not leave until he'd fixed what he had broken. Ricker wasn't foolish enough to think it a sure thing that he would be released upon the jail being finished, but doing nothing wouldn't help him either way.

There was no new wood or stone with which to build the jail, but there was no room to put it, either, with the remains of the former lying in a mass before him. With a sigh, he grabbed a cracked length of wood that had been part of the wall and began to move the rubble, piece by piece, into a large pile.

It wasn't easy work and it wasn't rewarding. He wasn't wearing gloves, so the boards bit into his fingers, leaving behind sharp splinters sunk beneath his skin. He had nothing with which to wrap his injured hand and the cut scabbed and broke open again, the wound burning when splinters snagged his broken skin and dirt mixed with his blood.

The sun traveled through the sky, and the constant haze did nothing to protect his shoulders and the back of his neck from getting hot under the sun. Other than the eyes that continued to watch him, no one approached and offered him either company or respite. He didn't imagine he would have been very good company, in any case.

More than once, his thoughts turned to Shadow or Mortimer, and he wondered where both were. He couldn't ask about the ghost, but he tried a few times to ask his various watchers about the boy. None had a word, kind or otherwise, to say to him, and he still had no answers when the sun sank below the horizon later that night, and the air cooled.

There were no torches lit for Ricker to see by, but he tried to continue working despite the darkness. He didn't want to return to sleep and risk seeing something more from his past. He tripped three times over boards he couldn't see in the darkness, and once over the chain that bound him. Finally, he simply gave up and used his hands to feel out a place where he could sit that wouldn't ram a nail through his backside.

The sound of his breathing seemed abnormally loud with his eyes open yet unable to see. The only other sounds were that of the wind rustling and chickens clucking nearby. Not too far off, he could hear the cows in their pasture, their deep, slow mooing echoing eerily through the night.

Ricker kept his eyes open despite the utter darkness making him blind. He wasn't going to fall asleep. He wasn't going to dream again. He didn't want to remember any more. He *wouldn't*.

Five minutes later, he was asleep.

The sounds of children crying reached slowly through the fog of his own despair. Beyond the fearful wailing, he could feel the stickiness of dried tears on his cheeks, and the aching of his eyes. He wondered at what had called his attention. The children's desperate sobs had surely been going on for a while and that couldn't have been what had woken him from the deep fog in which he had buried himself.

"Ricker."

The voice stopped his breath for a moment and Ricker had to remember how to breathe. His lips quivered and he drew in a deep breath, looking around. There were children pressed up into a corner of the dimly-lit room. Twelve and thirteen years old, the four of them were cuddled together, arms flung over each other, seeking whatever protection and comfort they could find.

Their faces were all puffy and red from crying, the tears still dripping from their chins. He could see the snot reflecting the dim light of their room as it ran from their noses or was smearing across a lip or sleeve. He felt no sympathy for them. All the fear they felt was well-deserved. How dare they think to come away from their actions unscathed by even remorse—

"Ricker."

That voice again. "Lottie?" he whispered, looking about him. He saw no one but the children, though. Only shadows.

Something warm slid across his arm and Ricker looked down. His breath caught in his throat at the sight of the body. He couldn't tell if it had been a boy or a girl, but he could tell it was a child. The fifth child... that's right, Lucas had always spent time with five other children... not four.

There was a sick sucking sound as he removed his hands from where they had been buried in the child's insides. His skin was slick with blood and he could see steam rolling off of his arms, the blood still hot.

He felt his whole body shudder. The heat of the blood coating his arms seemed hotter still as the chill swept through him, coiling like a serpent at the base of his spine. His hands shook as he stared down at them, trying to remember what had happened, what he had done. He wanted them to pay for doing what they did to Lucas, for leaving him like that, but not this... not this...

"Oh, Ricker."

"Lottie," he called, his voice a plea, weak in his throat. He looked up from his hands and searched the room. The children shrank back from his cage, still crying, but he couldn't hear them. He listened for the voice he thought he had heard. Could it have been her? It must have been her.

"Lottie?"

Ricker blinked open his eyes, his wife's name still on his lips. The sun had risen above the horizon and he squinted at it, breathing deeply. He felt the tears slip from the corners of his eyes and slide into his ears. His breath shuddered through his throat.

The sound of footsteps against the ground alerted him that someone else was there and Ricker pushed himself quickly to his feet, wiping his hand across his eyes to clear away the evidence of tears. He cleared his throat as he turned around, expecting the innkeeper, or someone there to watch him continue clearing away the rubble of the jail.

Instead, he found Eleanor standing before him.

She looked different than she had a few days before, when he'd last seen her. Her eyes were bloodshot, the skin beneath them dark from lack of sleep. Her hair was pulled back roughly, tangled, and it looked as though she hadn't taken care to wash it for a few days.

She was dressed in brown cowhide pants and boots, and a loose long-sleeved shirt that had once been white but was now stained with dirt and what looked like blood. Most noticeable of all were her eyes. When he first met her, Ricker had seen the innocence in her gaze that he knew would leave her only painfully. There was no innocence there now that he could see, and the taking of it had left some scars behind.

His right hand was clenched tight and, looking down, he could see the skinning knife he had kicked aside the night before wrapped tightly in her fingers. He eyed it a moment before meeting her gaze.

"Eleanor?"

"I want you to help me kill them." Her voice was rough, but her tone sharp, assured. The lack of hesitation didn't put Ricker at any sort of ease.

A thousand answers to who "them" was danced through his mind in an instant, but Ricker silenced them. He studied the girl's face. He recognized the pain in her gaze, and the loss. He had felt both too many times to not be able to read it in others. There was rage there, too, burning on the coals of a sorrow so vast and strong, it surely tore through her like a river.

"Who?" he asked.

"The PlagueWalkers."

Ricker glanced back down at the knife in her hands. There was no evidence that the knife had been used, and it was still sharp, as he could attest to himself.

"I take it your father didn't listen to reason."

"I want a blade, Weaponsmith, strong enough to cut off the Mark of a PlagueCursed."

Ricker's eyebrows rose in unison, his surprise not at all hidden. "You do know it's not possible to sever the wires of a DeathSpeaker."

"Do I look like an idiot to you?" Ricker didn't dignify the question with an answer. "We've been having trouble with some PlagueWalkers who lived a few towns over. They still live there, I s'pose, 'cept they aren't really living anymore, you know?"

Ricker did know. PlagueWalkers were nothing to trifle with. There very existence was a mockery of life, mimicking it even as they brought death to everything they touched.

"I'm losing business having those... things wander aimlessly. I'm going to deal with it, seeing as they won't."

Ricker presumed "they" were the people of the other town. Farm-rivals. "And you want to remove their eyelids?" Ricker could imagine it. The man waltzing into the town with blade en tow, poking out the eyes of the PlagueWalkers' bodies and watching their brains ooze out of empty eye sockets.

"PlagueWalkers are faster than you would think," Ricker said warningly, "and they don't travel nearly as far from their bodies as most people believe."

"I've seen them wandering around my village and that's far enough away from me to get close to them. I'll deal with them and don't you worry none about it. All you have to do is build me the blade."

Ricker remembered trying to convince the man that messing with PlagueWalkers was a bad idea. Asides from the possibility of being killed yourself before handling them, there was the fact that any left even remotely alive would hold a grudge. The innkeeper had been adamant in his plan, however, and wouldn't hear a word against it, however experienced a word it was. In the end, Ricker had simply gone to the forge and crafted the weapon like he'd been asked. And then, of course, everything had gone downhill.

Damn ale.

"Reason he might have, but not to me." Ricker looked at Eleanor and saw her swallow, as though struggling against something. "They took my mother," she said, her voice cracking with emotion. "They killed her."

The sound of a scream echoed through Ricker's head. He'd left upon that sound and had known somehow, at the time, that it had belonged to Emily Miller.

"The PlagueWalkers."

Eleanor nodded. "My father cut off their eyelids to stop them being PlagueCursed."

Ricker closed his eyes at the sheer foolishness. He'd thought the innkeeper was going to *kill* the PlagueWalkers. Had circumstances been less dire, had he not just learned of the Miller woman's death for certain, had he not just woken from a dream about the night he went mad, he might have laughed. The temptation to let go into laughter was still there, but Ricker thought that if he did, he might well cross a threshold he could not pass back through. If he stepped fully, willingly, into the madness, it would surely take him again.

After all that he had done, he wasn't sure Lottie would come again to pull him back.

He heard the clink of metal on metal and turned to find Eleanor had pulled a ring of keys from her pocket. She caught him watching.

"I stole them from my father last night, when he was looking for the monk boy."

"Mortimer," Ricker said, as Eleanor stepped up to him. He bent low so she could get to the back of the collar and heard the clicking sound of a key sliding into place. "How is the boy?"

"Frightened." There was a loud snapping sound and the collar swung open on a hinge he hadn't noticed. He grabbed it and pulled it off, letting it fall to the ground. "He was locked in one of the stables. It took me a while to find where Papa was keeping him." She slipped the keys back into her pocket and returned the knife to her hand. "I hid him somewhere he would be safe, but Papa is looking for him." She met Ricker's eyes, her own a storm of rage. "Now, will you help me?"

Regardless of how unlikely it was for the innkeeper to look for Mortimer in the hayloft just above the stable he had supposedly escaped from, Ricker didn't feel well leaving the boy there with no allies nearby. Ricker was certainly not the safest person for a child to be around - a fact that his subconscious seemed more than happy to remind him of – but Mortimer would be much safer with him than in a town filled with people who had no love for PlagueCursed.

Convincing the boy hadn't been a problem. Ricker was more than a little shocked when, upon seeing him, Mortimer had run up and wrapped his arms around his waist, looking for all the world like he was about to cry. He had no explanation for the way the child was acting, and Mortimer couldn't tell him. That frightened look upon his face was all that kept Ricker from pushing him away. If it made the boy feel safer, Ricker could let him hug him, just this once.

They'd stepped out of the stables to find two men waiting for them, though. Ricker had reached for his blades, thinking this would end their quiet escape, only to find his blades gone, and to realize he still only had on his pants and boots.

"It's all right," Eleanor said quietly, and stepped around him. "James, Peter, did you get everything?"

A tall, blonde-haired boy dressed in dirt-crusted pants and missing a shirt, held a bundle of clothes up for Eleanor to see. Taking notice, Ricker recognized his cloak as the fabric wrapped around the rest and stepped forward to take it from him.

"Thank you."

The boy nodded, but it was the other one that spoke. His dark hair was wind-swept backward and his pants were muddy from the knees downward, but he was wearing a green shirt and holding a brown cloak out to Eleanor. "Your pa's running around the southern pasture. Peter said something about spotting a boy hiding among the cows and he took the bait."

"Good." Eleanor swept the cloak around herself and pulled the hood up over her blonde hair. "Thank you, Peter," she said, looking at the blonde boy.

Peter shrugged. "I doubt it will keep him busy for long, but hopefully long enough. There's a wagon ready for you at the eastern pasture." He gave her a sad, concerned smile. "Be careful, all right?"

Eleanor nodded, but Ricker could see the boy didn't believe she was concerned about being cautious. He resisted the urge to sigh as Peter and James glanced at each other before taking off in the other direction, presumably to try and stall Eleanor's father some more, to be safe.

When it came down to it, he wasn't as worried about the innkeeper as he was about Eleanor's state of mind.

If she detected his concern, she didn't let on. "Let's go."

The wagon made their journey shorter than it would have been if they had walked, but Ricker found the lack of commentary during their journey disturbing. It was only after some time thinking about it that he realized he was missing Shadow, and the thought prompted the question of why the ghost still hadn't shown himself.

Ricker oscillated between concern for Shadow's uncharacteristic absence and anger that the ghost had abandoned them. He couldn't seem to decide which emotion should be prevalent and he felt as though he were spinning on a mad carousel as he flew quickly through an emotional kaleidoscope. He knew part of his inability to focus his feelings was due to the nightmares he had recently been suffering – nightmares that were less manifestations of his subconscious than they were memories of the worst times of his life. How he had managed to forget...

He couldn't think on it. Not now. PlagueWalkers. He had PlagueWalkers to deal with, and one alone was more than enough to require all of his attention. He needed to focus.

They had entered a village about the size of Eleanor's, but where hers was well-kept, if worn, this one was in shambles. The houses were barely standing, though it seemed a collapsed state didn't keep people from using them. There were cows and chickens in this village, as well, but no fences to keep them confined. They roamed the village freely, leaving their droppings wherever they were when the need struck them. Worse still was the emaciated state in which they appeared to be. It was not so much that they weren't well-fed but that they were sick.

Diseased.

"They have the plague," Ricker murmured.

"There is a lake, north of the village," Eleanor spoke quietly. "It is known to the locals as Plague Lake. They fish from it daily, for their own meals and trade."

Ricker glanced at her sharply and she caught the look, nodding. "Most of the people who pass through our inn are warned against coming here because all the inhabitants, save the PlagueCursed, are dying from the plague."

She shrugged one shoulder. "Eating the fish can't hurt them, of course, since they're already dying or immune, so they see no trouble in doing so. But while we can warn those who come through our village, those that come from another direction have no warning. And we can do nothing to warn those that buy their trade."

Ricker grimaced. It was a cruel trick, to capture fish diseased from toxic waters and trading them as safe to eat. Unless one was a PlagueCursed and immune, or already plagued, eating the fish would sicken them with Dark Plague.

It was no wonder the disease couldn't be eradicated. People were knowingly passing it along to others for their own profit.

"We've tried to convince them to put up a fence and signs, but they'll hear nothing of it. The leader of the town, Smith, is not a particularly nice man and he doesn't care for anyone coming into the town who is at risk for getting the plague. He thinks they deserve whatever they get for being able to still catch it."

A few cows called out from where they stood along the road, emaciated, their scabbing bodies already covered in flies.

"Are these from your farm?"

"The cows and chickens?" At Ricker's nod, Eleanor said, "Papa decided to pull a deal with Smith when he found out the man wasn't going to be decent about putting up signs and a fence. He'd give him some stock every six months if he kept those of his town well and clear of ours. Smith held up his end of the bargain, so every six months, a couple of men from the town and I will bring a couple cows and chickens over to seal our side of the deal."

She looked at the cow leading their wagon sadly. "We'll have to leave Claudia here. She's probably already infected."

Neither of them said it, but the truth of it burned in Ricker's mind.

He had dragged Eleanor along with him, into a town filled with death and plague. She was probably already infected, too.

Claudia stopped when Eleanor pulled on the reins and the wagon shambled to a halt. Ricker glanced at the building next to them. Like all the rest in the village, it was halfway to falling down. It stood out from the rest, however, as it appeared to be the largest in the village.

Ricker climbed out of the wagon after her, but put a hand on Mortimer to stop the boy from following him.

"What is this place?"

Eleanor turned to look at him, her hands stuffed low into her pockets. Ricker could see that her arms were shaking.

"This is where they keep the PlagueWalkers."

Ricker didn't ask how she knew that. He could see the fear burning in her eyes right alongside the rage. In that precarious state, it was amazing what someone could do to achieve what they desired.

"You said there are three?"

"Yes. They're kept together, near the back of the building. They look just like they're sleeping, but..."

"But they're missing their eyelids now."

He heard her swallow thickly beside him. "Yes."

Ricker didn't mention that he knew what a PlagueWalker's body looked like. He thought the girl might have known that, since she'd asked him to help her.

"I can lead you to—"

"Stay here," Ricker said, placing a hand on her shoulder. She looked up at him, startled, and angry. He looked over at Mortimer. The boy was sitting quietly in the cart, but his eyes were wide and his hands were clenched tight over the side of the wagon.

He looked back down at Eleanor. "Stay with Mortimer."

"You think *you* can take on three PlagueWalkers by yourself?"

Ricker didn't say what he immediately thought – that if he hadn't agreed to help her, she probably would have gone after them on her own. He, at least, had experience dealing with PlagueCursed. She, on the other hand, had only the strength offered her by grief, which always seemed a lot, but was never enough.

He opened his mouth to try and quell her anger, no idea what he could possibly say.

"Ricker will not be alone when facing them."

Had Ricker been holding one of his daggers, he would have dropped it, the ghost's voice so startled him. Eleanor, too, jumped at the sudden words that seemed to come from nowhere and everywhere at once. Only Mortimer, who had seen the ghost slip into Ricker's shadow, remained still as the ghost spoke.

"Jumpy, Ricker?" The voice echoed in his mind, as though spoken through a tunnel, and Ricker realized these words were for him alone.

He yanked a blade from his belt, tightening his fist around the hilt as he resisted the urge to growl. His thoughts ripped through his mind on the wings of a snarl. *What are you doing here?*

"Following you." The way the ghost said it was surely *meant* to annoy him, and it annoyed Ricker still further that it worked in his favor.

I thought you'd stopped doing that. He tried so hard to make the sneer in his mind cover the hurt, he really did.

There was a silence that stretched for too long a moment. Ricker opened his mouth to call the shadow back, for surely he had left…

"I'm still here, Ricker." The shadow's voice echoed hauntingly.

Ricker's mouth snapped shut and the fear fled him, replaced by the hot burn of anger deep in his stomach. He focused on that sensation, letting it warm every part of his body that had been chilled with loss. He needed to be angry. He needed to be angry so he would stop being so afraid the damn ghost would leave him again.

"I am sorry, Ricker..."

"What are you?" Eleanor's voice broke through the spell that had settled over Ricker, pulling him back to the present. She was looking down at Shadow, her eyes wide with confusion, almost bright with curiosity.

"Mere remnants of what once was and cannot be again." Shadow swept the top hat from his head and performed an elaborate bow that had Eleanor's eyes lighting up, a smile twitching her lips. *"I have been traveling with Ricker for some years now."* The top hat was replaced delicately. *"I am a friend."*

"Do you have a name?"

"Shad—"

"You may call me Randy."

Ricker's mouth snapped shut with a click. He stared at the ghost in disbelief.

"It is best that none of us remain alone, and best, also, that Mortimer remain outside. If you stay with him, Eleanor, I promise to keep Ricker safe from harm."

Using what, exactly? Ricker thought.

"My witty, flapless tongue," Shadow echoed in his mind.

Eleanor looked from Shadow to Ricker, her teeth biting into her lower lip. "Can she really keep you safe?"

231

"She?" Ricker asked, confused. Realization struck him and he shook his head suddenly, bringing a hand up to ward off any explanation. "Shadow is very... clever," he said. "Whatever we might run into, Shadow's eyes are the best I could hope to have on my side."

"Ricker... I'm flattered. Truly." The ghost sniffled loudly.

Shut it.

He didn't say anything more about Eleanor calling Shadow "she." Sometimes Ricker thought the ghost existed purely to confuse him. With his ability to speak directly into someone's mind, it made comprehending him easier, as what one heard wasn't limited to merely the sounds that the human throat could make. He could show any thoughts or memories of himself or someone else, just as he could pick them out of Ricker's own head.

Unfortunately, due to this ability, it also meant he could manipulate the perspective of those he communicated with. It would be very much like him to use this ability to make Eleanor perceive that she was speaking to a woman, and not a man. Shadow had only just met her officially, after all, and wouldn't be spending any great amount of time with her while he had been invading Ricker's company for years.

With her mother having just recently been killed, and her father being the kind of person he was, Eleanor would have a better chance of bonding with a woman than with a man. With his form being as androgynous as it was, the ghost could easily manipulate Eleanor's perception of him to make her feel more at ease.

Clever of Shadow.

"I'm so glad you think so, Ricker. Now, if you're done speculating on matters you twist about in your tiny mind, perhaps we can begin our little murder mission?"

Ricker glanced up at Eleanor, who still looked unhappy at being left outside, but more comfortable knowing that Ricker wouldn't be left alone. Vaguely, it occurred to him what an amazing child she was, that she managed to worry for someone who was practically a stranger after all that she had suffered through.

"Such strength, gentleness," Shadow murmured, fluidly moving along the ground. *"Come, Ricker."*

With a final look at Mortimer and Eleanor, Ricker slipped into the building, gripping his dagger tightly in one hand.

The door swung closed behind him with an eerie silence that seemed to promise how little his actions would affect the whole. His footsteps echoed in the wide, empty passage, and in the dim light, he could see little but darkness lurking in each corner. He could hear the sound of numerous people breathing the slow, deep breaths of sleep, and if there were only three PlagueWalkers within this building, he wondered at the presence of the others.

"I imagine this works as a hospital, of sorts."

Shadow's voice was a soft echo, and if Ricker concentrated, he could hear beyond it in the near-silence and actually tell that he wasn't speaking aloud. Ricker remained silent, his footsteps as quiet as he could make them on the floor.

He heard Shadow sigh softly.

"I am sorry, Ricker."

233

Ricker clenched his teeth tightly but said nothing.

"I wouldn't have left you, but you were being watched."

"The innkeeper didn't stop you from hanging around last time we were in the town," he snarled. He felt more than heard the gentle rebuff and stilled his tongue.

"Miller left you to your own devices, confident that the collar he'd burdened you with would suffice to keep you from leaving. He sent no one to watch you, and not one of his people came of their own accord."

Ricker had seen at least three different people watching him, and it was only because he had tried to learn where Mortimer had been taken that he remembered the three so distinctively. More than likely, there had been others, but he had no count. At least three. At least three who were not, as he had thought, the innkeeper's pawns.

Whose, then?

"Someone far worse than a bigoted farmer in a position of power. They have the gem. Now they want Mortimer."

Why?

The sound of frustration the ghost let out was not comforting. *"I don't know."*

... you never told me your name was Randy.

He thought he could hear Shadow's smile. *"You had but to ask."*

There was a flicker of light and Ricker's eyes were attracted to the two glowing points of light on the floor in front of him. A sigh whispered across the shadows.

"Quickly, Ricker, let us deal with this PlagueWalker threat and be done with this town.

These people who hunt Mortimer know where you are, and that bodes well for no one."

~*~

Eleanor shuddered when the door closed behind Ricker, leaving her alone with the monk boy. She wrapped her arms around herself as a chill swept through her, and pulled her cloak tighter around her body.

She didn't like it here. It always made her feel ill, to come into Smith's town, among the dead and dying and hopeless.

She brushed a hand across her eyes, thinking about how this sorrowful town was now the final resting place of her mother, who had deserved so much more than to be killed for her father's foolish actions. To die protecting her from harm.

There was a loud slapping behind her and she turned to find the monk boy smacking the palm of his hand against the side of the cart. When he realized he had her attention, he pointed across the road from where their wagon sat. Eleanor followed the direction of his finger.

Floating a foot above the ground was a six-foot cloud of grey-purple light. There was a vague comprehension of a human being in the form, but the arms and legs seemed too long, somehow, and warped, as though they were less appendages and more pieces of fabric floating in an errant wind. The face, too, seemed warped, but if one looked long enough, it was possible to see a pair of eyes, and a wide, grinning mouth.

Eleanor sucked in a breath at the sight of the creature, knowing instantly what it was. The PlagueWalker – the very soul of the creature that

235

roamed the world in a sick perversion of life. A phantom that suffered sleep only in the body and who wandered in a constant rage, destroying all it touched with death and plague.

Somehow... somehow, Eleanor knew the PlagueWalker stood here not to threaten her as Ricker ended its life by destroying its body. No, the eyes of these creature burned in a mocking gesture, a triumphant gesture. They were wrong. Right in that three bodies of PlagueWalkers rested within the building, but wrong that there were only three in the village.

There was one more, a fourth. The one that had killed her mother.

The PlagueWalker turned, an ambiguous gesture of movement, and began to slide and slither at once through the air, away from them. Eleanor let out a sound, halfway between a sob and a scream, partway a call to stop, and partly a battle cry. She made no motions to think about her actions, no attempts to tell Ricker of her discovery. She did not wait for Mortimer.

Her feet kicked against the ground in her rage and she tore after the PlagueWalker, determined to follow it. Determined to find it. Determined to kill it.

Mortimer's head oscillated quickly between the girl and the door to the building. He had little time in which to make his decision, however, and jumped down from the cart in a tangle of robes. With a smack of his bare feet against the earth, he raced after Eleanor, leaving the wagon far behind.

The PlagueWalker remained constantly ahead of them by at least three yards, even though Mortimer did manage to catch up to Eleanor. The phantom was taunting them, however, always remaining well within sight as it moved throughout the town in a senseless pattern, backwards across streets it had already gone over once in the other direction. Barely two minutes had passed before Mortimer was hopelessly lost, no idea which direction was north, much less where they had left the wagon.

Eleanor was breathing heavily when the PlagueWalker finally reached a crumbling building, quite possibly the oldest in the village, and slipped through the walls like a ghost. She hesitated only long enough to draw a few breaths, before grabbing the door handle and pushing it open. Mortimer grabbed hold of her arm, to pull her back, to make her wait, but she shook him off.

She would see this through. She would kill the PlagueWalker.

The inside of the house was all but pitch black. The smell of dust and rot was heavy in the air, and there was a silence that hung like a great beast over them, waiting to pounce. Their footsteps were muffled by the soft floor beneath them, but Mortimer could feel Eleanor moving around, and every now and then, a board would creak loudly beneath their feet.

The scuffling sound of her fingers tracing the wall was eventually replaced by the creak of a door opening as she found a handle and pulled.

Light burst from a cellar, shining up the stairs and through the threshold, momentarily blinding them. Mortimer peered down into the disturbingly well-lit room, wondering why a room below ground would be better lit than the living quarters, which looked quite dead when bathed in firelight.

Eleanor didn't ask questions, however, and she didn't wait for Mortimer to make a movement. Her feet found the steps and she moved down them, unconcerned.

Biting his lip and looking around at the angry, leaping shadows, Mortimer was forced to follow.

The cellar was lit by a series of torches which lined the perfectly proportioned walls every three feet. There were four tables set up in the basement, all of which were occupied. One with a series of metal tools that looked as though they might have been new three centuries prior, and the other three with bodies.

The bodies were well-kept and, upon closer inspection, it was apparent that the three were still alive. They breathed deeply in their slumber, looking the picture of health, but for the blood congealed on their faces from their eyelids having been removed.

"The PlagueWalkers," Eleanor breathed.

Three of them. It seemed too coincidental that there would be two groups of three PlagueWalkers, and Eleanor realized that she had been lied to. The PlagueWalkers were not where she had told Ricker they would be. They were here, and she had been led right to them.

Eleanor turned around suddenly, a frightened look upon her face. She opened her mouth to apologize to Mortimer, or perhaps to tell him to run, but the face that appeared from out of nothing stilled her tongue.

"Clever girl, figuring it out so quickly." The man clapped his hands together mockingly. "I thought farmers were known for their talent at sowing seeds and their *lack* of intelligence, but you're an impressive one."

Eleanor backed away until she hit one of the tables. The man continued forward until he had stepped into the light, and Mortimer was able to fully see him. His pants were dark brown in color and his shirt a deep crimson, the dark colors allowing for him to hide within the shadows without causing him to appear a darker spectacle, as he would have had he worn black. His hair was a dirty blonde color and wavy, pulled back at the nape of his neck. He wore a pair of soft-soled boots and when he moved, he didn't make a sound.

He glanced over at Mortimer with a smile on his face, before looking back at Eleanor. "I did promise you the PlagueWalkers for your services as a delivery girl, and so..." He waved an inviting hand at the three bodies. "Have at them." He grinned a smile full of teeth when she didn't move. "Now, now, dear, I can't imagine you're afraid to get your hands dirty. After all." He grabbed hold of Mortimer and pulled the boy close to him. "You've led my prey right to me, like a good hunting beast." His eyes matched hers with wild amusement. "Now kill!"

Mortimer stared wide-eyed at the girl.

She had planned this? She had led him into the hands of the very people he had been constantly running from? He knew that Hester said she would catch him in the end, but no, no, this couldn't be happening.

He saw Eleanor turn around and face the prone bodies of the sleeping PlagueCursed, and he saw her slide her hand into her pocket. She brought out a small knife with a tiny blade that gleamed in the light of the flames.

"That's it, girl. Kill them, and avenge your mother."

Eleanor's hand shook. "You planned this." she whispered. "You bastard!"

She spun in a moment and leapt at him. Mortimer ducked instinctively, but Eleanor's hand swung at the face of the man holding him. He moved quickly, his free hand flying up to catch her wrist, as his other shoved Mortimer hard, knocking him from his feet.

He landed in a heap and looked up to see the man twist Eleanor's wrist until she dropped the knife. He ripped his own knife from his belt – a wicked, curved blade with a point that would slide easily through the girl's soft flesh.

He pulled up on Eleanor's wrist, forcing her onto her tiptoes, and swung the blade forward.

"No."

Mortimer did not shout the word. It was barely even a whisper. The sound was the mere susurration of air gliding over his tongue, but it was enough.

The man's entire body seized upon the sound. He twitched, as though an electrical shock had raced through his blood, and collapsed in a heap, his body stiff, as though he'd been dead for hours, not seconds. There was no moment in which the breath escaped his body or the light faded from his eyes. One moment he was there, and the next, he was already gone. The leaving had been lost, as though Mortimer's voice itself had stolen time.

Mortimer stared, not at the man, but at Eleanor. She, too, had collapsed at the sound of his voice, her body flopping to the ground. He opened his mouth, couldn't find breath enough to draw in air, and closed his lips.

He'd killed her.

He'd killed them both, but he'd killed Eleanor.

As he looked to the tables, Mortimer realized he'd killed the PlagueWalkers, too.

~*~

There was no witty commentary from Shadow as Ricker raced through the town. They'd reached the back of the building to find it empty of PlagueWalkers, and so they'd traveled the extent of the pseudo-hospital in search of three comatose patients. They'd found numerous people dying from plague, but none who were cursed with a Mark on their eyelids, or missing eyelids entirely.

When Ricker stepped out of the building to find Eleanor and Mortimer gone, he began to wonder about the latter.

They began to search the town, and though it was not large, it was also not small. The ground was tracked with many footprints and useless to study in hopes of determining which way the two children had gone. They were forced to simply look and, Shadow leaving to search within buildings as Ricker followed the roads, they covered more ground.

Surprisingly, it was Mortimer who found Ricker.

The boy was walking down the dirt road toward him when Ricker turned a corner. He might have run right up to him, had he not realized first that Mortimer was alone, and second, that the boy's head was hung low and his shoulders shaking, as though he were crying.

Ricker felt his stomach clench, as though trying to digest something he had not yet eaten.

"Boy."

Mortimer looked up, his feet halting in their movements. His eyes were red-rimmed and there were tears rolling down his cheeks, blue eyes all but bleeding sorrow.

"Eleanor's dead." He meant to ask it as a question, but the truth was too apparent. He saw Mortimer swallow, and the boy nodded.

"The Plague Walkers?" There had been three of them, after all, and while not confined to even the proximity of their bodies, they could easily linger.

There was a moment of hesitation, and Mortimer shook his head slowly, his eyes never leaving Ricker's. He looked both terrified and resigned at once, beyond the sorrow. Ricker studied him for a moment, looking for a different answer, so he could ask a different question. He didn't see one.

"You spoke?"

The boy nodded and looked down again, his face a rockslide of pain.

Ricker barely wondered at how weak his hatred for the boy was at the revelation. He was becoming accustomed to it. He felt, more than saw, Shadow return to his slide, the ghost's echo of touch in his mind both a comfort and a curse. There was a question there, but Ricker wouldn't answer it. He didn't yet know the answer.

He sighed softly. "Come, boy."

He drew the knife slowly from his belt.

242

XIV

The landscape was barren.

It seemed fitting, somehow, that the wasteland stretching miles before them spoke so firmly of death. Not for the first time, Ricker felt as though he was shrouded in it. What he had done... was both the easiest and hardest thing that he had ever needed to do.

The days had passed him by in almost complete silence. Shadow had still spoken on occasion, but trapped in his thoughts as he was, there were many things the ghost said that he likely hadn't heard. It was just as well. Ricker thought, perhaps, he was unequipped to deal with the ghost at the moment. He had so many other ghosts to keep him company.

He didn't know why the silence bothered him as it did. It was not as though it was any different from the way it had been before. Even once Shadow had joined his company, the ghost did not *constantly* speak, though sometimes it certainly did seem that way. But no, it wasn't the ghost's silence that so unnerved him.

It was Mortimer's.

And that didn't make sense, because Ricker had never heard Mortimer speak. Why it seemed so strange, so unexpected, that after continued silence there was yet more, Ricker did not know. For some reason, he had expected the child to talk to him.

But, of course, the boy wouldn't. Ricker had come upon him only after he had spoken and the silence had returned, bringing with it a sorrow Ricker was unsurprised by, yet hadn't expected. The boy remained silent as they moved away from the building where five people now lay dead, and his silence continued long after Ricker had cleaned the blood from his knife and replaced it at his belt.

It was confusing, understandable, and unexpected, all at once.

"If it is bothering you, then you should do something about it."

And what should I do, Shadow? I can't reverse time and bring Eleanor back to life.

"You could be merciful and kill him now."

Ricker glanced behind him. Mortimer was following him at a short distance, his shoulders low and his eyes focused on the ground. Dust kicked up around him as he dragged his feet, but he didn't seem to notice how it layered the bottom of his robes, or how filthy his bare feet were.

"You were kind enough to slit the throat of Eleanor's cow so it would not suffer through the plague." Ricker glanced down at the shadow cast behind him. Only then did he realize the ghost's voice did not echo in his strange telepathy, but could be heard easily. He was speaking so Mortimer could hear, as well. *"You intend to make Mortimer wait for his own death? So cruel, Ricker."*

"Shadow, don't be stupi—"

"Please."

The quiet tone froze Ricker's breath. He forced his legs to relax as he turned his gaze back to the boy, drawing a breath of air into startled lungs.

Mortimer had his hands clasped together so tightly that his fingers were bloodless. He had raised his head, his gaze focused on Ricker. Those blue eyes held an incredible amount of terror within them, but the boy's gaze didn't waver.

"Please." Ricker looked away as two errant tears slipped down the boy's reddened cheeks. "Just kill me now."

Ricker breathed slowly, his face turned away from the boy. "I'm not going to kill you, Mortimer."

Ricker knew from Shadow's silence that the ghost had already known this. The boy hadn't realized, though. Somewhere, in the back of his mind, Ricker wondered how Mortimer could have *not* realized what was meant by the fact that he was still alive.

By the fact that Ricker had used his name.

"But... you said, if I spoke..." His voice cracked on the last word and he stopped speaking. Ricker felt his shoulders tense at the sound of the boy trying to catch his breath, fighting back the wail of tears.

"I'm not going to kill you." Ricker fisted his hands at his sides, his back to Mortimer. Why was this so hard? Why was it so easy? He'd made his decision. It shouldn't have been difficult to do as he'd been planning since leaving the plagued town. He'd been hunting DeathSpeakers for years. It shouldn't have been so easy to give it all up.

It shouldn't have been hard, and it wasn't. It was easy.

It shouldn't have been easy, and it wasn't. It was hard.

"I'm taking you to a church," Ricker said, uncurling his fingers and letting them relax. He drew a deep breath. "Not the one you left. It's close by... a few hours away. You can live there. Silently."

He knew he hadn't needed to add in that last word. The boy had refrained from speaking since his wires had been removed. His remorse at the death of Eleanor had been telling in that he hadn't wished for it, that his words were not spoken with the intent to cause her death. He was speaking now, but that was done believing he was already doomed to die at Ricker's hand for speaking in the first place.

"But why?"

The boy's whisper was hoarse, and surely the words must have hurt, dragged through his untrained throat like rusty nails. Ricker wondered if the boy was purposely testing his resolve, testing to see if he would change his mind.

But why?

Because he was a child. Because he had been kidnapped from the only home he'd ever known, hunted like an animal, and even cornered, he hadn't spoken. Because he'd had countless opportunities to flee in the night, or to try and end the life of his captor.

Because he...

Ricker shook his head sharply, clenching his teeth.

"I don't want to waste my blade on your blood." He meant it to come out as a snarl. He meant it to be the no-questions end of the conversation. Instead, he could hear the weariness in his own voice, and he resisted the urge to sigh.

He was tired. Tired of lying. To Mortimer, to Shadow.

To Ricker.

He pinched the bridge of his nose briefly and began to walk again, his steps kicking up dust. Mortimer returned to silence and even Shadow refrained from speaking. Still, all of their thoughts were loud in the air around them.

Ricker had taken the time to kill Claudia, the cow that had pulled their wagon. If he had bothered to show mercy to a mere beast, then he couldn't possibly have considered Mortimer's death to be less in comparison.

There was another reason he wanted to spare the boy; a reason that turned his head and wet his eyes and quickened his breath. A reason that haunted him as surely as Shadow haunted him, but Ricker would not speak of it.

And Mortimer did not ask again.

The church was much smaller than the one where Mortimer had grown up. It sat on the crest of a steep hill, a small patch of color against the dusty backdrop of the wasteland around it. It was hardly an oasis in the middle of a desert, but the reddish-brown bricks that formed the walls seemed warm and welcoming.

A long, narrow stone staircase led up the hill to the single door that seemed the only entrance. They had not yet reached the base of the steps when the low creaking of metal hinges tore at the silence of the world.

Ricker glanced up to see the door open slowly. The metal door was a surprising foot and a half thick, made of solid metal, and locked by a mechanical wheel that only turned when the proper combination was entered on two separate dials. At one time, the door had been the guardian at the entrance to a safe, but banks were no longer necessary in this world that found a coin a useless trinket and paper notes only worth as much as the fire they kindled.

A man appeared, straining to push the heavy door open. The man stood out against the shining silver steel of the door in his red robes and scarf. Once the door was opened, he stopped just to the side of the exit, watching as a second man left the building and moved swiftly down the stairs.

Ricker and Mortimer stopped at the base of the stairs and waited as the man made his way down them. He was, like the man at the door, wearing crimson robes that hung from his left shoulder and wrapped under his right arm. He was wearing a black undershirt, the sleeves only reaching to his shoulders.

His sandals scuffed the dusty earth as he stepped down from the stairway, stopping in front of them. He folded his hands calmly behind his back.

"Assassin, I had not expected to see you again." He glanced at Mortimer for a moment, before returning his gaze to Ricker. "And certainly not in such controversial company."

"Priest." Ricker nodded his head slightly in deference to the title. "I believe your number was considerably diminished the last time we spoke. I understand that means you have some room in your congregation." He made a motion with his hand toward the boy at his side.

Once again, Mortimer found himself an object of the priest's study. From a distance, Mortimer had seen the dark skin of the man's head, but this close, he could see that the man *did* have hair. His head was almost entirely shaved, except for the base of his skull, where a short ponytail was tied. His hair was completely white, but the smooth skin of his face told him the priest might have only been a few years older than Ricker.

The priest's eyes were dark brown and above all else, curious. Mortimer wished they were kinder, but this man was not Father Fabula.

"Interesting."

Turning around briefly, the priest made a motion with his hand. It was apparently meant for the man waiting at the door, as he made his way swiftly down the stairs at the signal.

His robes and sandals were the same as the priest's, but his undershirt was brown instead of black. He wore a scarf made from the same material as his robes that wrapped around his neck and the lower half of his face. He said nothing when he arrived and his steps slowed. He merely stood in silence, his eyes on the priest alone as he waited for orders.

"John," the priest said, motioning toward the newcomers, "you remember Ricker."

The man eyed Ricker briefly and nodded slightly, but he seemed disinterested by the presence of either arrival. Ricker, for his part, didn't look as though he was having a grand reunion, seeing the man. In fact, having seen so many priests in this church, the only one he could have picked out as familiar among the lot of them was the only one who didn't offer his name.

"This is Mortimer. He'll be staying with us for a time." The man glanced at the young boy before him with no change in his expression. "I'd like you to take him to a room. And find him some robes that will fit him."

Mortimer glanced down at the robes he was wearing. The simple brown material was very different from the robes these men were wearing, and the edges were frayed and torn. There was dirt and blood smeared in various places across the

249

fabric and they were probably unsalvageable, but they were *his* robes.

His fingers curled in the wide sleeves and he felt his eyes beginning to burn.

Glancing up, he found that the priest was watching him. Mortimer looked away, folding his arm over his chest and tucking his head down. He wanted to go home. He wanted to go home and have Father Fabula be there waiting for him.

A tap on his arm drew his attention and Mortimer lifted his head slowly. John was making a motion for him to follow. Mortimer turned and looked at Ricker.

The assassin raised his eyebrows, then jerked his chin at the stairs John had begun to climb. "Go on, boy."

Mortimer felt the burning of his eyes increase as they welled with tears. He took a retreating step, swiped a hand across his eyes, and fled up the staircase.

Ricker watched Mortimer dash past John, bumping into the man on the narrow staircase as he felt up the stone steps. His robes whipped around him as he ran up the stairs and through the open doorway into the church.

He sighed.

"It is unusual enough for you to let a DeathSpeaker live, but to bring him here." Ricker turned his attention back to the priest, who was still watching the staircase, as though he could still see Mortimer fleeing up it. After a moment, he turned and looked Ricker in the eyes, curiosity burning, as always. "What does he mean to you?"

Ricker scoffed and jerked his head away, too quickly. "He doesn't mean anything."

He could feel the priest's frown. "I am not near as much a fool as those you commonly handle, Ricker. Lie to yourself if you must, but do not lie to me."

Ricker grimaced. He turned back to the priest, his mouth open his speak. After a moment, he closed it, shaking his head. He thought for a few moments, before frowning suddenly and looking at the priest. "I didn't tell you his name."

The priest smiled. "You never tell me things. This rarely keeps me from knowing them." Ricker grumbled something foul under his breath but the priest took no heed of it. "I have been expecting you for some days now, Ricker." He made an inviting motion with his hand and the two turned and began to walk around the base of the hill.

"The hour grows rather late for your conscience to finally gain the upper hand. What makes this boy different from the others?"

Ricker thought of all the DeathSpeakers he had encountered in his travels. He could count them if he wished, but he had no desire to.

He had no certain answer for the priest. He remained silent as the two made their way around the hill, the dust kicking up around their legs and the shadows lengthening as the sun began to lower itself predictably toward the horizon.

"It has been some years since I have last seen you, Ricker. Still, it is easy to recall your presence here. When we first met, you were drowning in sorrow and rage. Even now, the waves of these oceans lap at your heels, but you are rising above them." He stopped Ricker with a hand on his arm and turned to face the assassin. "That you brought Mortimer *here*, of all the places you could have taken him, assures me of this."

Ricker tried to avoid meeting the other man's gaze. "The boy and I made a deal. That is the *only* reason he still lives."

His smile was sympathetic. "If you really wished him dead, Assassin, no deal would hold you from that outcome, however well-worded."

Ricker didn't say anything. He thought about how well-worded the deal had been. Even dangling above a flesh-eating plant, he had managed to twist the promise in his own favor. He had still planned on killing the boy, but things had changed.

The two of them reached the staircase again, and this time they climbed it, the priest ahead of Ricker. It was, perhaps, telling that the man would willing place his back to an assassin, but Ricker was unsurprised by the gesture. He had met the priest many years before and the two knew a good deal about each other. Though, Ricker was often surprised by the moments in which it seemed he really knew nothing at all.

The halls of the church were narrow and not very well lit. Shadows clung to the sides and corners, and more than once, Ricker thought he had seen Shadow twist out through the darkness and disappear. The ghost had been surprisingly quiet since he had arrived at the church, but he thought he may have just been pleased that Ricker wasn't going to kill Mortimer.

The path they walked was a familiar one that Ricker had taken many times before. He didn't need to see the priest in order to know where he was going, and his mind wandered as his legs followed the way he knew.

They turned a corner to see open doorways on either side of the hall up ahead, lights shining out from their depths. Ricker slowed his steps, his eyebrows drawing down.

"Priest."

His steps halted. There was a moment when neither of them moved, before the priest turned to face him. With the lights behind him, his face was cast in shadow, but Ricker could still see his eyes. They seemed bright, somehow, in the darkness – ever-curious, but also sad.

The priest said nothing. He simply watched Ricker in the silence of the hall, waiting.

Ricker glanced down at the floor, his eyes searching for some hint on how to ask what he wanted to know. There was no great way to do it, no perfect answer to his many questions. After a moment, he sighed.

"When we first met... did I tell you how my son died?"

"You tell me so little, Ricker."

"But do you *know*?" He couldn't even dredge up the effort to snarl. He voice was quiet, a whispered plea.

"Don't you?"

Ricker looked past the priest, down the hall. He could see shadows moving in the lights – silhouettes of whomever the rooms belonged to. There was a murmur in the air that was unmistakably voices, individual words indiscernible. He wondered what the young priests who lived at the church talked about.

"I've forgotten," he murmured. His gaze returned to the priest. "I keep having dreams... of everything." Only the more recent ones were of Lucas, and he didn't really want to know why that was. He didn't want to elaborate. The priest didn't need to know that every time he closed his eyes, he watched someone else die. "I remember some of it, but some things…" He shook his head, at a loss.

"You never told me how Lucas was killed." Ricker's fingers twitched at the surprising use of his son's name. "But if you truly wish for answers, I can tell you where to go to find them."

Ricker heard a sigh, as gentle as a breath against his mind. He thought, for a moment, that he could feel the ghost's sadness, and he glanced automatically downward, searching for the shade.

In the darkness of the hall, wrapped in shadows, a still darker shade stood cast against the floor. The stillness of the ghost startled him, and he moved his own arm experimentally, to see if it would be mimicked by the shadow. It wasn't, and so he knew that he was no imagining the tailcoat and top hat. The ghost's glowing eyes were closed, but it was the silence that bothered Ricker the most. The narrow hall seemed like a coffin, tucked away in a tomb. The air was still and dead, permeating only by the sorrow that Ricker could all but *hear* rolling off of the ghost, forceful as a wave, silent as a scream.

"I have a map that will lead you where you wish to go." The priest's words seemed to pull Ricker back from the depths. He lifted his head to study the man and, against the darkness of his thoughts, the hall seemed bright indeed.

When the priest began walking again, Ricker followed. They stopped outside one of the rooms, looking in. There was a group of five boys talking amongst themselves. They, like all the priests in the church, wore red robes, but these five were young yet, not one over twelve. Their undershirts were white and each had a scarf wrapped around their necks.

Ricker studied them a moment and was startled to realize Mortimer was among them. His presence was given away by the black dots that were his Mark, and the lack of a ponytail sprouting from the nape of his neck. Ricker watched as Mortimer remained silent, listening as the other boys talked. Even without his ability to speak freely, they seemed happy to pull him into conversations, taking his responses from nods and shakes of his head, or the widening of his expressive eyes.

"He'll do well here," the priest said quietly, before turning to Ricker. "Are you going after the pendant?"

Ricker didn't ask how the priest knew of the jewel-that-wasn't. Of all things, that was of no surprise to him.

"I made a deal to return it to the place it was stolen from. After I have my answers, searching for the gem will be my priority."

The priest nodded, looking back into the room.

"I wish you luck in your travels, Ricker; in your search for answers, and for the gem."

"Thank you," Ricker said quietly.

"Come." The priest smiled at him. "Let us find you a map."

~*~

"The place that you seek is located to the northeast, buried in the bed of a long dead river." *The priest pointed out the area he had marked. The map was old and yellowed, but asides from a few*

torn edges, it was in good condition. It was also not a small map.

"The journey will take you days, but you will find your answers there. Good luck, Ricker."

"Thank you, Priest. And, please..." Ricker trailed off, looking at the ground. He didn't really have the right to ask that.

The priest placed a reassuring hand on his shoulder. His smile was kind. "We'll take good care of him. I promise."

The church was miles behind him, and Mortimer, as well. Ricker had walked for little over an hour, the sun sinking behind him, but he had eventually been stopped by the silence. He had studied his shadow before him as he walked, but there was no familiarity there. No glowing eyes or pretentious gait, and no smart remarks.

One again, the ghost had seen fit to leave his side. It bothered Ricker more than he had thought it would. Even just a week ago, he would have given anything to find a way to make the ghost leave. Now, things seemed wrong without the shade's presence.

Ricker glanced behind him, but with the sun in his eyes and the miles behind him, he couldn't see the church. The possibility occurred to him that the ghost had stayed with Mortimer, but that didn't seem right. Surely, if Shadow had intended to leave him, he would have at least said good-bye?

But no, the ghost wouldn't stay gone. That was the great, horrible thing about Shadow. He always knew how to find Ricker, and even if he left for a time, he would show up again, when least expected, and least wanted.

And Shadow had told Ricker he wouldn't leave him, wouldn't abandon him.

Not that he felt abandoned.

No, Shadow would be back. In fact, he was probably there now, hiding within the shadow of something else, laughing at Ricker's thoughts. He refrained from glancing around to find something else that cast a shadow in the receding light. They had come this way earlier that day, on their way to the church.

The strap of his satchel was stretched taut and Ricker tried to adjust it to lessen the tightness in his chest. Even with the crossbow satchel dangling off his shoulders, the feeling didn't leave, but Ricker swallowed the sensation, and everything else.

Wherever the ghost had disappeared to, he would be back. Ricker wasn't worried. Shadow always knew how to find him.

Epilogue

Hester stepped through the threshold, the twelve foot double doors pressed back against the stone walls. Her boots snapped against the marble floor as she made her way down the wide halls, her every step purposeful and her stride long.

The smell of oil was heavy in her nostrils and black smoke curled into the air from the burning tips of the torches that lined the corridor. The dancing flames sent shadows skittering across the floor like rats.

She ignored the shadows and the eyes that followed her. People stopped their conversations to stare at her, their own steps faltering as their attention was caught. She didn't look at them. Her eyes remained focused in front of her and no one tried to get her attention.

The side hall she turned down was filled with fewer people than the main hall. She followed it to a spacious, circular room, naturally lit by what little light could squeeze through the rectangular holes in the ceiling. These holes, each six feet long and two feet wide, had once contained a thick piece of glass. The glass had been shattered years ago, leaving the windows open to the elements, and nature had taken over its place. Vines grew thick and heavily over the roof of the building and curled, unrestrained, through the rectangular opening, fawning themselves across the ceiling. The bare spaces between the foliage let in sunlight in haphazard rays, and the large room was heavily warped by shadow for it.

At one time, the walls had been decorated with grand murals telling various stories, but the paint had chipped until only a spattering of color here and there remained. Furthest from the entrance Hester had used, there were numerous stone shelves that stood to eight feet in the air. Once, they had held nearly a thousand books, but the years and the unrestrained weather had destroyed all but a few of them. Of those that remained, perhaps three people within the building would have been able to read them. Hester was not among these people, and so she did not see the great loss that it was, to look back and find those bookshelves barren and dusty.

There was a single chair in the room. It was an armchair, with a wide seat and high back. Whatever color the fabric was couldn't been seen, as they were hidden by various coats and blankets and other articles of clothing that had been haphazardly tossed across the chair to cushion it.

Draped across the chair was a figure swathed in darkness, but her form unmistakably that of a woman. She had her back pressed against one air of the chair and a leg hanging over the other. A ray of sunlight danced upon a tangle of frizzy curls the color of blood, the heavy locks reaching to the middle of her back in their wild fray. The woman's attention had been captured by a thin chain of tiny beads she was twisting around and around her fingers.

Hester stopped a few feet from the chair, her attention focused solely on the occupant. She did not speak and made no notion to gather the woman's attention. There was no one else in the room but the two of them, and the woman already knew she was there.

"Hester." The woman chopped the name upon her lips, enunciating each syllable with cutting deliberation.

"Master."

"I see you've returned my ruby. Curious, that you haven't returned it to me before now." The soft clinking of the chain stopped as the woman's hands ceased their playful movements. She turned her head casually, and Hester could feel the invisible eyes sliding across her body, as a panther would trace its gaze across the flank of an antelope. "Curiouser still that you chose to wear it."

"It draws them closer, Master. They want it, as well."

"Of course they want it. They are greedy." The beaded chain was discarded as the woman moved, returning both feet to the floor and standing swiftly. She brushed a hand down her front, straightening her coat.

"I've heard tales of your attempts to fetch me my DeathSpeaker." She took the few steps that separated her from Hester with a leisurely gait and raised a hand, brushing delicate fingers against the feathers of an arrow shaft still protruding from Hester's shoulder. "Failed attempts."

She gripped the feathered end of the shaft lightly and pushed it toward Hester, watching as the woman's eyes narrowed slightly but she didn't move. "I see you did not escape unscathed."

"No, Master," Hester murmured weakly.

"I do hope you don't plan on bleeding to death before you've finished your task." The words were spoken casually, but the pads of the woman's fingers squashed the feathers against the shaft as she gripped the end and twisted it slowly, clockwise.

"No... Master."

"Very good." The woman released the arrow and turned around, stepping back to the chair. She paid no attention to the sound of Hester's breath shuddering lightly as she attempted to control herself.

"The hunter who was protecting my DeathSpeaker has left the boy in the care of monks. Odd that he would choose such a fate for the boy, being what he is, but it is not the hunter that concerns me. It is these monks." She settled back into her seat, folding one leg over the other and relaxing against the back of the chair. "I cannot abide my DeathSpeaker being raised to worship a false god when I am here."

Hester straightened as she felt her master's eyes settle firmly upon her. "They should give you no trouble, but... I've thought that of others." She studied her hand thoughtfully for a moment, before letting it hang leisurely over the arm of her chair. "Kill the caretakers, and burn the church."

Hester nodded in understanding. "And the hunter, Master?"

The flippancy of her dangling hand was replaced by a cold fist as the woman curled her hand over the arm of the chair. She said nothing for a long moment, and in the silence of her calculations, one could almost hear the ringing of a death knell.

"I have heard various things about this DeathBreather. It is of no surprise who he is; it was only a matter of time before I came across the Breathing Assassin in the hunt for my DeathSpeaker. But I have heard, too, that he speaks often as though he is holding a conversation with someone who is not present." Her voice sang with curiosity. "That perhaps he is being haunted by something more than merely a past filled with death?"

Her head tilted as she regarded Hester, waiting for the woman to admit to seeing such things.

"I have seen nothing strange about him, Master."

"No? No odd lights that seem to follow him, or a second shadow?"

Hester shook her head, but stopped when it began to make her feel dizzy. "I have fought him, Master, and there were no such things. He spoke to himself, as though speaking with someone else, when our fight had been interrupted. But I saw no one."

"Hm. It is possible he is merely mad." She stood again from her chair and moved to a nearby table, her fingers curling in a come-hither gesture to Hester, which was swiftly obeyed. A small, silver chalice rested in the center of the table. Hester held perfectly still as the woman removed the crimson gem from where it hung around her neck and placed the jewel delicately into the chalice. The glow from the ruby reflected against the inside of the glass and light rippled from within the cup, as though blood were running out over the sides.

The woman studied the gem as she spoke.

"The hunter has been the cause for enough problems to warrant a need for his removal. You may separate your regiment as you see fit between him and boy." She turned away from the gem to face Hester, her eyes fiery, though her voice remained calm. "You have proven yourself not to be without your own failures, Hester." She touched the arrow. "I won't abide by that a second time. I am fond of you, but fondness will only carry you so far."

"Yes, Master."

She stepped closer to Hester and she pressed her body tightly against the other woman. She felt Hester shudder delightfully beneath the sensation. "You feel so little in your cursed state, my Hester. I would hate to have to abandon you, but I cannot allow those who do my cause no good to remain. You understand, don't you?"

"Yes, Master," Hester whispered, her voice aching, her eyes following every movement of her master's fast.

"Very good." The woman leaned forward and kissed Hester gently on the lips, the sensation of touch on bare skin sending a fierce burning sensation through the whole of Hester's body. She pulled away and traced a gentle hand down the girl's cheek and Hester's eyes closed, a tear sliding down her cheek. "No one else can touch you without dying, Hester, but you will always have me. Do as I say, never fail me, and I will never abandon you."

Hester's lips quivered as her master's hand pulled away, and she opened too-bright eyes to find the woman had turned away from her. She straightened her expression and bit back the desire to call out to her master, to beg for the touch again.

"Separate your regiment as you see fit between the hunter and the boy. I want the DeathSpeaker brought to me."

The woman lifted the chalice in her hands and stared down into its depths. In the blood-colored light, her form shone like the vision of a ghost. The purple tailcoat seemed eerie with buttons that reflected the crimson light, and sharp shadows danced over the woman's face from the rim of the top hat that sat upon her wild red hair.

"As for the DeathBreather…"

She smiled down into the glass, and in the ruby's light, her teeth were covered with blood.

"Kill him."

DEATHSPEAKER
The God Stone

Mortimer was left in the care of the priests, but that doesn't mean he is safe. When he's visited by someone he watched die and the priests are murdered one by one, he is forced to run.

Not knowing where Ricker is or who he can trust, he wanders across a barren world he knows nothing of, his every step dogged by his pursuers.

They want him, and they'll have him. He is all they need to reveal the truth in the legend, and the final key to using the artifact.

The God Stone.

Made in the USA
Charleston, SC
07 November 2012